# PAST
# SINS

# PAST SINS

## CELIA ASHLEY

**Robin Maderich Publishing**
Zionsville PA
2023

ISBN: 979-8-9870681-4-4



Printed in the U.S.A.

Robin Maderich Publishing

Cover design by Robin Maderich

This book is also available in digital format.

# DEDICATION

*to fearlessness and love*

# AUTHOR'S NOTE

For the purpose of full disclosure, *Past Sins* was originally released in 2005 as *Midnight Hearts*, with a reprint in 2014. Changes have been made to the narrative, a new cover prepared, and the story has been given an updated title that better represents the substance therein, because despite the romantic element and adult content (earning it fifteen weeks on the bestseller list on Fictionwise in 2005), *Past Sins* is categorically a supernatural thriller.

There are countless readers in this world. Far more than might have read *Midnight Hearts* in the past, and by reworking and releasing the title under the new name, I hope to entice others to enjoy this gripping story. Like Mitchell's *Gone with the Wind* and Orwell's *1984*, which both were released with title and cover changes to reach and increase their audience, I hope to do the same. And no, I am not comparing *Past Sins* to either of those classics, but merely pointing out the strategy.

So, if you've read *Midnight Hearts* before, you have been warned here in the book's first pages of the reincarnation. And if you haven't, I hope you find yourself intrigued enough to read on.

Thank you as always for your interest and enjoy!

(P.S. In case you find yourself wondering at this story's conclusion whether I truly believe in ghosts, be advised I do. This story, however, takes them to the extreme for entertainment purposes.)

## *Chapter One*

*"Now hast thou but one bare hour to live,*
*And then thou must be damned perpetually,*
*Stand still, you ever-moving spheres of heaven,*
*That time may cease, and midnight never*
*come."*
Christopher Marlowe 1564-93
*Doctor Faustus (1604)*

Ethan closed the truck door of his pickup quietly, listening to the faint echo off the structure's stone front. Shoving his hands deep into his pockets, he rocked back onto his heels, gaze moving over the facade of the plastered fieldstone house in appraisal.

Commonly, and certainly not surprisingly,

early colonists built from whatever source was close to hand, and in eastern Pennsylvania it happened mostly to be river rock or fieldstone, a beautiful and sturdy building material. Hue, shape, the feel in one's hand, as familiar as the texture of Ethan's own skin after all these years.

He noted where the structure had been added to in a later period. From ground level the chimneys appeared in relatively good condition, though far from perfect. The roofs would probably need repair. Slate. That would be expensive, although he had a supply stockpiled from dismantled buildings. The porch addition might have to come down, he mused, giving it a quick glance as his hand came up to scratch the stubble at his chin. Stone should be re-pointed; woodwork repaired and repainted; windows glazed; shutters replaced. For the latter, he knew where he could find original era replacements.

Stopping himself, he looked around. No use tallying up repairs or restoration possibilities without first speaking to the owner. He strode up onto the porch and rapped on the door. After waiting a minute or so, he knocked again, a little louder. An unexpected chill moved across his skin. Goose bumps raised the hair on his forearms. Even though it still had to be at least eighty-five out in the sun, the cool shade beneath the porch overhang could be to blame.

He waited another minute longer, then discreetly tried the knob. Locked.

Given the day he'd had, he knew he should just go home. Instead he hesitated, tipped his head to listen. On the distant road he noted the hum from an engine as a well-tuned car sped past. Nearer he heard the breeze in the treetops, a few birds, and little else. He couldn't detect the slightest sound from inside the house. Granted, the walls were likely a foot and a half thick, but the door wasn't.

Executing a quarter turn on his heel Ethan shoved his hands once more into his pockets and gazed the porch's shaded length. From the corner of his eye he caught movement in the nearest sidelight and spun back.

"Ms. Madison?"

The narrow window beside the door shimmered, reflecting the moving leaves along the driveway. Just to be certain, however, Ethan knocked on the door again. Receiving no response, he peered into the glass, trying to be nonchalant about it. The foyer revealed a well-used rug and an antique table with a set of car keys but no purse. Maybe she'd forgotten the appointment and gone out with someone for the afternoon. He couldn't see anything moving about inside, not even a curious pet.

Turning away from the door, he glanced at the window sills and frames before starting toward his truck. The woodwork needed scraping and painting. Despite his best efforts, he added another note to the list in his head, calculating time, manpower, visualizing paint colors. He drew a deep breath, slowly releasing it.

"It's not like you need the work," he said out loud, thinking longingly of a hot shower and fresh clothes, but making no  move to return to his vehicle. Finally, wrestling a small wire-bound notebook from the jeans pocket he tore out a sheet and leaned on his thigh to write a note. He slid the note between the doorframe and the door directly above the knob, hoping it wouldn't blow off. Not likely, unless another storm came up. Right at the moment the air felt as still and heavy as oil. Even the momentary chill he'd experienced had vanished.

The porch floorboards creaked beneath his feet as he turned toward the steps, echoing in vibration clear down to the opposite end. He stopped, leaning his weight a few times on the one booted foot, concerned about the joist integrity beneath. Movement caught his attention at the porch's far end. He sucked in his breath before laughing out loud. Oh, yeah, this porch would have to come down or be completely overhauled. At the far side, a white rocker had begun a slow back and forth movement from the shifting boards. Not a good sign.

Ethan leaped the two steps to the slate walkway, strode back out into the drive and began a full circuit of the house, jotting down notes on the pad. At least he would be prepared if he ever met the property owner. No one could fault him for trying. Despite the neglect of the home's condition, he noted gardens meticulously tended, weeded and freshly mulched. He'd performed preliminary research on the property and the woman who had been living here had passed on the year before, so perhaps the new owner hadn't deliberately disregarded the property, only required someone else to effect the much-needed repairs.

Spotting the barn, which looked to be in remarkably good condition, he went over to the building and stuck his head inside the wide-open doors, calling out. The atmosphere in here felt heavy as well, fetid with mustiness and what was likely the scent formed by years of animal husbandry. The barn at this time housed no animals, only a lawn tractor and garden tools just within its doors. He called Perry Madison's name again, for good measure. Something exploded in a fluttering rush and shot over his head, close enough for him to hear the whistling wings in passage. Coming up from an instinctive crouch, he pivoted on his heel to try to catch a glimpse before the bird flew into the woods behind the house. It seemed huge, perhaps a barn owl startled from its daytime roost, but he'd been too busy ducking to get a good look.

Nothing showed in the hazy sky above the treetops. Narrowing his eyes to scan the trees themselves for a bird just settling, he found it difficult to locate anything in the thick foliage until something caught his eye lower down, drifting a distance away along the trail into the woods. He stepped out from the shadowed door of the barn.

"Hello!"

If the woman heard him, she gave no sign. He headed across the rough grass toward the trees. Apparently Perry Madison had opted for a stroll in the woods on this deucedly hot day. Maybe she wasn't one to wear a watch, to give a damn about the time or the fact she had scheduled a meeting with him. Really, he ought to just turn around and head back to his truck. He very nearly did, but when he caught sight of her again, pale in the shadow and quickly gone, he decided not to. She really ought to know exactly how forgetfulness inconvenienced others.

As he stepped into the cool shade beneath the trees, he caught sight of her yet again.

"Hello?"

And that quickly, she disappeared over the rise. Dammit. Increasing his pace, he followed. Before long he noted the occasional footprint on the damp path, the depression of a slender, hard-soled shoe. At least he knew now he wasn't imagining things. There had been a moment, a brief one, when he thought he might be.

## Chapter Two

Listening, Ethan frowned. He recognized water, a noise that had been subliminal for some time but which had picked up in flow and volume when he continued on the path onto an easy but stony ascent. Now, he bounded up between the rocks before him. Renewed perspiration broke out between his shoulders blades. At the crest he hesitated. A fortuitous pause, as the trail ended at a steep drop. A swift-running creek ran below him. On the opposite side, falling water tumbled from the hillside's rocky face into the stream below. The prismatic spray from the nine-foot drop glimmered luminous in the sun. Water on Stone, the property was called. It had been aptly named.

Ethan looked about for a way to descend. Rocks provided sufficient handhold as he clambered down to the stream bank, his work boots skidding in the mud. Shifting the notepad about in his pocket, he sat down on a boulder jutting out over the swift water. He closed his eyes, permitting an envelopment of his senses, reveling in the cool moisture hanging in the air and clinging to his skin. The noise from the waterfall prevented him hearing any other, drowning out birdcall, the breeze moving through the trees on the crest, sounds from human habitation nearby. It felt in effect like absolute solitude.

After a few moments in which his breathing and heart rate steadied, Ethan opened his eyes again. Shifting his feet, his boots brushed against something in the moss. He bent to take a look, stared, frowned, and stared again. A furrow formed on his brow.

Women's sandals lay on the mossy soil. One lay upside down, the well-worn sole muddied. The other showed the outline from a small, narrow foot in its wear, the leather slightly discolored by mildew, as if the shoe had been lying for some time in the elements. For how long he couldn't be sure, but the humidity over the past few days could account for its condition. Hooking a pointer finger through the strap, he lifted the sandal and set it beside him on the rock, finger still curled in a fierce grip. The discovery seemed ominous, somehow.

Raising his gaze, he glanced around, eyes narrowed in assessment against the sudden glare as the sun began its descent toward the horizon.

"Hello?" he called. He glanced over his shoulder, to the ridge, then back toward the creek and the falls. "Hello?"

The falls rushed silver-green from an opening in the hillside, an underground spring swollen by the recent rains making a tumultuous exodus. In the dark cleft below and behind, Ethan spied movement. Something vaguely human appeared, swaying from side to side and barely distinguishable, like a watercolor painting washing away before his eyes. Ethan stood up. The sandal fell unnoticed from his hand, tumbling on the moss-covered bank.

A woman stood there, steadying herself in the sun, one hand on the rocks, the other raised to push sodden, cinnamon-colored hair from her face. He couldn't be sure she was the woman he'd seen ahead of him. He'd not been close enough to distinguish features. If it was the same woman, he couldn't imagine how she'd managed to get into the creek and behind the falls when he'd been no more than a minute or two behind. While he watched, her head lifted, eyes blinking, seemingly unaware he stood across the creek.

Dressed in a sodden, sleeveless white shift, the woman swayed at the ledge's edge. Ethan's gaze shifted away from the garment's saturation, a condition that seemed to reveal more than simple nakedness. Yet, she stood in dangerous proximity to the rocky edge. Ethan had no idea how deep the water might be, muddied by the rains, nor if rocks lay beneath the surface.

The woman's head snapped to look across the tumbling expanse directly at him, her eyes large and unfocused, her pale countenance a semblance of startled confusion and what might have been fear.

"Hi," he shouted, lifting his hand. "I'm sorry. I didn't know anyone was here."

She said nothing. He kept his eyes on her face, strode closer to the water, pausing at the steep bank.

"Are you all right?" he called. "My name is Ethan. Ethan Taylor. I—"

"What?"

Arms crossed over the front of her body, her gaze had become suddenly sharp and focused.

"Ethan Taylor," he repeated in a shout. To her right, mist moved across the stone, circling round her. She lifted a hand to wave it away, the focus in her eyes briefly lost. Her expression changed again, mouth opening, but any words vanished in the water's heavy thunder. Unexpectedly, she extended a bare foot as if she intended to step onto something more substantial than air. Subsequent to her imprudent move she tumbled forward and down into the creek in an ungainly arabesque.

Heart thudding in shock, Ethan leaped from the bank, ignoring his own concerns about hidden rock, fighting a swift current to his waist as he waded out to the point she'd gone under. Spotting ballooning white fabric and tangled hair, he reached for her shoulder below the creek's surface and hauled the coughing woman to her feet. Fighting the current, he wrapped his hands around her upper arms to keep her from being swept back down. Water dripped from her clumped lashes down cheeks nearly white. Freckles stood out as though inked onto her skin.

"Are you hurt?" His gaze checked for overt injury and found none. Feeling the creek's chill through his soaked jeans, he didn't wait for a reply. He scooped the woman into his arms and carried her to the bank, where he lowered her onto the warm stone he'd just vacated. Gasping, she bent over her knees and hugged herself for warmth.

He waited for her answer, observing a little color returning to her cheeks and lips. She glanced up at him through the tangle of her hair, pushed wet locks from her brow with a trembling hand.

"I—I don't think so," she said, voice hoarse, teeth chattering.

Wordlessly Ethan stripped off his shirt and wrapped it around her. She glanced at him again in grateful acknowledgment.

"Thank you," she murmured after a moment.

"No problem," he said, crouching down beside her. He folded his hands together between his dripping knees. "What were you doing in there?"

"Swimming."

"Oh yeah? You were doing a piss-poor job of it, then."

"No doubt."

He snorted lightly, without amusement. Following her focused gaze, he frowned at the falls, the dark opening behind.

"That can't be the safest place," he remarked, turning back to her. "Even without the recent rain."

A small shudder jerked her shoulders beneath his shirt. She looked down, away from the torrent. Unwrapping her arms from her waist, she grabbed the dress hem and twisted it fiercely, tendons standing out along the backs of her hands. Water puddled the mossy soil at her feet. Bending forward, Ethan retrieved the sandals from harm's way, holding them up by the narrow straps.

"Are these yours?"

The woman stared at the shoes. Her gaze slid from Ethan's hand to his face. For the first time he saw her eye color. The gray of a winter sky, he would have called it. Eerily pale but charming rather than cold. The way they regarded him now, however, unnerved him.

"Who did you say you were?" she asked.

Ethan wiped his palm on his thigh. Uselessly, as the denim and fingers hand remained soaked. He held his hand out.

"Ethan Taylor. And you?" he asked, although he knew. It seemed unlikely anyone but the owner of the property would know a place existed behind the falls large enough for a person to fit into, let alone enter there.

She grasped his hand with chilled fingers. "Perry Madison," she said. "And you're early."

"Actually," he answered, releasing her fingers, "I'm late."

She tipped her head to one side, her damp hair swinging away from her shoulder. "What?"

"I had my secretary call you to explain," he said. "Didn't you get the message? I had a flat tire."

She frowned at him in concentration. "What day is it?"

"Thursday. The fifth. I'm sorry," he said in sudden understanding, "I guess I should have called you this morning to confirm and to remind you. I don't—"

"I didn't forget," she said, reaching for her sandals. Bending, she studied them a moment, scraping at the mildew with a flick of her fingernail before putting them on. "I have the appointment marked on the calendar."

Standing, her eyes went again to the falls in mute consideration. She sucked in her lower lip, teeth sinking into soft, pale flesh. Her cheeks filled with hectic color, then paled. Beneath his shirt she started to tremble. Ethan took a step nearer. A subtle scent reached him, making him think of something he shouldn't. He dismissed the startling thought as quickly as it came.

"What's wrong?" he asked, disturbed by arousal's residue still percolating through his veins.

Troubled, he backed away. She inhaled audibly, wet fabric lifting in a way he did not want to notice. She raised her head to look at him, gray eyes wide, pupils large. Her hands clenched into fists at her sides.

"I don't know," she answered and dropped, folding like a damp rag to the earth.

## *Chapter Three*

A strange, cold pressure prevented Perry from lifting her eyelids. After a moment, she brought her hands up, clawing, fumbling, panic filling her as she struggled with what ended up being nothing more sinister than a washcloth over her eyes. Dangling the dripping cloth, she stared at it in confusion. She heard a voice nearby. On a phone it seemed. The contractor. Ethan Taylor.

Sitting up, she struggled through clouded vision to view the room around her. As her eyesight cleared from the washcloth's weight, she spotted movement in the shadowed corner at the sofa's edge.

"She seems to have come around. If you hold on, I'll check."

Perry watched the man move toward her, a cell phone to his ear, damp, disheveled dark  hair pushed back from his brow. He crouched on the floor beside her. Staring at him, Perry shoved herself a little closer to the sofa back.

"Hey, how are you feeling?  Do you remember who I am?"

She so much didn't want to answer him, would rather have pretended total amnesia. "Yes."

"Who am I?"

Persistent man. "Ethan Taylor."

He nodded. "Do you know where you are?" he continued, apparently prompted by the voice on the phone.

"On the sofa. In my living room."

"Do you remember how you got here?"

The answer to that didn't come quite as readily. She frowned in concentration, squeezing the washcloth. Ethan Taylor took the cloth from her hand, shoved it in an empty glass on the coffee table. The wet splotch left behind spread into the existing dampness in the fabric draping her legs.

"I'm on the phone with a friend who's a doctor," Ethan explained. "He needs an answer to my last question."

"Right." Perry drew a deep breath. He nodded again, encouraging her to speak. Why was he asking her these questions? Lifting her gaze, she glanced briefly at his face before shifting focus over his shoulder toward the window. Leaves hung listlessly on the maple just outside, crooked shadows barring the aged glass indicating evening. When had that happened?

"Your vitals seem fine. However, my friend and I have been discussing the possibility you might have hit your head? Did you? I don't see any signs of it, but that really would be cause for a trip to the hospital."

Attention recalled, Perry reached up, pushing her fingers through her damp hair, checking her skull for tenderness.

"My head doesn't hurt," she said, bending her neck to eye the mud on her clothing. Over her ruined dress she wore a man's shirt. His shirt. Yes, his shirt, because he didn't have one on. Made sense. Sort of. Somehow she recognized the scent of him locked into the fabric, nearly overpowered by the smell of...what? The creek. Right. And something else.

Standing abruptly, she took a step away from the man. He shot to his feet as well, putting a hand to her arm in support, fingers altogether too warm considering the fact his jeans were soaked and he stood beside her shirtless. She shied away from the sight of his torso, muscular and lean.

"You carried me?"

He dropped his hand from her arm, cradling the phone against his collar bone, muffling their conversation from the person on the line.

"I did," he said.

"From the falls?"

"Yes."

"All that way," she whispered.

"All that way," he answered, repeating her words in a manner that made her cringe inside. Not angry, not condemning. Concerned, perhaps. Perplexed. Maybe even a little amused, now she'd hadn't gone and died on him.

But dying had never been a part of it. Or, God, had it?

Under cover of his shirt, she slapped her arm, grabbed the flesh over her wrist, twisting hard. Not dead. Not dreaming.

"I'm sorry," she said. "I'm sorry you had to do that."

He shrugged, a fluid movement lifting his naked shoulders. "Leaving you to tumble back into the creek wasn't exactly an option."

Perry heard a muffled question come through the phone. Ethan lifted the instrument to his ear, asking the doctor to repeat what he'd said. Perry stared at him, a chill coursing her skin that had nothing to do with her soaked clothes. She tucked her shaking hands beneath her arms, clutching her abdomen. Reality, memory, left her breathless.

"She's up, standing here looking at me."

His gaze met and held hers for a moment before sliding away. Dark eyes. He had very dark eyes, and long lashes. With the return of appalling lucidity, she tried to remember what *his* eyes looked like. It occurred to her she'd possibly never seen them at all.

"She remembers me carrying her now."

"With nauseating clarity," she muttered. His head snapped back toward her, mouth opening, but his friend spoke again.

"I don't know," Ethan said into the phone before addressing her. "You're not pregnant are you?"

Perry shook her head.

"Ill?"

"No." She figured out the next question before he spoke it. "I haven't been taking any drugs, and I don't drink."

"Never fainted before?"

She drew a deep breath, releasing it slowly. "No."

At his expression, Perry's shoulders jerked beneath the borrowed work shirt still draped around them. She lifted her chin. "I'm going to put some dry clothes on."

"Will you be all right?"

"Yes. I don't need any help." She handed him his shirt. He took it, letting the garment dangle from his fingers, then lowered his hand to his thigh. Wet jeans clung closely to his body. Too closely. Not his fault, Perry reminded herself. He wouldn't have been in the creek if not for her.

Turning away, she strode to the base of the staircase, paused there, glanced back. "I have nothing dry to offer you, but I'll bring you a towel. I'm sorry."

"Don't worry about it," he said. "A towel is fine." Spinning on his heel, he spoke once again into the phone. Perry's gaze lingered on the lean contours presented by his back, wondering at the physical feat, carrying her unconscious body all the way from the falls. Dismissing it because she had to, she turned to climb the stairs.

In the hallway above she paused to listen to his calm voice, unruffled as he finished his call, as if he made rescuing abruptly-unconscious women and carting them home in their soaking wet summer dresses commonplace. She looked down, fisting the damp, dirty fabric in her curled fingers. She remembered putting the dress on, walking out the kitchen door to take a stroll in the woods.

Three days ago. Three days without food. No wonder she'd fainted.

Perry rushed into the bathroom, pushed the door closed with both hands and leaned her head against the painted wood, fighting nausea as she fumbled with the old latch on the knob. The antiquated state of everything in the home was the reason she'd called the contractor. She couldn't imagine what might be going through his mind.

Yet, she wondered if Ethan's arrival hadn't prompted *him* to withdraw. She couldn't remember. Not clearly. Not everything. She squeezed her eyes shut, shocked by memory's heated fragments. Her stomach rolled again in disgust and fear as she recognized what she'd done behind the falls, what she had allowed, what she had reacted to, most certainly by the arousal she still felt rippling across her skin despite the interim crisis.

With a heavy exhalation she spun from the door, yanking her wet garment over her head and tossing it across the claw foot tub. Snatching a towel from the rack she scrubbed hard at her damp skin, part of her wanting to jump into a scalding hot shower and wash with the most abrasive soap she could lay her hands on, while another part of her wanted only to return to *him*, to feel again the contrast of cold stone and heated breath, mouth, hands, skin, moving her to remarkable heights.

"Oh, God," she whispered, pressing her face into the towel. Things like this didn't happen. Not to real people. Not to sane people. Not to people living ordinary lives, returning home to the house they'd grown up in because a person who meant more to them than almost anyone else had died.

Lifting her head, Perry wrapped the towel around her body, cracking the door open to peer into the hallway before darting across to her bedroom. Yanking open drawers, she searched for warm and concealing clothing, finally grappling still moist skin into panties and jeans. She slipped the baggiest sweatshirt she could find over her head, not caring about the day's temperature or that she'd be breaking into a sweat very shortly. In her present condition she didn't need Ethan Taylor looking at her in any way but professional.

Grabbing a clean towel from the hall closet, Perry descended the steps. Self-consciously she crossed the floor to where Ethan stood pulling items from his pockets and laying them on an antique table's marble top. He frowned at the wreck of a narrow, spiral-bound notepad.

"I don't suppose this will help much," she said, offering him the towel. He glanced up, taking it with a nod of thanks. He'd put his shirt on, half the buttons left open, the garment hanging loosely over his torso. She looked away, observing sidelong the vigorous scrubbing of his jeans before he finally gave up. He straightened, expression rueful.

"I am embarrassed beyond words," she said.

"Don't be."

"Please," she said, "if I can't have my dignity, at least allow me my shame."

He laughed. The sound stunned her, straight to her bones. Stepping back, up against a chair arm, she gave him a wry smile.

"Heck of a first meeting."

"I would say I've had worse," he answered, "but I'd be lying."

She nodded. "Great. Honesty's good."

He laughed again. Her blood sizzled quietly in response. She ground her teeth together as her body yearned out of control in betrayal of common sense and propriety.

Ethan wrapped the towel around his shoulders, eyeing her sidelong as he flipped through the ruined notebook. "I can't believe how quickly you managed to get into that water."

"Well, I was falling. Gravity had something to do with it."

A slow smile turned up his mouth. "Not quite what I meant, but it doesn't matter. I'm just glad you're all right."

"You should have called for someone. You didn't need to carry me. However, I appreciate that you did."

"Don't worry about it," he murmured. Clearly, he wanted her gratitude dropped. Perry drew a breath through her nose, lowering her head. Her gaze fell on his boots.

"Crap. Your feet must be floating in there."

His lips curved again. "There's a tide going on every time I move my toes," he agreed. "I have a pair of sneakers in the truck. I'll go put them on. That is, if you still want me to have a look around?"

Despite an urge to scream 'no', she realized she felt some comfort in his presence and, as long as he remained willing, the estimate needed to be made. "Sure," she said. "Would you like a cup of tea?"

"That would be perfect."

Perfect, she thought, marveling at his casual tone, behaving as if he had not carried her unconscious body the better part of eight hundred feet. Bewildered and still grateful, she turned away to pad on bare feet to the kitchen. He followed, pausing in the center of the floor. She glanced over her shoulder at him, finding him standing with his hands in his pockets, scanning in professional assessment the room's condition. She was struck by his impressive height, his thick, dark hair far closer to the ceiling than hers. Perry tore her gaze away as he turned to look at her.

"You're sure you're going to be all right?"

"Positive."

"Do you faint a lot?"

"I told you I never have before," she said.

He grunted. "Will you see a doctor about it?"

"You take this whole rescue-of-a-damsel-in-distress thing pretty seriously, don't you? But yes, I'll probably give the doctor a call tomorrow." She hoped the word 'probably' got her off the hook for an outright lie. Maybe now he would let it go.

He stood a moment longer as if wanting to say something else. She turned from him toward the sink, reaching for the cold water tap on the faucet.

Flipping open the kettle's lid, she turned on the water to fill it. As she leaned forward she felt the brush of her nipples against her sweatshirt interior like a caress. Her hand on the kettle lid shook. Why hadn't she taken the time to put on a bra?

*You know why.*

The kettle slipped from her fingers into the old enamel sink with a crash, water splashing over the counter and onto the front of her shirt. Crying out, she backed away, straight into Ethan Taylor. He grabbed her upper arms to steady her.

"I'm fine," she said, trying to keep the hysteria from her voice as she eased herself from his concerned grasp. "Really. The pot just slipped."

She waited until Ethan moved away from her before permitting a panicked shiver. She swallowed, nauseous, uncertain. By Ethan's silence, she understood he hadn't heard anything. She'd almost hoped...well, it didn't matter what she'd hoped. He'd heard nothing. Only she could hear.

"Maybe you should sit down," suggested Ethan. "I could make the tea."

Perry shook her head, willing herself to be calm, breathing deeply, deliberately. Refilling the kettle, she set it on the stove, lighting the gas beneath. She took down two cups from the cabinet and two tea bags from the jar as if undisturbed. Head tipped to one side, Ethan watched her, his dark hair across his eyes.

"Would you rather I came back another time?"

She shook her head again, not speaking. Not daring to speak as she concentrated on the task at hand. She needed another person in the house with her, just for a little while, until she'd regained control of the situation.

"I'll be right back then," he said. His sloshing boots retreated to the back door, which opened and closed quietly. The teapot soon began a shrill whistle. Hastening to turn off the flame, Perry poured hot water into the cups. Clutching her own, she moved to the window, holding the vessel close beneath her chin. Fragrant steam rose to her nostrils.

Ethan had paused outside in the yard, stretching himself to ease some stiffness in his back. Perry sighed guiltily, knowing the cause. His partially open shirt flapped in the breeze along his long torso, revealing evidence of daily physical labor. He worked hard. He looked hard, every inch of him, and not from some regimen in a gym. She watched him cross the yard toward the driveway with a particularly arresting locomotion, his stride easy and long, almost feral.

*You find him attractive, do you not?*

Perry paused with the mug to her lips. A chill tripped in electrifying swiftness along her spine. She lowered the mug to the counter.

"And if I do?" she said, voice harsh, angered by her fear and distinctly uneasy to discover herself answering the voice aloud. She wondered if it was bravado or only a natural progression.

*We may use him.*

Perry's hand jerked, knocking against the cup. Heated liquid sloshed over the mug's ceramic sides. The plurality of the reply had not been lost on her.

"We? I don't think so," she hissed. "You leave him alone. Go away. Do you hear me? Get the hell away."

And it did. *He* did. She felt suddenly aware of her skin as her own again, her pulse beating normally, her breasts no longer tingling, the seam in her jeans no longer presenting itself as inordinately intimate. Snatching a paper towel from the roll to dab at the spilled tea, she contemplated what this return to near normalcy might mean. Did she possess any control over this nightmarish seduction? Possibly. There were just too many unknowns, though, to be certain.

She had her cup, as well as herself, firmly in hand when Ethan returned. From beneath her lashes she recognized his extraordinary good looks through her own perception and within reality's normal context. Relief flooded through her. She could control this. She could. A knowledge of power surged through her veins like adrenaline.

"Shall we get going, then?" she asked, handing Ethan his cup as she led the way from the kitchen. Ethan followed close behind, swinging a long-handled flashlight in his other fist. She smelled the light spice of his cologne—as well as the more robust fragrance from his efforts in carrying her—

and all settled in her mind without undue alarm. Yes, she definitely had control now. She welcomed Ethan's proximity, her consciousness regarding his height, the breadth of his shoulders, the rumble in his voice as he asked a question while they climbed the attic stair, knowing any mild reaction she had to him as a male was her own.

Crossing the attic floor, Perry stood in the center under the peak breathing in old paper, cloth, dust and disuse. Nostalgia struck her as she looked around in the mote-filled sunlight filtering through rippled panes in the windows at either end in the narrow attic room. Boxes and crates set under the rafters were smoky gray with undisturbed dust. Clothing, crates filled with books, old furnishings, had been jammed in every square inch to either side of the cleared passageway down the center.

Every last item belonged to her now. The possessions she viewed as her own filled an area in the barn, with the exception of those things she'd brought inside. She hadn't been inclined to enter the attic since her grandmother's passing. Though the house and its contents were left to her in their entirety, she suspected relatives might come forward in time to make demand based on value despite the legal wording in her grandmother's Will. One day she would perform a thorough inventory of the attic contents and sort them all out. But not today. Not tomorrow. Not any time in the near future. She couldn't bring herself to even start the process.

For a few minutes she watched Ethan shine the flashlight on the roof beams, checking, she supposed, for leaks and damage. Every so often he would grunt and slip the flashlight beneath his arm, jotting notes on a new pad he didn't place in his damp pocket. He stuck the pen behind his ear.

"Is it bad?" she questioned.

"Not really," he answered, glancing at her as if just recalling her presence.

"Okay. I guess that's good then."

"Interesting assortment of stuff in here," he said, sweeping the light across the floor. "Some is worth money. Actually," he added, peering closer at an object hidden from her view, "some of these things might be better off in a local museum. Did all this come with the house?"

"You might say that. Several generations of my family lived here, if you count me. When my grandparents bought the house, though, a lot of what you see had been left behind by the previous owners."

He looked startled. "This was your grandparent's house?"

"My grandmother was the last to live in it. She passed away last year. She wasn't up to taking care of a lot of what needed to be done. Unfortunately, I didn't come home as often as I should have and didn't realize."

"It happens," Ethan said. "Families are like that. You don't realize what's going on sometimes until it's too late to change it."

She blinked at his empathetic tone. *Don't feel sorry for me*, she thought. *If you knew what I'd been doing you'd feel nothing but abhorrence.*

"My family's not very large. I was the only direct descendant left. Nana left everything to me."

He glanced around the attic. "Quite the undertaking. Do you plan to catalogue all this? I know some people with the historical society who might be willing to lend a hand."

Perry followed his gaze, suddenly recalling a time she'd been in the attic searching for some item belonging to her mother. Her fingers tightened on the mug. How old had she been? Ten? Eleven? Spinning on her bare heel, she stared into the darkened spaces beneath the eaves. The hair lifted on her nape.

Nothing. There had been nothing then, there was nothing now.

And yet she knew an altered reality existed. She had been living it, for three days. Three. Freaking. Days.

"That would be great," she replied stiffly. "Maybe when your crew is here they could haul it all downstairs to a more convenient location."

At her tone, all movement from Ethan's side of the attic ceased. She turned back in his direction. He straightened, ducking his head beneath the rafter just in time to avoid collision. "Are you saying the job is mine? I didn't even give you an estimate yet."

"Oh," she said with a self-conscious snort. "Right. Although, frankly, you're the only person I called so far." She started across the floor toward him, halting after two steps to spin away toward the far window instead. She didn't want to be misread. A residue of whatever a man could scent on a woman when aroused wasn't something she wished him to misinterpret. Better to keep her distance.

"You came highly recommended," she added at his continued silence. "I sort of figured I'd be giving you the job, no matter what." Leaning toward the aged glass she stared out at the barn, her view distorted by the large rippled pane. She placed her mug on the sill.

*Take him. He's willing.*

Perry sucked in her breath. "No!"

"Did you say something?"

Glancing back at Ethan, Perry shook her head. With a wave of his flashlight Ethan resumed his inspection. Perry turned back to the window. She pressed her forehead to the glass, feeling its cool surface against her skin and the curving bone beneath. Perspiration dotted her brow as she recalled her insatiable need in the cave, the hours and hours of sweet torment. The implication in the kitchen, of using Ethan Taylor, chilled her skin. A part of her, dark and shaming, yearned for it. The conscious, moral segment of her thinking self cringed, quite repulsed.

"I told you to leave him alone," she whispered, quieter now so Ethan wouldn't hear her. Maybe she couldn't give the job to him, after all. Bad enough she'd been responding to spectral stimulation. She wouldn't let that happen to anyone else.

*You will welcome him.*

Perry shook her head against the window glass, slick with her sweat. I told you to leave us alone, she thought fiercely.

*Us? You ally yourself with him?*

Perry lifted her head. She heard a loosened floorboard squeak beneath a soft tread. A chill danced along her spine.

*You are allied with me. I will make him do as I choose.*

No! Perry screamed silently. Breathing hard, she placed both hands on the window frame, steadying herself. No, she thought again. You will not.

*My heart.*

The word 'no' formed in Perry's mind again, and stilled to nothing.

*We will use him.*

Appearing silently behind her, Ethan's hands slipped beneath her shirt where her flesh lay bare and heated. Slid beneath and up, cupping her breasts. His fingers toyed with her nipples, already hard, tugging at them gently, teasing them. He pulled her back against his body.

She went willingly, unthinkingly, feeling the strength in him. Her own hands remained gripped on the window frame as if to the only point of safety as his fingers tugged on the fastening to her jeans, unzipped them, trailed down the front of her belly into her undergarments, pushing her legs apart with his knee, pushing his fingers in exploration of the soft flesh between.

"Please," she whispered, "stop."

"Perry, did you say something?"

Her body jerked, heat flaming across her skin. Spinning on her heel she stared across the attic to the far side where Ethan Taylor stood examining the window ledge opposite. Crossing her arms over her chest, she fought the trembling in her limbs. "No, nothing," she said, flushing with shame. "I——I have a call to make."

She rushed down the stairs without looking at him again. Racing to her bedroom, she leaned against the mahogany dresser, palms flat against the wood, breasts rising and falling beneath the sweatshirt.

The towel she had earlier used had fallen to the floor and after a moment she bent to pick it up, holding it close to her face. Her skin's temperature slowly cooled cocooned in damp terry.

*We will use him. He will be more than willing, I promise you.*

"Shut up!" she cried. "Go away!"

She didn't control it, control him. Beneath the falls she'd surrendered herself, surrendered her free will without true understanding, unable to stop once she'd begun. Maybe too late to stop any of it.

## *Chapter Four*

"All right, Ethan, I'll look forward to your call."

Ethan shook Perry's hand again. For the third time. And, once again, was reluctant to let her fingers go. He could only assume some chemistry had started seeping into his senses. Usually he played it pretty cool. Not evasive or aloof, but cautious. With good reason.

She looked small in her oversized sweatshirt, vulnerable. Her auburn hair, dry now, drifted around her face in the rising breeze. Still pale, the freckles bridging her nose stood out like tiny, spattered, mocha droplets on her skin. A pretty woman, but not exactly the type he'd been dating on and off. More like—well, more like someone he might want to get to know better.

Reluctantly, he released Perry's hand. She crossed her arms, shoving the fingers he'd been holding into her sleeves' baggy folds. He thought he saw her shiver. Highly likely, given her dunking in the creek.

"Vitamin C," he said.

"What?"

"Vitamin C," he repeated. "Ward off any cold. Or whatever."

She blinked. He received an impression he'd amused her.

"Works for me," he added.

"Thank you."

He took a step backward, setting his weight on the loose, porch floorboard.

"I'll need to get under here and check out the support," he said, indicating the floor with a quick head bob. He glanced to the side, toward the rocking chair. Without his weight pushed down in succession on the board beneath his foot, the rocker remained unaffected. Maybe it wasn't as bad as he'd thought.

"Whatever you think. Just let me know and we can discuss it."

He nodded, walking backward down the steps. "Goodnight."

"Goodnight. And thank you for rescuing me. If there's a chiropractor bill, let me know."

He was still smiling when he got in his truck. Backing it around to head out the driveway, he couldn't resist a quick look at her on the porch in the dirty side mirror. She had already opened the front door and stood on the threshold, a dusty, sunlit aura from an inside window enveloping her. She raised a hand to wave at him. He waved back, arm out the window, and pulled away.

His thoughts were still on Perry when he pulled into his driveway. Gathering paperwork from the seat, he tucked it under his arm and then leaped from the truck. He crossed the graveled drive, striding toward the front door as he sorted through mail he'd retrieved from the box. Bills. Junk. Something that looked suspiciously like a wedding invitation. He didn't do weddings. Not anymore.

He unlocked the front door and slipped inside, taking a moment to deposit the mail and paperwork on the hall table. The filter in the cichlid tank bubbled lightly in greeting. Fish were the easiest pets to have given the hours he worked. Easy to feed, lights on a timer, the noise of the filter keeping the house from being too quiet. A dog or a cat would have done the same thing, with a lot more animation, but without someone else in his life he couldn't hope to properly care for a pet like that. Fish were it.

Dropping pellets into the water, he watched the cichlids' antics for a moment before heading into the bedroom to strip off his still damp clothing. Lifting his head, he caught sight of the photograph on the dresser. A laughing, lovely face. Near the end, he hadn't thought laughter possible. Of course, he hadn't known they were near the end. That knowledge came later. But she was the reason he avoided the dating of anyone vaguely suited to him. Women like Perry.

Inhaling, he stared a few minutes longer at the photograph, his hands on the dresser, one finger tapping a slow rhythm as he considered. With a small nod he turned away, crossing the bedroom floor to snatch the phone from its stand. Carrying the phone into the front hall, he leafed through papers until he found the paperwork with Perry's information on it. He dialed her number.

"Perry, hi, it's Ethan. Am I interrupting anything?"

"No," she answered after a split second's silence. He plunged on.

"I know I said I'd call or come over with the estimate in the next day or so, but I was wondering if you'd like to have dinner."

Silence again, then, "Instead of you coming over?"

Now why would she think that? "No, in addition to my coming over. Or calling. Just for dinner. I thought it might be nice."

"Oh, Ethan, I—"

"No is fine. I don't usually ask potential clients for a date. In fact, not ever. If it makes you feel uncomfortable or you're just not interested, you can say so."

"Tonight?"

He sucked a sharp breath through his nose, lifting his hand to glance at the watch on his wrist.

"Sure. Tonight would be fine. Late dinners are less crowded. Do you want to meet me somewhere halfway? If I drive back there to pick you up we might be out of luck. I'm not certain how late we can get served."

Dammit, was he rambling?

"Name the place and I'll meet you there," she said.

So he did, feeling a grin break over his face. Returning the phone to the bedroom he hurried into the shower, because he hadn't allowed himself much leeway.

*Chapter Five*

Perry parked her car in the lot, deposited the keys in her purse and sat for a moment behind the wheel, staring toward the small twinkling lights embedded in the trees and lining the restaurant porch. Leaving the house had been hard. She kept waiting to be stopped, to be prevented from joining the normal world. When she had been able to shower and dress and walk out the kitchen door, she had found herself hoping the whole incident had been a dream. A nightmare, actually. But she damned well knew it wasn't.

Ethan's pickup truck occupied a parking spot nearby. It would have been nice to arrive before he did, to be the first seated. His eyes on her as she crossed the floor would make her feel awkward. She didn't want that.

Pushing open the door, Perry stepped out onto the pavement, standing beside her car as she smoothed her dress over her hips. She had dressed carefully, despite her haste, in a fashion more demure than he might have expected, considering his first sight of her by the falls. A simple dress, flat shoes, hair plaited in a single braid down her back. She hadn't bothered with makeup, but she rarely did. She wanted nothing to call attention to herself. If she had known the wallpaper color in the dining room, she would have found something to match.

Perry reached back into her purse for her keys, telling herself the smart thing to do would be to go home. She liked Ethan. That could be a problem for him. She wasn't at all certain liking anyone, allowing herself any emotional attachment, was a wise idea. Ethan Taylor seemed to be a good man, an honest and likeable man, a very down-to-earth sort of guy. If she let herself get any closer to him, she would have to tell him the truth. How did one explain something like this? And even without explanations, if she and Ethan became friends, more than friends, if *he* spoke the truth, Ethan might find himself an involuntary participant in her nightmare.

Closing her eyes, Perry swore softly beneath her breath. Quite frankly, she had half a mind to lock herself into a small room somewhere with no plans to ever come out. Of course, she'd be no safer there.

Shoving her keys deep down into her purse again, somewhere too far to reach with ease, she strode in determination across the parking lot and into the restaurant. At the podium she paused, forcing a smile at the man raising his brows inquisitively at her.

"Good evening, madam," he responded. "Are you meeting someone?"

"Yes. A Mr. Taylor. I believe he's already arrived."

"He has," said the man. "Follow me."

Wending their way between tables, the man led her to a booth near the back illuminated by a shaded bulb above and a candle near the wall. Ethan rose as she approached, standing a head above the host. Ethan extended his hand to assist her into her seat. His gaze moved slowly and discreetly over her. Nevertheless, Perry felt his scrutiny. She slid into her seat, yanking her skirt down over her thighs.

"I hope a booth is okay," said Ethan. "I'm not much of a table man myself. I don't like being out in all the commotion. Not that there's much at this hour, I guess."

Perry's lips curved. She didn't care to be in the middle of commotion either, although she couldn't prove it by the incident earlier at the creek and after. Steering her mind away, she accepted the menu being handed to her, watched as Ethan resumed his seat opposite.

"You look very nice," he said, before she could get a word out in greeting.

"Amazing what a shower can do," she answered.

"Don't be nervous, Perry. 'Thank you' works. You do look nice. Accept it."

"All right. Thank you."

He made a noise in his throat, like a contained and rumbling chuckle. His dark eyes reflected the candle flame despite the shaded bulb burning closely overhead. The natural and probably expensive dye of his shirt, a pale yellow linen, accentuated the tanned skin on his face and arms.

"See anything that interests you?"

Uttered in regard to the menu he nodded toward in her hands, his question nonetheless brought a flush to her cheeks. Ducking her head, Perry hastily skimmed the restaurant's offerings.

"Have you been here before? What do you usually get?"

Everything looked so good. As it would. After all, she hadn't eaten in three days.

Dear God.

"Are you all right?" he asked. He seemed to possess an uncanny ability to perceive the slightest change in her mood. More likely, though, he responded only to the abrupt and unexplainable alterations to her pallor. She nodded at him in assurance. Nevertheless, his study remained intent, even when he leaned back in his seat.

"Do you like fish?  The sea bass is excellent."

Perry nodded again, several times and with much more enthusiasm. "Yes, I think I'll have that. I think I'm going to have a baked potato with it as well?  I know the menu says it's served with rice, but I need something with loads of butter. Oh, and I'll have both the salad and the soup."

Across from her he laughed. "A woman with an appetite!    Have whatever you like, Perry. Something to drink?  I could recommend the apple martini."

"I've never had one. I don't usually drink."

Ethan closed his menu. "Don't feel you have to for my sake. Lemonade, then?"

"No, I'll take the martini. You've intrigued me. Hopefully, I won't get drunk."

"On one?"

"You never know," she answered. "I'm a lightweight."

He laughed again. She smiled at him, her eyes moving to his left hand. Though tanned, she saw no sign he'd recently removed a wedding band. She hadn't asked him his marital status, naturally, assuming he wouldn't have invited her to dinner if he had a wife. Yet finding his finger lacking any overt sign reassured her.

The server arrived in the middle of Perry's mental note. Ethan ordered for them both, then handed the girl the menus. Once she departed he sat forward with his hands folded on the tabletop.

"I'm glad you came out," he said. "You look far more relaxed than you did at the house."

*With good reason*, she thought. At least here, he was safe. They both were. She felt like herself. Even though *he* hadn't spoken to her again after Ethan's departure, she'd been expecting it every minute. Enmeshed in the stark eroticism of her experience behind the falls, she knew she would have been willing to yield herself again in order to achieve that lofty physical rapture. She couldn't let that happen.

Folding her hands in her lap, Perry focused on the man across from her.

"And I'm glad you asked me," she said. She couldn't remember the last time she'd gone out to enjoy the company of friends, let alone a male companion. Since her marriage's demise, she'd avoided the latter, and since her return from the middle of the country to the East Coast, the former as well. She told herself she possessed too many loose ends to be gathered and repaired, and that the time would come again for a normal routine, a real life. But, truthfully, since returning to live in her grandmother's home she had isolated herself, embroiled in her work and now—this other matter.

In recollection, a shiver danced down her spine, and not altogether in revulsion or fear. Across from her Ethan removed his jacket from his chair back, handing the garment around the table edge.

"It is a little cold in here," he said.

"Thank you," Perry murmured, slipping the jacket over her bare shoulders. A good man. Yes, Ethan Taylor was a good man. He wouldn't be used. She wouldn't allow it.

"I'm glad you stuck around to check the house out. Like I told you earlier, you came highly recommended. I've heard nothing but positive feedback about your work."

Ethan shifted in his seat. "Thank you. I like what I do."

"How did you get started in the business? Besides all the back-breaking work, it must be fascinating."

The martini arrived at that moment, and Ethan's water with lemon. Abstemious. She liked that, too. Lifting her glass, Perry took a small sip.

"Wow," she said. "That is tasty. Strong. But tasty."

"Will it make you drunk?"

"Uh, let's hope not," she answered, smiling.

He lifted his glass, tipping it in her direction.

"To a normal, relaxing evening," he said. "Here's hoping I never have to carry you anywhere again."

She laughed despite herself. "Good God, amen to that," she agreed.

"Not that I minded. You don't weigh much more than a pack of shingles."

"Really?  Having never lifted one, I wouldn't know. However, getting back to your profession, is it the physical work you like, or the chance to reproduce history?"

His mouth quirked. "Is this like…an interview?"

"What? No! I'm only curious. I promise."

"Well, then, funny you should zero in on both like that. Because it is both. I like physical labor. Call me crazy, but it's true. It's cleansing and rewarding and beats the hell out of paying for a gym membership, since performing a lot of the actual labor myself puts more money in my pocket. And, yes, I've always had an interest in history."

"Me, too," she said, turning to find their salads arriving. Conversation halted for a brief interval, then resumed as the server disappeared.

"What is it you do?" he asked. "I don't believe we discussed it on the phone when you made the appointment."

Perry drizzled creamy Italian dressing over her

salad, spearing a bit of lettuce with her fork. "Well," she said, "I write."

One eyebrow arched. "Write? What sort of things do you write?"

"Whatever I'm hired to put into words," she told him, popping the tomato and lettuce into her mouth. She chewed and swallowed while he waited patiently for her to go on. "Lately, it's been mostly business manuals. Pretty boring stuff, actually."

"Someone has to do it. Ever try your hand at fiction?"

She glanced up at him. "I have," she admitted.

"Published?"

"Yes."

"Anything I might have read?"

"I doubt it," she said. "Unless you're a more romantic sort than you look."

"I beg your pardon?" he countered.

She laughed and explained. "I've written a couple of historical romance novels. I don't think you would have read them."

"You'd be surprised," he retorted. "Try me. Did you use your own name?"

"In a way," she said. "I use my last name first, just the initial, then my middle name, and first name last, as a pseudonym. Sort of corny, but it works."

Across the cloth-covered table Ethan puzzled this out. With an astonished expression, he slowly lowered his fork. "I don't believe it. *Honorable Intentions*, right?"

Perry sat back, mouth dropping open. "You've read it?"

He looked sheepish. "One of the ladies I dated briefly left the book on my sofa. I must admit I was curious, especially when I noted the time period. So, yes, I read it. Pretty hot stuff."

Perry made a face at him. "That would be all a man would remember," she said dryly.

Ethan folded his arms on the table top, leaning forward. "Oh, that's not true. Actually, I recall the writing was very detailed, well researched and engaging. Plus, it was a darned good love story."

He remembered the love story. What an unusual perception for a man. She stared hard at him. She could see him being impressed by the research, considering his profession, but to be aware of the story's depth? For the briefest moment Perry felt as if she'd fallen a little bit in love with Ethan Taylor. It was nice to have one's work appreciated for the reasons one intended. And then she laughed.

"I'm happy you enjoyed it," she said. "Hot stuff and all."

He grinned, waving the last remark aside. "Have you another on the way soon?"

Perry shook her head, smiling crookedly. "I've been busy with the stuff that pays the bills because, as of yet, the fiction is not. Besides, since moving into my grandmother's house I've been, ah, somewhat distracted." He seemed to be waiting for further clarification. She remained silent, picking up her fork once more.

Across from her he nodded, accepting her reserve. Glancing up at the light, he wrapped the cloth napkin around his fingers, reached up and loosened the bulb, effectively extinguishing the lamp. Only the candlelight remained to illuminate their table.

"Much better," he said.

"Much," she agreed.

"Me, not romantic," he scoffed, picking up his fork.

Perry smiled again. Her stomach rolled, hard. She felt giddy and blamed the martini, but when she looked at the glass she found it still nearly full. Ethan resumed his salad. Perry observed each bite, grateful for the subdued lighting that would keep her attention from his notice. It really had been a long time since she'd spent any time in a man's company outside business, let alone on a date. Dinner was a good start. She liked Ethan's friendliness, his confidence, and the fact he didn't seem entirely aware of how darned good he looked. An interesting man who also seemed interested in who she was, what she did, to whatever depth their brief relationship would allow. Still, she couldn't help but wonder how quickly the interest would vanish if he learned the truth.

Looking up suddenly, he said:

"I offer a history of the house. Prepared and bound, as part of the job. Did you know that?"

Perry shook her head. The soup arrived, giving off a delicious aroma. Perry leaned slightly closer to her plate and closed her eyes, inhaling deeply. "Wonderful," she whispered, then slitted her lids to view Ethan from behind her lashes. He watched the server walk away, not with any interest, but as if waiting for a chance to speak again. For the first time she noted the tiny laugh lines at his eyes and etched to either side of his mouth. They made her smile.

"So this report," she ventured, taking a spoonful of soup from the bowl's edge, where it was coolest, "you prepare it yourself?"

"Yes."

"Then you've learned a lot of the history of the house. I wonder if there is anything in your report I've not uncovered myself."

He swallowed, dabbing his mouth with his napkin. "Since I didn't know if I had the job the report's not complete. However, we could go over what I've gathered together, if you'd like."

The manner in which he tendered the offer seemed particularly personal. No hidden meaning lurked behind. His desire to spend time with her was obvious. Well, if nothing else, Ethan would be an ally when she needed one. When? If. She had meant if, of course.

Ethan extended his hand across the table. "Dance with me?" he asked.

With his eyes he indicated a back room where a

live trio had been playing soft music that did not interfere with the conversation and digestion of the diners. A small dance floor gleamed in the low light from several recessed overhead fixtures. On the dull reflective surface a lone couple swayed gently in each other's arms to the blended sound from the three musicians.

Perry hesitated, opening her mouth to tell him no, preparing to use as an excuse the fact their food would get cold. But her gaze shifted back to the two dancers, a man and woman intent on their embrace, the knowledge in each other, their unawareness anyone else existed in that moment.

Perry drew a deep breath, let it out. She knew she wanted that, too, even if only for the duration of a few slow minutes.

Slipping her hand into his, she stood, dropping her napkin onto the table beside her bowl. Ethan's free hand moved to rest lightly on her waist as he steered her toward the dance floor with a word to the server of their imminent return, and to leave the soup bowls there. Perry felt his fingers through her dress, through the light cotton fabric. His hand lay gently where her waist met her hip. His skin was warm.

For a moment Perry listened for the voice, telling her the things this man would do at its bidding. When the only voice greeting her was Ethan's own, she smiled and stepped into his arms. He drew her close.

"Your hair smells good," he murmured.

"Good shampoo," she whispered with a laugh.

He smelled good, too, like freshly laundered clothing. Beneath she scented his own masculinity and closed her eyes, breathing deeply his fragrance, a man of flesh and blood.

## Chapter Six

Perry turned the key in the kitchen lock, feeling the vibration from the moving tumblers through her fingertips. Shoving open the door, she stepped quickly inside, pushing it shut behind her. For a moment she held her breath, listening for any sounds in the empty house. Walking from the car, the distant creek had seemed intolerably loud, almost menacing. Here, behind thick, stone walls, she heard the mantle clock ticking, cooling timbers settling, the refrigerator's gentle, mechanical hum. No creek. No voice. No thought invading her mind. Only the memory instilled by a remarkably pleasant, exciting evening in Ethan's company.

Relaxing, she hung her keys on the peg beside the door. She hummed as she crossed the floor, remembering Ethan's hand in the small of her back as they danced, his breath across her cheek, his voice rumbling in her ear. Contented, Perry climbed the stairs, pausing outside her grandmother's old room. Looking into the darkened space, she realized she only remembered her grandfather vaguely, and she thought most memories came from photographs. Flicking on the light switch, she gazed about the room she hadn't touched except to clean since her grandmother had gone into the hospital. Everything needed to be sorted through and packed up. Perry would much rather have left it undisturbed, almost as if her grandmother would return any moment. But she couldn't leave things go like that. She needed to take responsibility.

Sighing, Perry turned off the light and headed toward her own room, but halted in the hall only a few feet away. Rushing back into her grandmother's bedroom, she slapped her hand along the wall in fumbling haste to turn the light back on. Rushing to the rug centered on the floor, she circled, searching for whatever had belatedly sent alarm signals dancing into her brain.

Everything looked to be in order, yet a chill stippled her arms, drifted up her bare legs beneath her dress's fluttering hem. Could he be here and she not know it?

No. She had no sense of him. None at all.

Catching movement from the corner of her eye she spun to the window, staring at the billowing curtain. She realized she ought to be reassured. Fat chance. That window had been closed. Perry rarely opened it, afraid she would forget and rain would get in to ruin the window seat and the handmade quilt folded on top. Breath straining through her nostrils, Perry rushed to the window and yanked down the sash, scrabbling across the top for the latch. The drift of curtain subsided abruptly.

She stood motionless for a moment, waiting for her racing pulse to slow, listening to the noises in the house. She hated that the smallest creaking in a floorboard should suddenly sound threatening. She didn't frighten easily, and had no plan to become a timid creature at this stage in her life.

Calming, it occurred to her Ethan had probably opened the window while checking the house. After all, she hadn't been with him every second. Any creak or groan or ticking clock meant nothing but an old house settling and an ancient timepiece marking the hours.

Even the voice meant nothing, she thought with determination, if she refused it.

But could she, if he sought her out again?

She had to. If not for her own sake, then for Ethan's. She liked him. She enjoyed his company. He needed protection, to be kept free from the clouded world she'd wandered so willingly into.

Having lost some elation over the evening, Perry headed to her room. Shutting the door, she turned on the small television set for noise before stepping from her dress and into an enormous, soft tee shirt. She climbed into bed, tucking the sheet under her chin. Rolling onto her side, she pulled her knees up until she felt like a ball beneath the covers. Tonight, she would sleep with the tv on.

In the morning Perry rose with a determination that everything return to normal, to the way it had been before the three lost days. She would try not to think about what had taken place, because remembering meant wanting, and she couldn't want that. Not anymore. She never should have.

She interpreted the fact she'd slept without interruption as a positive sign. Even prior to the lost time she'd not been sleeping well, disturbed by half-remembered images, waking often, sweat-soaked, disoriented. Aroused. How had she let those conditions go on without questioning them? Maybe Ethan's doctor friend was right. Maybe she'd picked up some strange illness. Was hallucinating even. Nevertheless, the possibility an illness could create such powerful hallucinations did nothing to ease her mind.

Carrying a plate with buttered toast and a cup filled with steaming coffee, Perry headed into the small room off the kitchen she had temporarily set up as her office. Temporarily threatened to become permanent, yet the choice had its benefits. Golden sun filled the room in the morning and many of the potted plants and herbs her grandmother had so lovingly tended had managed to survive Perry's less competent care to scent the air with wonderful, green fragrance. Setting plate and mug on the desk, Perry woke up her laptop and sat down. The papers she'd been working from littered the desk's left side. Mug to her mouth, Perry flipped through the untidy pile in an  attempt to return them to the order she'd had them the day before.

No. Not the day before. The last time she'd looked at these papers had been Monday morning. Monday morning when she'd decided she needed a break, and went out for some air before the day became too humid...

Lowering the mug carefully, Perry pushed back from the desk and stood. She walked to the window to stand in the warm sunshine, eyes closed, shoving her shaking hands deep into her pockets. In the living room the mantel clock whirred, ready to chime the hour. The sound made her jump. She bit her lip.

She remembered *he* called to her by a name, a name not her own, it seemed to her now, yet she knew she'd answered him. Not consciously at first, aware only the wind had taken on an unusual cadence, stirring the leaves, There'd been a sudden absence of birdsong, too. Yes. How suddenly the morning chorus had stopped, and the sounds from the far-off highway as well, vanishing in the subliminal calling that had made her recognize a yearning for companionship, for a man to be with. Made her recognize that need, then amplified it like breath on an ember.

For three days she had been almost literally aflame. She had no other words to describe what she recalled. An urgent, vibrant desire raging through the silver twilight of the cave behind the falls and on into the thunderous night without ceasing, without recognition of time's passing. Even now she trembled in memory, both in fear and in lust.

Pressing her forehead to the glass, she clenched her hands into fists in her pockets, nails digging deep. Her tee shirt vibrated with her pounding heart.

When she'd finally put her dress back on and wandered out into the sunlight she knew she would have drowned when she dropped into the creek, if not for Ethan's fortuitous presence  nearby. In that moment, she hadn't possessed the will or the strength to save herself.

Lifting her lids, Perry gazed blankly through the curtainless window. Did one call a priest for something like this?  She hadn't been raised a Catholic, but she didn't think it would matter. Yet, could she bring herself to confess the details? Admit what had taken place?  Alarmingly, part of her clung to those timeless hours lost in exquisite arousal with savage, irrational possessiveness.

Yanking her fists from her pockets, Perry rubbed her eyes. Returning to her desk, she picked up the coffee cup and took a swallow from its contents.

"Oh, yuk."

The steaming brew had gotten ice cold while she'd been jettisoned back in memory. Sticking it in the microwave wasn't an option. Time to dump it down the sink and get a new one.

As she stepped from the potting room, she heard the mantel clock chime the last gentle note of the nine o'clock hour. She looked down into the mug in her hands. Cream and coffee had separated, congealed, as if the cup had been sitting on her desk for hours, rather than the sixty seconds or so it took the clock to signal the time while she stood by the window.

Hurrying back to her computer, she checked the day and time. Friday, 9:02. No lost time, then. Thank God. But what was up with the coffee?

Frowning, she carried the mug to the sink and dumped the contents. She lifted her gaze to the window. Outside, the sun shone in a warm haze over the grass, unlike the house, which seemed suddenly dim and cold. Oppressive. Maybe if she just went out for a quick walk, she'd feel better.

She'd gotten halfway down the flagstone walk behind the kitchen before recognizing her actions were nearly an exact repeat of that other morning, four days earlier.

"Crap."

Stopping dead, she listened, remembering the breeze in the leaves. Today, leaves hung limply in the humid air, yet she could still hear the whisper through the foliage. She felt the noise on her skin like a feather-light caress. The beginning of seduction.

Her eyes closed in memory. She tipped her head, exposing her neck to the sensation of movement, non-existent sweat trickling along her skin. Her respiration stilled, breath held for one heartbeat, two. Beneath her clothes her flesh quickened in response.

"No."

Jerking her head down, Perry tugged on her clothing. Anger replaced arousal.

"No."

Hurrying back up the pathway to the house, she went inside only long enough to grab her purse and keys, and then headed for her car.

## *Chapter Seven*

The clacking adding machine drowned out the drone from the window air conditioner as Ethan tallied figures for his estimate for Perry. At a tangent, he wondered who really used these antiquated devices anymore. Wondered, too, why he needed to run the figures through for the third time.

As if he had any need to wonder. His mind kept wandering to the night before. He wouldn't have expected it, and yet he couldn't deny the chemistry. He just needed to keep his head where it belonged.

Swiveling in his chair, Ethan added the new figures to the form on the monitor. Almost done. Then he could call her and offer to bring it over.

Later, of course, as he needed to get on the road shortly to meet Tom at the job site. He knew it was too soon to ask her to dinner again, but maybe she'd consider meeting him for coffee or something.

Mouth curving, Ethan flipped through the catalog at his elbow, searching for the right hardware. Beyond the air conditioner's racket, the work trailer seemed unusually silent. Ruthie had a family issue at home and had asked to work from there, so all calls directly to the office had been forwarded to her. Calls must have been at a minimum, or at the very least didn't require his response, because his cell phone sat on the desk without a single chirp. Even Tom had chosen to give him some peace for a few hours.

Jotting down several part numbers, Ethan made a notation to double check the price. He turned his head as the metal steps outside the door rattled. Through the jalousie window he saw someone approach and lift a hand to knock.

"Come on in," he called, before a fist made contact. The door opened.

"Hi."

Ethan lungs deflated in a rush. "Perry! Good morning."

He stood. Perry remained in the open doorway, eyeing him as if her welcome were anything but certain. She looked just about as sexy as the night before, despite being dressed in a baggy tee shirt and a pair of jeans with a hole in one knee. He'd never been particularly fond of red hair or freckles, either, but hers moved him to thoughts he hoped she couldn't read in his face.

"Come all the way in," he said, stepping around her to pull the door closed behind. He scented her hair, her skin, as he reached past her for the door handle. She smelled good to him in a way that was entirely visceral, causing a gut reaction that seemed premature considering their brief  relationship. He moved away to the water cooler.

"Drink of water?  Coffee?  I could make a fresh pot. Sit down. It's great to see you."

"I don't want to interrupt anything," she said, taking a tentative seat on the client chair against the wall.

He indicated the office.  "Nothing going on here. Except your estimate. It's almost done. Is that why you came?"

She looked around, then back at him. "I...no. Well, yes, sort of. If it was finished, that was a bonus. I just needed to get out of the house and figured I'd try and find your place on the chance it was done. And that doesn't sound right either. I don't want you to think I didn't want to see you." She subsided with a puffing breath, looking down at her hands clasped tightly in her lap, the knuckles showing white.

Holding a cup midway to his lips, Ethan frowned. "Everything all right?"

She nodded. Unconvincingly.

Setting the water on his desk, Ethan sat down, scooting his wheeled chair closer to hers. "Are you sure?"

She looked up, pale eyes wide. "Yes. Really, I am. I had a great time last night, Ethan, but I wouldn't normally just show up at your business. I did need to get out of the house for a break, and I am curious about the estimate, but the fact I enjoyed your company makes me feel like I'm stalking you by coming here. Crazy, huh?"

He laughed, shaking his head. "Not at all. I'm glad you came and I promise I don't feel threatened by it at all," he added with a wink. "Unless you're planning on killing my rabbit or something."

"What? You have a rabbit?"

"No. I have fish."

"Oh. I have plants. Plants that belonged to my grandmother. I used to have a dog, a retriever, but my ex-husband took custody of Boxer."

"Huh," he said, smiling at her. He watched her mouth curve and thought about kissing it. Her lips looked soft and like they might just fit perfectly against his own.

Abruptly, he pushed his chair back over to the desk.

"Would you like to see what I have so far?"

She got up and came over to stand beside him, leaning on her hands on the desktop. He tried not to be distracted by her arms and their lovely, strong shape. With a few clicks of the mouse, he brought up a series of photographs to start with, showing her by example what he expected to accomplish.

"Is all of this your work?"

"It is."

"Beautiful. You are a stickler for detail, Ethan."

His skin shifted at the way she said his name. Quickly, he brought up several more photos. "These are the pictures I took last night of your place before I left. You can see some of the architectural details are very similar to what I just showed you. And that the porch is not original to the structure. I still need to get a look under it before I can make a final—"

"Wait. What's that?"

Her arm shot past, finger extended to the monitor's right side. Taking her hand, he moved it aside, leaning forward to look.

"I...don't know," he said, squinting at the narrow, irregular, white oblong smearing the edge of the frame. He knew what it looked like. During certain extracurricular studies in college, students constantly came forward with similar photographs, thinking they'd captured something unearthly on film. Ninety-nine point nine percent of the time all they'd captured was dust or reflection or a piece of lint or hair right against the camera lens. The school hadn't been handing out degrees in paranormal studies, of course. They gathered more like a club, headed by a professor. It had been fun, enlightening, prompted serious consideration sometimes. Ethan glanced over at Perry. "A spec of something on my lens, I guess. Why?"

Her fingers circled into a fist, shoving deep into her pocket. Ethan shifted focus to her face, the freckles standing out on cheeks gone pale.

"Why?" he repeated.

She shrugged. "No reason. I thought maybe something was hanging down from the porch ceiling. Another thing to add to your list of repairs."

"Nah," he said, "it's nothing. Look, the next photo doesn't have it."

"Okay."

He glanced at her sidelong, at her stiff stance. Was she someone who tended to get spooked by the possibility of the supernatural? She'd grown up in the house, she'd said, so surely she would have encountered something as a child, if anything existed. He smiled at her in reassurance.

"Your grandmother left you a very nice home. It appears to be sound. A little restoration and the place will be a beauty."

"Thanks."

"Do you want to see the damages now, or wait until I've completed the estimate?"

She laughed, shaking her head. "You may as well hit me with the whole thing at once."

"I'll do that. Tonight? I've got to head out shortly to a job, and will probably finish the estimate up this afternoon."

"Tonight works."

"I'll stop by."

"Um..."

"Or we can meet somewhere. Coffee.  Or ice cream. You like ice cream?"

"Love it."

"All right. It's a date—no. Is it? Well, actually, yeah, it is a date. I'll call you?"

"Yes."

"Perfect."  He stood. Not for the first time, he realized he towered over her. He liked that. It made him feel like he could keep her safe from anything. Yet he knew there were certain things no one could be saved from, no matter how hard you tried.

"You okay?" Perry asked.

"Yup."

"I'll see you later, then."

He nodded, walking her to the door. As she reached for the handle he wanted to grab her, to pull her back in and hold her, protect her, not let her go. She'd seemed terribly vulnerable when she first showed up. But protecting her wasn't his job. He had to remember that.

She stepped outside, turning on the top step to face him. "Thank you," she said.

"For what?"

"For everything so far."

He stared at her a moment, feeling a coldness deep in his core begin to thaw. It had been a long time since he'd realized the ice was still there.

Lifting his hand, he hooked his fingers behind her neck, then bent to press his lips to her brow. She moved, raising her head, and he kissed her mouth next, feeling her tremble like the residual vibration from a powerful heartbeat. She stepped forward into the kiss with blood-sizzling responsiveness. Breathless, he broke away first.

"Well," he said.

She bit her lip. The sight of her doing that made him a little insane.

"I'll see you later?"

"You'll see me later," she said.

## Chapter Eight

*The moon, not yet full, rode high in the sky. He could see it, though, nearly round, the silver shine reflected in the shimmer from falling water. He watched the sphere move across the sky with anticipation, confused by his inability to clearly decipher time. How long had he been waiting for her here in the liquid dark? In their place, theirs alone where no other came. Yet he could not remember how many days had passed since last she had been here with him, her body warm and willing, belonging only to him despite the fact his brother had taken her to wife.*

*Frustration made him moan. He had imagined himself in the house, too, his brother's house where he did not dare any longer to go, and his brother there as well. Or had it been a dream? How odd. In his dream he could sense his brother's lust, that chaste man of God who denied his wife the pleasure of their marriage bed. Could feel it and sought to use it, as if he might step inside his brother's skin, his brother's life, become the man who possessed the one woman he wanted. The only woman he had wanted in life's entirety.*

*Pausing in his restless pacing he stared down at a vein running through the rock at his feet, a deep earthy red, like her hair. Hair so long and thick and bountiful she used it to cloak her nakedness from his eyes the first time he had come upon her bathing in the creek. Before, he had thought himself alone in his yearning, but he had seen the lust reflected in her eyes when she turned around and found him there, watching.*

*The water had been cold, so goddamn cold it had near shriveled him to nothing—that, and the fear he would be discovered standing in the stream beside this woman whose damp hair clung to her bare skin more jealously than a lover, the wife of his preacher-brother, the girl he had known since they both were children together and now grown to beauty beyond imagining. Opening for him without a word of protest or greeting. A subtle movement, the parting of her legs. An invitation that left him breathless and nearly weeping.*

*He could still remember. Yes, he could still remember.*

*What he did not recall was how they had come to be here, in the cleft behind the falls, but it did not matter. She had been his from that moment on, as he had always been hers.*

*Turning his head as a dog would when questing for a scent, he drew a deep breath and listened. She was here. No, not here, but nearby. The sound of her voice came faintly to him, an echo from long ago memory. Carrying across the pasture and into the woods, a thread of speech, a single word, and then nothing. How he heard her voice through the crashing noise from the falls he could not tell. But she had not come to him, even though she knew he waited. She had gone into the house instead. How he knew that he could not say either, except he could see her there in his mind's eye, moving like a wind drifting through the darkened rooms. Lonely, longing for him with a passion that made her tremble...*

*No. No!*

*Abruptly he threw himself against the cave wall, moaning, his pain soul-deep. Something had changed.*

*Something had changed.*

## *Chapter Nine*

Dashing her hand across her eyes, Perry swallowed hard, padding barefoot across the hardwood floor to the shut window. She desperately wanted the fresh night breeze blowing into the room, but she knew she would hear *his* voice in the creek's subdued noise, calling her by that other name.

The hair stood up on her nape and along her forearms at the thought, the calling to her, claiming her as his own. Her nipples grew hard beneath her shirt and she sucked in her breath, trying to push away the wanton longing she couldn't shake. She didn't want to feel this. It was wrong. Had always been wrong, and unnatural, and should have been scaring the living hell out of her. In her present state, the most she could manage was disgust.

At least she didn't feel him in the house. Hadn't since the day Ethan had come to look around. Resistance came at a price by night, though, nights both sleepless and straining.

Turning, she looked at the bedside clock. Ten o'clock. Two nights ago at this time she'd just been returning from a late run to Helen's Dairy Barn with Ethan, estimate in hand and the memory of a very enjoyable evening uppermost in her mind. And then the barrage had begun. The seeking, the distant calling. By morning she felt as battered as a cornstalk under the flail.

Perry made a sound in her throat. Desperation, maybe even fear at last. The phone rang.

Through the third ring she stared at the night stand as if finding a ringing telephone totally alien, and then she snatched at the receiver and pressed it to her ear. "Hello?"

"Perry, did I wake you?"

Ethan. She reveled in his voice's deep timbre, the slow, easy drawl some Pennsylvania men, native-born, possessed.

"Perry?"

"Yes, Ethan. Sorry. I heard you. You didn't wake me. I was just lying here with the television on," she hedged.

He hesitated before responding. "Are you feeling okay, then?  I was stretched out, too, watching the ten o'clock news. For some reason I started to worry about you."

Perry envisioned him spread at his length on a deep cushioned sofa, his feet crossed at the ankles, one arm hooked behind his head, a television on across the room with the volume muted. She smiled into the phone. "It's nice of you to worry about me," she said.

"We're not exactly strangers anymore.  Are you sure you're all right?  No more fainting?"

"None," she said.

"You're not just saying that to shut me up, are you?"

"I have no desire to shut you up."

Perry sat down on the mattress edge. She dug her bare toes into the small area rug beneath her feet.

"Good. I'm going to ask one more question. Have you seen a doctor yet?"

Perry curled her toes a little deeper into the rug as if clinging onto a hazardous incline. "I..."  She hesitated. "I don't think I need to."

"You don't sound very sure."

Perry clutched the phone until her knuckles hurt, toes curled into commas in the rug's sturdy weave. *Time to jump*, she thought.

"Ethan," she said. "Do you believe in ghosts?"

She counted her heartbeats in the silence following her question. He didn't need to agree with her. She wasn't looking for that. She only hoped speaking the words aloud, grouping these particular sounds together, might somehow diminish their meaning.

"You're not laughing," she said at last.

"I wouldn't do that," he said. "I can tell you're serious."

Her eyes lifted to stare at the immobile curtain and the window glass reflecting the room's contents, ignoring the sounds outside.

"I am serious."

"Understood. And I do believe in ghosts. Or at least I spent a lot of time searching for proof of them, many years ago. Why do you ask? Has something happened?"

"Yes." She hardly recognized the strangled syllable issuing from her mouth.

"Tonight?"

"Not yet."

He was silent again.

"Ethan?"

"What do you mean 'not yet'?"

Dipping her head, she took a deep breath. "It's hard to explain. Except to say that nothing's happened yet."

"Is it a residual thing, then? Something that repeats itself on a regular basis?"

Perry frowned. "I don't think I understand."

"Some hauntings are considered residual, where an event seems to repeat itself over and over and it really doesn't matter if you're there are not. Other events are more interactive."

She stood up, began to pace around the room.

"We'll call it interactive, okay?"

"Really?" He sounded intrigued, not as if he thought her crazy at all. "All right, then. Are you afraid?"

She paused in her pacing to consider. Was she afraid? Or was she more frightened of herself, of control's loss, her synergistic reaction to a being she ought to believe didn't exist at all? Still, her present conversation with Ethan made it seem like her world hadn't totally tilted off its axis.

If only she could avoid telling him the whole truth.

"Sometimes I am," she admitted.

His breath left him in a rough exhalation, followed by what sounded like his stubbled jaw across the mouthpiece. Unmistakably, she heard the noise of a zipper sliding.

"What are you doing?" she asked.

"Getting dressed."

"You weren't dressed?"

"After ten at night? Hardly. My social life isn't such that I would normally be going out again. However, I thought I might come over for a little bit."

"Now?"

"Hold on," he said, and put the phone down. A second later he picked it back up. "Yes, now, if that's all right? I know it could probably wait until tomorrow, but you might want to talk about what's happening while it's running fresh in your mind. I'd like to hear about it."

"Are you an expert on this sort of thing?" she inquired archly. "You said something about looking for proof when you were younger. Don't tell me you're one of those ghost hunter people."

"Nothing wrong with 'those ghost hunter people', as long as they approach the case with a healthy skepticism."

"I'm not a case."

"I didn't mean you were. However, I think I know enough to help you try and gain some understanding regarding your situation. And to be truthful," he concluded, "I'm curious as hell."

"Well, at least you're honest."

"Always," he said.

*Well, then,* she thought, *you're one up on me.*

"I'll be waiting for you," she said, and hung up.

## *Chapter Ten*

Pulling up outside the house, Ethan parked in nearly the exact place he had before and exited his truck. Above the house heavy clouds nearly blotted out the sickle moon visible earlier in the night. No lights had been put on at the front of the house, although he saw faint illumination behind the curtains in a window upstairs. The back light shone over the pathway and the kitchen itself appeared fully illuminated, the interior glow spreading over the ground outside through the window by the sink. Ethan strode across the grass to the flagstone walkway, mounting the single step onto the low concrete slab before the kitchen door. Lifting his hand, he prepared to rap on the doorframe with his knuckles.

Slowly his fingers opened, lowering onto his thigh as he leaned a little forward, peering through a dusty screen and the large glass pane beyond. When he first walked up he thought he had seen Perry moving around the kitchen. The kitchen, though, was unoccupied, a kettle on the stove emitting a forceful rush of steam. He could hear its piercing whistle muted only slightly by the windowpane. Inside the house the summons had to be annoyingly shrill. Concerned, he knocked once in hasty announcement before he turned the knob and stepped over the threshold.

The door swung back against him, the edge catching his forearm and almost knocking the manilla folder he carried from his hand. Cool, damp precursor to the coming storm, a vigorous gust blew at him through the house, no doubt from an open window somewhere, strong enough to sweep the hair back from his brow before racing in an eddying circle across the lawn at his back, lifting and scattering the hay spread at some point to mulch a newly seeded patch.

Stepping inside, he turned on his heel to shut the door and found himself shouldering it against a change in the wind's direction. At this peculiar but not infrequent phenomenon, Ethan realized the coming storm would likely be a nasty one.

Dropping the manilla folder onto the table, he strode quickly to turn off the gas beneath the kettle.

"Perry?"

Ethan removed the kettle from the heated burner. It had continued to mutter with a staccato chirp. Returning to the door he bent to gather the debris blown inside by the wind and tossed it in the trash.

"Perry?"

Brushing his hands on his jeans, he tipped his head to listen.

"Perry?" he called again.

A floorboard creaked above his head, a faint crack and vibration. In that old house he knew the sound could have been generated from any point above. Exiting the kitchen, he announced conversationally that he had turned off the teakettle. No one answered him.

Bounding up the steps two at a time he called Perry's name again, heading for the room where he had seen the light. Two doors down, however, he abruptly felt the full force from the rising wind tugging at his shirt. Halting on the threshold, he looked to the open sash. A figure stood on the window seat, silhouetted dark against the night, arms wide, hands pressed flat-palmed to the deep wall on either side. A garment billowed in the rushing air, whipping long, auburn  hair into a tangled mass.

"Perry!"

Horizontal lightning embedded deep in the clouds flashed across a face turned toward the room's center, not the night outside, startling him to no small degree. Perry's briefly illuminated features contorted in an incomprehensible emotion that did not seem wholly to be fear. She remained unaware of his presence.

He ran across the room, grasping her about the waist with both hands. A small cry escaped her and she released her hold on the window frame, toppling toward him. He caught her under the arm before she fell. Through the thin fabric of an oversized tee shirt he could feel the heat off her skin, as warm as if fevered.

"Perry, it's Ethan," he said at her blank and startled look.

She shuddered. Her eyelids lowered, the thick lashes a smudge on her cheekbones. He fully expected her to go limp in another faint, but after a moment she opened her pale eyes and focused on his own.

"Ethan," she said, "I didn't hear you."

"Nor the teakettle, apparently," he said, studying her face for strain. "What were you doing in the window?"

Perry turned, pulling away from his grasp. She brought both hands up along her arms above the elbow and hugged herself as if cold, which was entirely possible. The rising wind had ushered in cooler temperatures.

"I was going to put on some clothes before you got here, I swear," she murmured. "I don't make a habit of appearing half-naked before men I barely know."

"Just this one," he said.

"It would seem so."

He drew a deep breath, concerned by her tone as well as the irrelevant conversation. Reaching out, he stroked the tangled hair from her shoulder and dropped his hand to his side.

"Would you mind very much telling me what the hell is going on here?"

In another lightning flash he saw her bite down on her lip, hard. She nodded and sat down on the window seat. Ethan closed the window, then lowered himself beside her, stretching his legs out.

"You can see the creek from this window," she said. "I could always hear it, but I never realized you could see it before. Can you imagine? All these years and I never noticed that."

Ethan turned for a better look. From the high vantage point one could see through the trees a dull gleaming motion, no more than a spectral glimmering between the boles and shadowed foliage. No doubt in a time of full moon the water would be brighter, but in the approaching weather's gloom it moved like pewter reflected in glass.

Dipping his head to ask her a question, Ethan immediately forgot what he had been about to say. The heat of her reached him where he sat, making it momentarily difficult to concentrate.

"Perry—"

"He's out there," she stated in a hoarse whisper.

Ethan started, glancing again to the deeply

shadowed woods and the hint at the creek's deceptively slow-moving surface. He remembered well the water's force against him, impeding his progress as if it sought to pull him down with Perry in his arms.

Angling his head he glanced down at her face, the gentle profile, the mouth curving in something less than humor.

"Who?"

"My ghost," she said.

Once again he raised his gaze to the murky view outside the window. She sounded very sure. He thought again about the years in which he had volunteered as part of the study into the paranormal when still in college. Although they hadn't proved the factual existence of spiritual entities in residence, neither had they disproved all events. Much in the world remained unexplained, making him intensely curious still. Perry, on the other hand, did not seem curious at all, but most definite in her statement. Plainly, her experience disturbed her, but he couldn't be certain she felt any fear. In fact, when he looked at her, the gleam in her pale eyes appeared anything but timid.

"Where did you see this ghost? In the outbuilding? How do you know it's there now?"

She drew a deep breath, exhaling through her nose. Outside the window the trees began to thrash beneath the wind. In the distance, still too far away to be anything more than a pulse in the clouds, lightning flashed again.

"It called me," she said. "He called to me, from down by the creek."

The hair lifted on Ethan's arms, his nape. "Called to you how? By name? How did you hear him?"

Her chin tilted up, head tipping back. Her eyes closed. Ethan suddenly wanted very much to take her in his arms. It would have been an easy thing to do. He would not even have had to move, just reach out and draw her against him. He forced himself to keep his hands at his sides.

"Like that," she said.

He leaned forward, frowning. "What do you mean?"

"He said, 'I can make him take you in his arms. It will be a simple task to undertake.'"

Ethan bolted up from the seat. Stalking to the room's center, he stood with his back to her, wrestling with the words she'd spoken.

"I'm sorry," she said behind him. "I actually didn't want to tell you, but I think I have to."

What the devil was she saying? That this spirit, this entity, sought in some way to manipulate his actions? Why? He had felt nothing—well, not nothing. He'd felt exactly what she told him the spirit had said to her.

In an attempt to calm his frantically circling thoughts, he paced to the far wall and back, breathing deeply. He halted a single stride from

Perry, arms folded across his chest.

"Ghosts, or whatever you wish to call them, cannot hurt you. They cannot control physical objects. Not in that way. Their thoughts, if they have them, are relegated to the past where they dwelled, not in the present. Or, if they are interacting in the present, they still cannot control *you.*"

Perry watched him from shadowed eyes, her countenance combining hope and disagreement. "What about the stories where objects float and people have blankets yanked off them in their sleep?"

"I am aware of no occurrences scientifically proven to date," he stated firmly, more for his own benefit at the moment than hers.

She shook her head, her hair tumbling about her shoulders.

"Do you need scientific proof? What I just said to you startled you considerably, and I can only imagine why. There's more, Ethan. A lot more. But I don't think I'm ready to talk about it."

Perry sat with her legs close together and her hands folded with unusual primness in her lap. For all her stillness, though, she seemed to vibrate. He could feel her energy like an electrical charge held captive within an insulating sheath.

"Are you all right?" he asked.

She nodded, looking away from him.

"Ghosts can't hurt you," he repeated. "They

cannot touch you."

Her gaze shot up to meet his, clearly reflecting her doubt, then returned to mutely studying her interlaced fingers.

"They can't," he said. "Your own fears, however, are a different story."

"Yes," she said, "I know."

Lifting his hand, Ethan rubbed the smooth place between his brows. Could what she suggested be possible?  More likely, she had read his intentions in his body language and spoken them aloud. But to what end?  It seemed less likely she would be involved in games like that. She impressed him as open and honest and, yes, sane. Though he'd possessed a momentary doubt regarding the latter, it had been quickly dispelled.

"Can you sense the spirit still?" he asked.

"No. Not now."

He nodded, oddly relieved. "Do you ever feel it here in the house?"

Slowly she stood up. The tee shirt shifted about her body, sliding along her thighs. He knew even without close examination she was naked beneath. He deliberately steered his mind clear from that circumstance.

"I did the other day," she answered. "For the first time. It was while you were here."

"And it spoke to you then?"

She nodded.

"What did it say?"

She stared at him for a long moment. His gaze drifted to her mouth. He briefly contemplated what it would be like to kiss her. Her lips looked soft and full and agile. Parted slightly, he could see the exposed and gleaming edge to her teeth.

Abruptly, he returned his attention to her steady stare, doubting himself, now, questioning his own natural inclinations. He didn't like it.

"Is it—"

"No. He's not here now. I don't know why, but he isn't. As to what he said to me the other day," she stated quietly, "you really don't want to know."

Ethan stood silently, unwilling to comprehend. Something had been occurring in Perry's life, but what exactly that something might be he couldn't fathom. His experience with such matters had only been limited to his college years. And he had never heard of anything like this.

"Go get dressed," he said. "I'll finish preparing the tea you started."

*Chapter Eleven*

Perry clutched the cup filled with steaming chamomile tea between both hands. Across from her, seemingly recovered from revelation's shock, Ethan had opened a folder he'd brought with him and began spreading certain documents over the tabletop. The overhead kitchen fixture, usually less than flattering, treated his handsome countenance with uncustomary grace.

"The Historical Society permits me access to a great many documents not allowed to the general public," he said. "I have more research to conduct regarding your home, but what we have here is probably the skeletal history of the last one hundred and fifty years. The house is a good deal older. I'm still working on that."

Perry nodded, sipping her tea with her elbows on the table. It had pleased her to watch Ethan moving about her kitchen, making tea for her and for himself. He had not hesitated to search through the cabinet for cookies, which were now arranged haphazardly on a plate on the table between them.

"Everything in here is a copy of what the Society possesses. There are some letters, death certificates, bills of sale, certain chronologies compiled early in this past century. Some old photographs. People have, naturally, passed away in the house over the years, but from what I can tell they were none of them unexpected nor violent, although they don't have to be, I suppose. Still, there's more to be studied. I've been a little short on time these past few weeks."

Extending her hand, Perry drew a photograph nearer, spinning it so it faced in the proper direction for perusal. "When was this taken?" she asked.

Reaching across, Ethan flipped the corner up. "Nineteen-twenty-four," he said. "No porch yet, although I believe it was probably added on soon after. And there's a second huge oak in the front, see? But I didn't even see a stump when I was here in the daylight."

Perry made a face. "There isn't one. A lot has changed over the years. Look beyond the roof line. There are no trees to be seen at all. I guess it was all field then."

"Either that," he said, turning the photo around so he could see where she pointed, "or they were just smaller. Most of those in the back may have been saplings at the time this was taken."

Picking up a cookie, Perry bit into it. "What else?" she questioned around a mouthful of crumbs.

"Here's the barn around the same time. It's actually in better shape now. See? And here, this is an old John Deere tractor in front of that shed that needs to be taken down. I haven't yet figured out who the fellow sitting on it is, though. And this one is of a young boy fishing at the creek, taken sometime in the early fifties. I—what?"

"Nothing. Even that's changed. The sides are steeper now, unless that was taken somewhere I don't know about."

"No, you've probably been right there. The constant flow of water erodes the banks. I'm sure you've probably noticed changes just from these recent storms we've had. Some of the places I've worked I've found evidence that the bed of a creek has shifted over time to run another course entirely."

Compressing her lips, Perry nodded again. "Are there any of the waterfall?"

"Not that I've found," he said. "Why?"

"I think that's where he, uh, well he doesn't live there, of course. But he exists connected to it, somehow."

Ethan sat up, interested.

"How do you know?"

How did she know? A legitimate question, but one she would have difficulty answering. If she told him that she would have to explain all of it. A blush crept up her throat to her cheeks at the very idea. In addition, she suspected he might be appalled at the knowledge she had permitted what had taken place. Permitted?  It was not as though she just let it happen to her. She had wanted every moment of that strange, unearthly passion.

"I just...I just do," she faltered and rose abruptly from her chair. Crossing to the counter she pulled the honey pot close, dropping a dollop into her cooling tea. The thick golden liquid sank to the bottom of the cup in a congealed mass. Behind her Ethan sat in silence. After a moment she heard him shuffling the papers, returning them to the folder.

"This will keep until a better time," he said. "Let's go sit where it's more comfortable for a few minutes. If you want to talk to me, you can. And if not, we'll just finish our tea and I'll explain some of the procedures you can expect in the next few months with the house. Then I'll go home. Okay?"

Perry closed her eyes. No, it wasn't okay. Now that he was here she wanted him to stay, despite the peril present if he did. It wasn't as if she wanted to share her bed with him. Not right now. She just wanted his companionship, his presence in her home. She wondered if he would sleep on the couch if she asked him. She had a feeling he would, but it would be damned uncomfortable presenting that scenario to him. She wondered as well what would happen if *he* returned in the night. That, she could not risk.

The kitchen light flickered just as thunder rumbled overhead. She hadn't noticed the lightning with the room so glaringly illuminated. At the table, Ethan swore. She spun about in time to see him sliding back his chair.

"I don't know what I was thinking," he said. "I left the window open in the truck. I'll be right back."

She watched him rush out the door with the unnerving perception he would not be coming back. That Ethan, in point of fact, had already gone from her life, leaving her devastatingly alone, a feeling akin to what she'd experienced beneath the falls when *he*—the entity—had departed. She knew, with sudden clarity, this emotion was not her own.

"Go away," she said, squeezing her eyes shut and clutching the cup's handle so tightly she thought it might snap. "Leave me alone!"

She received no reply.

A scant two minutes later Ethan returned, shaking himself like a dog. The shoulders on his shirt were soaked, as well as his hair. At his back before he shut the door Perry witnessed large raindrops pounding the flagstone walk.

"Ye gods!" he cried theatrically. "T'is a night not fit for man nor beast!"

Despite her misgivings, Perry laughed. "I'll grab the plate and your tea," she said. "Your towel is still hanging on the knob of the powder room. I think you need it."

With grunting assent, he snatched the towel from the door and dried his hair, following her from the room with the terry draped about his shoulders. Switching on a lamp as she passed, Perry sat to one side of the sofa. Ethan hesitated only a moment before seating himself at the opposite end, stretching out long legs in blue jeans, crossing his feet at the ankle. Lifting his mug to his thigh, he settled his other arm across the back of the couch. He looked, Perry decided, very much at ease.

"There's something about this room," he said. "I like it. I like the way it feels."

Perry looked around, at the eggshell paint on the plastered walls, the outdated furniture, the books and photos and knickknacks. For a moment she saw the room the way she used to see it, years ago as a child living with her mother and her grandmother, three generations of Madison women together under one roof.

"Me, too," she answered him. "Always have."

He nodded.  Behind him lightning flashed, bright on the window panes and swiftly followed by a long rumble of thunder. The aging glass rattled. Once again the lights flickered. Wordlessly Ethan switched his cup to his other hand and reached to the side table, picking up the long lighter Perry kept there and touching its flaming tip to two candles.

"Just on the off chance we might need them," he murmured, resuming his former position. "It's not like I'm romantic or anything."

Smirking at the jest, Perry settled into her corner, tight against the cushions. The lights promptly went out. She made a small noise, less in consternation than exasperation, and tucked her feet up under her. In between the vivid bursts of electrical charge outside from the storm, the candles flickered, their light reflecting off the ceiling rosy in hue.

"There's one thing you never asked me," Ethan said.

"Asked you about what?" She didn't want to talk about the whole ghost thing. Not right this minute. She felt absurdly contented; figured it a reaction to Ethan's comfortable self-assurance, but she didn't care. The peace she felt in his presence was something she needed. With the lights out, she had the sense she'd been cocooned in safety. She wanted to hold onto that for a little while.

"Why I went into the woods that first day, when you didn't answer the door."

"I figured you were nosy," she said with a smile.

He chuckled. "Maybe I was. But when I saw you—"

"God, I can't even begin to think what you must have thought of me, then," she said. "Finding me in the creek like that, my fainting. Carrying me back here. I'm sorry."

"Stop apologizing. Especially now. I think I

understand a bit better. I guess that's why you didn't see me."

Perry frowned, thinking for a minute. Had she not seen him at first? He was probably right. She'd been dazed, not really noticing her surroundings when she first came out from behind the falls, overwhelmed by all manner of sensation: lust, loss, a dull horror. She didn't want to think about it or talk about it. Not yet. She knew Ethan had come over to discuss the whole business, try to shine a light into her darkness. Upstairs, in her grandmother's room, they had touched on the truth. She wasn't quite ready to let him know more.

"Right," she said.

Taking a small sip from her tea cup, she set the dainty vessel on the coffee table, then tipped her head against the sofa back. Wind-flung rain pummeled the windows and fell with a slight hiss down the chimney to the empty hearth. The twin candle flames wavered in an errant draft, then held steady.

"Everything's so quiet," she said. "Even though you aren't aware of all the little noisy assaults in your daily life, you are once they're gone."

He murmured agreement, turning his body a little to rearrange the candles. He pivoted back. "This doesn't bother you?" he asked.

"What? Being without electricity? No. For one thing, it's only temporary. For another, I rather think I prefer it. I was born in the wrong age."

He smiled with his mouth closed, a deep creasing to either side indicating humor. His dark eyes reflected the candle flames. "Well, me too. But what I meant was something else."

Closing her eyes, Perry did not wait for him to rephrase his question. "If you mean am I bothered by sitting here in the dark in the middle of the night with you, the answer is no."

"That wasn't exactly what I meant either," he said after a moment, "but I'm glad to hear it."

Perry peered out at him through the lashes of her right eye. His smile had vanished. With his hand over the cup on his thigh, he stared at the fireplace or something in the vicinity. His face had lost all readable expression.

"What did you mean then?"

He sighed, the exhalation visible in his chest's extended rise and fall. "Does it bother you to be pursued by something you don't understand? Because that is what you are saying is happening, isn't it? This—this haunting, or whatever we're going to call it. This spirit is, for some reason, seeking you out."

Perry closed her right eye again, turning her head toward the ceiling.

"Yes," she said.

"Do you have any idea why that might be so?"

The reason, she mused, is because I am quite willing to give it what it wants.

"Perry?"

"Ultimately, no," she stated quietly. "I have no idea. I know what he wants from me, but I don't know why. There must be some reason, wouldn't you think?  Assuming the world is a logical place. I am, however, beginning to doubt the possibility that is the case."

He made a noise of amused agreement in his throat. "Do you think it might be something else?"

"If you're asking about my mental health," she murmured without opening her eyes, "I can't say. I feel sane enough."

He was silent for a few seconds while thunder boomed, then spoke again, his voice an echoing rumble. "What happened upstairs?  Why were you standing in the window like that?  And when you told me what it had said to you, did you know somehow what I was thinking?"

Perry considered his questions carefully. She knew she had come downstairs and put the kettle on before hurrying back up the stairs to dress. As she passed her grandmother's room some thought had drawn her inside to the window. She'd opened it. She was not certain why, but she did not think it had been of her own accord. After, she'd slipped into a state she did not care to describe to Ethan. It would have been very difficult to do so, even if she were inclined.

As to what Ethan had been thinking, if it was anything near to what *he* had shown her, what *he* had implied, well, that was a dilemma of its own.

"I had no idea what was going on in your mind," she said, avoiding a direct answer. "I guessed, however, by your reaction, that I was not far off the mark. But it wasn't me who knew."

"You're saying you believe this spirit might direct my actions somehow?"

"I don't know," she whispered. "I'm not saying it. He is. Can a spirit do something like that? You're a lot more knowledgeable about such matters. This is new territory to me."

When he didn't respond, Perry sat up. The flames at his elbow bent in a draft, casting his face in shadow. Perry started to lower her feet to the floor but stopped, drawing them back up under her. It was an old childhood fear, placing her feet on the floor in the dark beside the bed. She remembered she used to cry, so frightened that something beneath the frame and mattress would reach out and take hold of her. Recollection made her wonder why she hadn't been frightened of her present situation sooner.

Because, she told herself, lust could be a very powerful motivation to forget those things one ought to fear. In its own way that type of mindless passion resembled insanity, a madly fleeting, but consuming heat. One could burn to ash in it and never flinch away.

"Would you consider professional help?" he asked her. He reached back to the table without looking to slide one candle closer to the edge, lighting the area between them more clearly.

Perry studied his face, all gilded planes and shadow in stark contrast. "You really don't believe me then."

"I'm not suggesting a psychiatrist. Don't look so devastated. I'm still in contact with some of the people from college I was involved with doing research. I thought you might speak to one of them—"

"Research?"

"Into the paranormal. You know, those 'ghost hunter people' as you referred to them earlier. Although that wasn't exactly what we were doing. At any rate, this is way beyond my purview. In comparison to a great many I worked with I was just a dabbler. But if this is truly a case of a spiritual entity, you need someone who knows what they're talking about. And even if it's not, and it's something else, at least you'll know."

"Like, me being crazy," she said.

"You're not crazy, Perry. But you are scared. I can see it in your eyes. When did you sleep last?"

Perry sucked in her breath, then realized it was just a lucky guess, uttered in innocent concern. "A few days, I think," she said.

Ethan nodded, as if he suspected no less. "Would it help if I stayed here tonight? I can sleep on the couch—actually, you can sleep on the couch. I'll park my butt over there in that overstuffed chair with the ottoman. And in the morning when I'm at work I'll make a few calls to see what I can find out."

"You don't have to do that," she said in ineffectual protest. As if he had read her mind, he was doing exactly what she'd been afraid to ask him. She watched him lean forward, setting his mug beside her own before he stood, stretching with a low groan. Perry eyed him from beneath her lashes, waiting for the voice to speak to her, to taunt her, discovering only mental silence, blissful and complete.

"All right," she agreed. "Thank you."

"Blankets?" he asked, arching a single brow.

"In the chest over there," she indicated. "They'll smell like cedar though."

"I won't mind if you don't," he said, and walked over to lift the lid. Perry's gaze followed his lanky stride, held, turned away. A second later a lightweight blanket fell over her head, tossed there by Ethan's quick arm. Shaking it out to cover herself, Perry stretched out along the sofa cushions, pillowing her head on her forearm. Ethan crossed to the aforementioned chair and sank down into it. Unlacing his boots he dropped them to the floor, then snapped the blanket flat over his legs, his feet propped on the ottoman. The sudden gust of displaced air caused the candles to gutter deeply, but they remained lit.

Leaning back into the chair cushion, Ethan interlaced his fingers behind his head. His tee shirt sleeves slipped down, each arm flexed by position revealing a lean muscular curve, a notable evidence of natural strength. Perry dragged her gaze away, lifting her eyes to his to bid him goodnight. She found him watching her lazily, his long, dark lashes lowered, his smile languid.

"Go to sleep, Perry," he said.

Warmth rushed through her at his tone, nearly forcing her into a sweat beneath the light blanket covering her. Obediently, she burrowed her head closer onto her arm and closed her eyes. Across the room he made a noise, something low and ill-defined. She thought it might be laughter.

## Chapter Twelve

Lifting the one candle with life left in it, Ethan poured the wax pool into the other container. That wick had burned itself out a quarter of an hour ago. In his other hand he held the folder he'd retrieved from the kitchen, all copies and notes returned to it once more. He'd found nothing there to suggest a reason for a haunting. He hadn't thought so, but as he hadn't been able to sleep it did no harm to look through the information again. As the mantel clock chimed the hour delicately, Ethan bent to place the folder on the floor, looking across, and not for the first time, to where Perry lay sleeping.

At some point she'd rolled onto her back, the

light cover pulled up close to her chin, her cinnamon brown hair flung in a riotous mass over the pale sofa cushions. Despite her position her mouth remained closed, perhaps from the blanket's pressure rolled beneath her jaw. He knew if he were lying there he'd be snoring like an old hound. But then again, maybe not. No one had yet complained about him creating any nighttime disturbances to their slumber. It just seemed to him anyone sleeping on their back would have to go off into a chorus of strange noises at some point.

Come to think of it, Perry wasn't really making any sound at all. The storm had long ago passed on without the return of electrical service. The house remained relatively quiet, just the occasional squeak and groan, and water from the sodden leaves outside dripping earthward. Ethan stared hard to assure himself she breathed. Locating the evidence he turned away, his gaze drifting around the room.

He had meant what he said to Perry, about liking the room. He felt comfortable in it, at ease, almost as if it welcomed him. He supposed it might be something about the wall color, furniture placement, the little mementos of someone's life— not Perry's though–scattered about among the furnishings. Or, he mused, it might be Perry herself.

Once again he found his eyes drawn back to her. He studied her curved lashes, the rosy smudge coloring her cheek. While he had been sitting guard over her during the past hours he had been waiting for the strangeness of the circumstance to hit him. But it hadn't. Despite his reason for staying he experienced no major discomfort in that knowledge. The fact they were only recently acquainted didn't register at all. He felt very much as if he had known her far longer than a handful of days.

As for Perry, he had a notion she felt similarly. If she didn't, then she was a lot more trusting than he would have expected any woman to be in this day and age. Two dates and a business connection didn't mean she really knew him. Yet there she lay, sleeping as carelessly as if long accustomed to his guardianship and his presence.

He didn't quite know what to make of the tale she had told. He didn't doubt her belief in it, but he had never come across anything resembling contact like this. As for the spirit—if it truly existed—exercising any control over him, he had to admit he had initially been unnerved by her proclamation, but after time and consideration felt confident such a thing couldn't happen. His attraction to Perry was obvious to the both of them. Her words in her grandmother's bedroom had merely been coincidence or some unconscious recognition on her part.

Frowning, Ethan tossed back the loosely knit blanket lying across his legs and stood up, stretching his arms above his head. Come the morning he was going to be damned tired, he knew, but he really couldn't sleep. He had tried for about forty-five minutes and then given up. It would not, of course, be the first time he arrived at work bleary-eyed, although it didn't happen often. No doubt some of the guys would even have a crude remark or two to make, but he had never been one to talk much about his private life and fully intended to ignore any comments passed.

At a noise from Perry, Ethan lowered his arms, turning toward her. She had rolled onto her side again. The blanket lay in a heap on the floor. Despite all good intentions, Ethan's gaze tracked slowly from her head to her bent knees and back up again as he recalled the various stages of undress in which he had witnessed her since their initial meeting. If it had been intentional on her part it would have been downright laughable. As it happened, though, he felt no desire to laugh at all, but something totally to the contrary.

Remembering the way she looked when she walked into the restaurant two nights ago, wearing that simple cotton dress with her hair pulled back, legs and arms bare and not a skim of makeup on her face, he felt something inside roll over and spring to life, and not wholly in a sexual context even if his body was, at the moment, betraying him to the contrary. Giving a sharp tug to the sudden restriction in his jeans, Ethan crossed the floor to the window. He hooked his arm over the frame and leaned his forehead against the cool pane, peering out into the sodden wee hours of the morn.

A lone firefly clung to the glass, body pulsating with neon green light. Ethan stared at the tiny creature, trying to recall what he'd heard about them. Didn't the female carry the chemical that caused it to glow, to attract a mate? A firefly's version of seduction. Pretty blatant. With a display like that, though, a guy didn't have to worry about mistaking the signals.

He didn't think when the time came he would have to worry about mistaking any signals with Perry either. She possessed a certain something, an honest, wholesome sensuality. No matter what she did it managed to shine through like her own glowing chemical. When she was ready, she would turn to him and let him know straight out. She seemed like a woman who claimed her man in no uncertain terms. He liked the idea of that very much.

Of course, first they had to get her through this mess, and there was that little matter of the work he needed to perform for her on the house. He'd never dated a client before. If the guys were going to bust his ass about a noticeable lack of rest, how much more fodder for their speculation would they gain upon witnessing them together? For him, at any rate, his attraction to her was so pronounced he knew the symptoms were bound to be recognized by someone in his crew in short order and not one would have any trouble guessing the reason.

Groaning quietly at his particular predicament,

he redistributed his jeans again. He had to stop thinking about her for a minute and concentrate on something else instead. As soon as he determined that necessity, however, he pictured her breasts in the soaked white dress, the nipples straining against wet fabric. And after that, the fabric parting and her breasts rounded in his hands, his mouth moving over her milky skin, his tongue circling the rosy aureoles, his teeth clamping down ever so lightly on her taut flesh and the cries escaping her, swift and low.

His breath rushed out through his nostrils, clouding the glass. The images came to him swiftly, almost against his will, making sweat stand out along his forehead. He felt as if he already knew her intimately, every inch of her open to him. He ached to be inside of her.

Whispering a desperate expletive, he raised his head just in time to catch a reflection, a movement in the room behind him.

Heart jerking in his chest, Ethan spun about. Light from the lone candle flickered over the walls and ceiling, creating more shadow than illumination. Perry had awakened and sat pressed into the far corner of the couch, the blanket from the floor clutched beneath her chin. What he'd seen hadn't been her, though. For one thing, there hadn't been enough time for her to dart across the living room to the staircase and then return unseen.

"Perry?"

She stared in his direction, pale eyes wide, the color in her cheeks high. He crossed the room in two strides and sat down next to her. Reaching out he took her hands and pulled them away from her throat, down toward her lap. The blanket fell to the floorboards, unheeded once more. The heat emanating from her skin nearly burned him.

"Perry?" he called her again. Her tongue slipped out to moisten dry lips. "Perry, look at me. What just happened?"

"He...he was here," she whispered.

A chill slithered down Ethan's spine. He resisted the urge to turn his head and look behind. In a low breath he uttered a quick prayer, the first he could recall speaking out loud in years.

"Was?" he asked. "Or is?"

"I think he's gone," she said, her voice still subdued, almost husky. "I'm not sure, though. Can you feel him?"

"Can *I* feel him?"

Ethan looked at her, at the smoldering heat in her gaze lurking beneath the confusion on the surface. Once again she seemed overly animate without the slightest motion, as if somewhere inside she'd begun spinning at a dizzying pace. He knew, God, he knew if he reached out and touched her, anywhere, let alone where he could see the pulse beat at the side of her throat, that whatever tender thread kept her glued to the couch would be severed. He could envision her flying up against him, the vibrating passion, her mouth on his own, the moist warmth of her melting over the shaft of an erection that was growing increasingly more uncomfortable. The image hit him so hard he felt nearly overwhelmed. Was this what she meant when she asked if he could feel him—it, he corrected—this damned spirit haunting her?

"Christ," he muttered, not in blasphemy, but in pleading. He stood up quickly, striding over to retrieve his shoes.

"I think we're going to my place, sweetheart," he said as he bent to put them on. "I'm getting you out of here, at least for tonight."

When she didn't answer he glanced at her around his arm. She shook her head.

"I don't think I can."

"I do," he answered tersely.

"It's my home," she said. "I can't leave it."

"You can and you will. Is there anything you need to bring with you? I'll make those calls first thing and see if I can get anyone interested in whatever the hell it is that's going on here."

He thought she would refuse yet again, but instead she relented. She folded the blanket over the sofa arm.

"Where are your shoes?" he asked, glancing pointedly at her bare feet as she rose. She looked down and shrugged.

"My sandals are by the door," she said.

"Toothbrush?"

"Upstairs."

"Never mind. If you get desperate, use mine." At the face she made, he amended, "There's probably a new one floating around from my last trip to the dentist." He wanted as little delay as possible to their departure. He felt edgy, unnerved, even a little angry. As he finished tying his sneakers he couldn't think why that might be, except, damn it, if he was going to fuck her it was not going to be at the bidding of some twisted entity.

With a sharp intake of breath, he swore at the crude and rather chilling turn of his thoughts. Perry deserved more respect than to be thought of in those terms, even in his own mind. As for the latter part, that did not bear dwelling on at all, at least not for the time being. He felt far too vulnerable for that speculation.

"What's wrong?"

Straightening, Ethan turned fully around to face her. A good-looking woman, sexy, pleasing to him in many aspects, it was only natural for him to want her. Nothing else going on here. The night's strangeness had caused his thoughts to run rampant, that was all.

"Nothing," he lied. "There's nothing wrong besides the obvious, Perry. Get your shoes. I'll grab the candle to light the way."

She headed toward the kitchen a pace ahead. Suddenly, he didn't even want her that far away. It didn't feel quite safe.

"I'll follow you in my car, I guess?" she asked as she moved through the shadows toward the place she had left her sandals lying.

"No," he said. Too quickly. He felt like something watched him. Drawing a deep breath, he steadied himself.

"I'll drive," he said, "and bring you back when you're ready."

To his relief she made no protest.

## *Chapter Thirteen*

Lights from the dashboard gently illuminated the pickup truck's cab. Outside, the still-clouded sky made the night even darker than usual beneath the trees overhanging the roadway. After traversing puddles, some fairly deep, and skirting fallen branches and various debris, they sailed out onto the main highway. It seemed to Perry that Ethan looked a little too intent and drove a little too fast. Something about his posture, close to the wheel, white-knuckled, the occasional deep and heavy respiration, made her wonder what he might be thinking. She didn't ask, afraid to distract him from the task at hand.

He said little, glancing her way every now and then. His dark hair stood in disarray, the nearest sleeve on his shirt rumpled, turned back on itself. Wordlessly, Perry reached out to smooth it down. She could feel the muscular ridge and curve beneath her fingertips. Not daring to linger long, she lowered her hands into her lap.

"I don't know that it was necessary for me to leave," she ventured finally, when he had slowed the truck to the speed limit.

"No? I can't imagine why not. I saw it tonight, Perry. Or something."

"But you were the one who said ghosts can't hurt you," she reminded him.

"I know what I said," he replied, his tone curt.

"I never felt like I was in danger," she went on. "Not physically. I don't think he has any desire to harm me. At least, I didn't."

"You've changed your mind?"

In the interior lights' amber glow, Perry closed her eyes, leaning her head back against the seat. The truck slowed further. A turn signal dinged in a tiny repetitious note.

"I don't know," she answered quietly.

"Then why did you leave with me?" he asked.

"Because I knew you wouldn't leave unless I came with you." Perry lifted her lids. The truck bounced into a driveway and began a slow crawl along its length. In the near distance Perry saw a darkened house with a single light burning on the porch. Ethan said nothing until he had pulled up outside the huge garage and killed the engine.

"This—" he began, and shook his head. "This is crazy. Are you saying you were afraid for me?"

"Yes."

He drew a long breath in through his nose, discharging it slowly. His hands dropped from the wheel. Yanking the keys from the ignition, he began to tap them thoughtfully on his thigh.

"Why? Why were you afraid for me and not for yourself?"

Releasing her seatbelt, Perry pivoted on the seat to face him. His gaze held steady on hers, awaiting an explanation. And she owed him one. She knew she did. Nevertheless, she couldn't fathom where to begin.

"You said you saw him," she started.

"Saw it," he corrected. "I didn't say him. What I saw didn't have any real form. You, however, have referred to it as him from the onset. May I ask how you are so certain what gender this entity might have possessed while animate?"

Perry swallowed hard, knowing how irrational she would sound. Besides, she could see Ethan was near to drawing his own conclusions and that he didn't care much for the path down which they were leading him.

"He looked—looks nearly as plain to me as you do now, slightly shadowed, parts a bit brighter than others. Not anywhere near as solid, but not transparent or smoky or whatever one might expect. And often I just hear him, and don't see him at all."

Ethan blinked slowly, assimilating her description; possibly envisioning it. The keys stilled in his hand.

"But you feel him," he stated quietly.

"I...yes," she said.

"And you fear this spirit is seeking to utilize me for fulfillment, for gratification? Because that is what you're telling me, isn't it? That when you feel him, you don't necessarily mean you sense his presence. You mean he touches you in some manner that is intimate."

Perry nodded, not trusting herself to speech. Her cheeks flared up. She pressed her fingers against them, feeling their heat. Bowing her head, she stared at the glow from the porch light across her knee.

"Willingly?"

"What?" Her head jerked up.

"Are you a willing party to this?" he asked. She couldn't see his eyes, their expression. "I don't understand. How can you possibly feel anything at all?"

"It's...it's like reading a passage in a book that moves you," she struggled to explain. "You experience what you read, even though it's not real. I'm sorry, I don't know how to make it any clearer.

"The first time, I didn't even realize what had happened, I just perceived the changes in me afterward. The episodes became addictive, out of my control, although I didn't understand that until the other day. Almost hypnotic, where a word is all that's needed to put you in a certain state. But when you came upon me at the creek, I had been gone from my home for three days. God," she whispered, and started to cry. She didn't mean to, because it seemed like a play for sympathy, but she couldn't help herself. She felt mortified now she had confessed the truth aloud, Frightened, too, and desperately certain Ethan would turn from her in disgust, rescinding his friendship as well as the promise of something more.

For a long time he didn't say anything, staring through the windshield at the blank garage door. Forcing herself to stop crying, Perry wiped her eyes with the back of her hand.

"Three days?"

She nodded. He didn't look at her.

"You're sure."

"Yes."

"But I—"

"'But you, what?"

He shook his head. "Nothing. I don't know what I'm thinking. I don't know what to think."

Neither did she. What to think. What to tell him. How to take back the words she'd let loose between them. Well, that last part she knew. There was no taking those words back. She cared too much about him already to even try, because the only way to do that would be to lie.

"You can't go home until I have someone

check into this," he said.

Perry leaned against the seat. At least he hadn't made the sign of the cross in her direction. That was some consolation.

"It's my home," she said.

"I know that. But surely, you must see you're not safe there? Spirits can't hurt you, but you could hurt yourself in that state."

His voice seemed flat, emotionless. Perry sat very still.

"Three days," he whispered again.

"Yes."

He licked his lips as if his mouth had gone dry, head tipping back on his shoulders. He reached up to the visor, pulled out a single paper tucked against the roof. After turning it over several times in his hand he put it back. Perry didn't think he had any awareness he'd done so.

"And you have some reason to suspect this entity wishes to use me to get to you. That seems to be allotting a sentient personality to something which should just be a shade, as it were, of the past."

"I'm only aware of what he said to me," she told him. "I had never heard him in the house, until you were in it as well. Does that mean anything?"

Ethan shrugged. "I don't know."

Perry watched him and waited. She wondered if she should just exit the truck and find someplace else to stay. Of course, she had walked out without money or identification or anything but the clothes she'd had on. In fact, she didn't even have the keys to get back into her own house.

"Ethan?"

"Hmm?"

"I'm sorry."

"For what?"

"For getting you into the middle of this."

"I got myself into the middle of this," he stated. Convincingly, even. Perry bit her lip to keep from crying again. She felt too emotional, too vulnerable, too much like she was falling prematurely for a man she barely knew. All that, and she just realized as well that she'd spent the last few months in a brittle nightmare she'd been unable to recognize.

"And no matter what you might believe," Ethan said suddenly, turning in his seat, "I am not being made to want you through some force outside my command. I'm doing a bang up job of that all on my own."

"I—what?"

He laughed, a short sound with little humor in it, and reached with astonishing speed to slip his hand against the back of her neck and pull her closer. His mouth came down across hers. The keys hit the floor. His other hand settled against her waist. The contact sent a shiver along her skin. She opened her mouth to the pressure of his.

For their first kiss it proved exquisite, long and slow and with just enough control to make her tremble. She could feel his warm  breath cross her skin as he exhaled through his nose. His hand on her waist remained stationary, firm, bracing her when she wanted nothing more than to rise up and meet him as his tongue slid over hers in a languid caress. She moored her one hand to the seat edge and slid the other into his sleeve, curling her fingers around the straining muscles in his arm. A low noise vibrated up from his chest into the hollow of her mouth. Her own breath grew short. Despite his efforts to keep her anchored she tightened her grip on his arm and arched against him. He pulled his head away.

"We're three dozen yards from my front door," he said in a husky undertone, "and this seat doesn't go back any further. Let's go inside."

Silently, Perry opened her door and got out, not quite steady on her feet. The world seemed to be spinning at an accelerated pace with her body oscillating in its center. The chill common to the darkest hours before dawn touched her skin, arousing her still further. Her nipples were hard, the flesh between her legs slick in almost instantaneous reaction. Ethan wanted her and she wanted to be with him just as badly. It frightened her a little, considering recent events, to think in a few minutes she would be surrendering all restraint to him, to a man she barely knew, to a man such as he appeared to be.

He came around the truck and took her hand in

a gentle grip, leading her across the graveled drive and up the steps onto the porch. She blinked in the glare from the brightly burning fixture. He opened the screen door. She held it for him, her other hand never leaving his as he inserted the key into the lock. He pushed the front door open. In an action that seemed one of habit he reached inside to switch off the overhead light, then stepped over the threshold. She followed.

The darkness inside his home felt welcoming, relaxing her with its sensation of anonymity. She could scent something not quite familiar, although pleasant, permeating the foyer where they stood. Wordlessly he pulled her forward, slipping his arms behind her back and cupping her buttocks with his hands, forcing her up against him. Quite obviously, he was as physically ready as she.

Perry wrapped her arms around Ethan's neck. He kissed her again deeply, holding nothing back. Sliding his hands down her thighs, he lifted her without apparent effort to his waist. She wrapped her legs around him, steadied by his arm beneath her hips and across her back, her mouth locked onto his own. He took a single step to the wall.

She thudded against the barrier without harm, protected from full contact by his arm. Through the thin fabric of her lightweight sweats she felt him straining against the confinement of his jeans. She rolled her hips, pulling herself closer with her legs. He made a noise in his throat, sliding his hand into her waistband and down over her buttocks to skim along between her legs. His mouth moved down, hard, to the side of her throat.

"You're soaked," he whispered against the pulse beating rapidly there. "God, you're drenched."

He pushed his fingers inside her, catching her as she arched back and away from him. With another word, something unintelligible and intemperate, he turned and carried her through the darkened house to a closed door.

"Get that, will you?" he said. "My hands are somewhat occupied."

Trembling, Perry reached behind and turned the knob at her back. He flung the door inward with his knee.

His bed's firm mattress gave only a little to the pressure when their two bodies dropped down onto the quilted spread. His movements were certain and easy as he pulled his shirt over his head in a single motion, then took his time with hers, removing it carefully from her entangled hair. He slipped her bra straps down her arms, pressing his mouth to her shoulder's curve while his fingers trailed over the roundness of her breast not yet exposed. With one hand in his hair Perry kissed his head.

Raising himself up on his elbows, Ethan pulled her undergarment down in tantalizingly leisure, his breath moving across her skin, curling over the tight flesh of the nipple nearest his mouth. He touched his tongue to the tip, the damp residue of that brief caress chilling in the drifting air created by withdrawal. As Perry watched him, dimly visible in the pale illumination cast by the bedside clock, she witnessed his lazy smile, the smile that made her heart turn over, and then he repeated his prior action, this time holding her nipple with his teeth before licking it in a swift and delicate motion. Perry's breath escaped her in a rush.

"Ethan," she murmured in throaty plea.

"Perry, I know," he answered. "I know what you want. I know what I want. This could all be over in two seconds if we let it, that's what kind of fevered pitch you've brought me to without even trying. But I didn't imagine it to be this way the first time with you."

"You've given it that much thought, have you?" she teased, running her fingers along his arm and down his back. He leaned forward, planting a kiss between her breasts.

"I have," he said. "And as we haven't known each other all that long, you can imagine the torturous evolutions my mind has been going through. I figured if we reached this point we would spend all night at it. Unfortunately, I haven't got all night any longer. I have to be getting ready for work in little more than an hour."

"I don't mind," she whispered.

"Hmm, I'm certain you don't. I have a feeling you'd climax in a heartbeat."

At his words she arched against him and he slipped an arm behind her back, drawing her up along his body, bathing her in his skin's heat. He stroked the hair from her brow and kissed her there, then trailed his fingers over her shoulder and cupped her breast in his hand, rubbing his thumb back and forth across the stiff peak as he observed the effect his tender attention had on her body. Perry closed her eyes, all sensation drawn to that single contact. Absolutely right. In a heartbeat.

When she opened her eyes she found him holding himself very still, his hand resting against her.

"Perry?"

"Yes?"

"I'm taking a shower."

"What?"

"A cold one. I don't know if that really works, but I'm hoping it does."

Perry struggled back on her elbows, propping herself against the headboard.

"I don't understand," she said.

Ethan swung his legs off the bed and sat up facing her, his thigh pressed along hers. She sensed a slight tremor, like a shiver, racing along beneath the skin.

"I want to wait," he told her quietly, taking her hand. "Do you mind?"

Perry looked down at his fingers interlaced through her own.

"I—no, I guess not. Is something wrong?"

Lifting her hand, he pressed her fingers to his mouth. "Not at all," he said against her bent knuckles. "I just think it would be most fair to you if we waited."

"Fair to me?" she echoed.

"Yes. And to me as well. Taking into consideration what you've told me, I can't help but wonder if you...if you are this enthusiastic because of me, of us, or because of what you say has been happening to you."

"You don't believe what I've told you, then?" she countered, wounded by his statement. Rejection had not yet set in.

"To the contrary, I do believe you. And I feel I would be taking advantage of you in your present state. Also, I really would like to know that it's me who makes you come like that. Next time. I think we should wait until we gain a better understanding of what's going on."

Stunned, Perry groped around in the dark until she found her discarded shirt. She pulled it on over her head.

"You really are quite the gentleman," she said without sarcasm.

"Disappointed?"

"Not at all. Here I am, half naked in your bed and more than willing, and you refrain from genuine thoughtfulness. Give me a few more minutes to mull over that behavior and I might find myself falling for you in a big way, Ethan Taylor."

He laughed and stood up, bending from the waist to kiss her on her crown, pushing back curling tendrils with his flattened palm. "You just hold that thought, Perry," he said, and walked out.

A few minutes later she heard water rushing through pipes in the wall toward the shower head in the nearby bathroom. Pushing wet lathered skin from her mind, Perry yanked the quilt up around her shoulders and rolled toward the opposite side of Ethan's bed, closing her eyes as bona fide tranquility settled over her.

## Chapter Fourteen

*Rising from his knees, he moved to the curtain formed by falling water and stepped through it onto the ledge. The moon, which appeared not to have progressed at all across the sky, shone pale and luminous, reflecting in the turbulent water at his feet. He stared across the creek to the forest and the cleared pasturage beyond, knowing that there lay the path which would lead him to her. How many years had it been since he wandered that way, since he was welcome in the house where he had grown from infant to child to man?  As the eldest of many sons, the house belonged to his brother now. He, himself, had been the last to leave it, and then unwillingly. He would have liked to stay.*

*At what point had the man who had cast him from his home taken Lily to wife? When the congregation had begun to question his brother's lack of a helpmeet, he supposed. When the speculation had been at its worst. The parson's choice of a bride had been deliberate, even with many vying for the position. Lily had been the prize over which he and his brother had long battled. He could still taste the bitter gall that had risen to taint his mouth when he heard tell of the betrothal.*

*He had been long away, he knew. Too long for someone such as Lily to wait. That night before he marched with the others to Philadelphia carrying the banner of political upheaval like a badge of honor, full of fire and determination, he should have asked her then to marry him. He had been afraid though, afraid she would say no. It had been better to bear a hope in him to that city of strangers and pandemonium, rather than the certain knowledge of her refusal.*

*His mouth twisted in remembered pain. His heart clenched tight. Enough, he told himself. Enough. Time to claim what should have been his all along. Lily was his by right. His brother did not want her; she had served the purpose for which she had been chosen. The whispers had been silenced. What more did that self-righteous man of the cloth want?*

*Lily desired to leave. But she feared telling his brother the truth, yet would not walk away without revealing it. He had offered to go with her to speak out, knowing they would both be condemned for their behavior, that they would have to live their days together sinning in the eyes of God and man, but she had refused. The time would come, she had told him, when she would know what to do.*

*Sometimes he felt afraid for her. He remembered the night she had come to him, bleeding. What his brother had exercised had been unnatural and cruel. He had helped her to wash herself, to cleanse her of the act's residue. It had been hard to do so without wanting to go straight up to the house and lay his brother low. He had been angry enough to kill him.*

*No, Lily said, let it be. Just promise me you'll never stop loving me.*

*An effortless promise to make, one from which he could not be forsworn.*

*Stepping down into the creek he started across, the moon glittering in his eyes. Her name tumbled sweet on his lips as he fought the current, moving without noise, without the slightest splash, toward the far bank. He reached for the rocky outcropping, to drag himself up and out from the water, and felt the slick surface slip repeatedly from his grasp. Frustrated, he pitched himself across the stone. The water dragged him back. He tried again and again, and yet again, flinging himself in desperation, feeling neither bruise nor cut nor the force of his battering. And then, just for a moment, he remembered. Too fleeting to hold, like a gossamer strand of a spider's skein waving in the silver night. He remembered and he forgot, and when he raised his head he was staring once more through the curtain of falling water. Beyond, the moon continued to shine, fixed like a pearl in filigree in the dark, webbed branches of the trees.*

## *Chapter Fifteen*

"Hey, boss, you look like you haven't slept a wink."

Ethan glanced up. He set the register in his hand back down on the desk. Gray light fanned into the office through the open door, misted and pale.

"Morning, Tom," he said.

"Eight o'clock and the boys are all set to go. It's back to the Brady place this morning, right?"

Wordlessly Ethan nodded, spinning his chair to reach back to the filing cabinet. He grabbed a purchase order and spun forward again, holding it out. "Pick this up on the way, will you? I'm staying here in the office for a while."

His foreman stepped inside, taking the extended paper. With a quick glance at it, he slipped it onto the clipboard in his hand. For a moment the man looked at him, sandy brows arched.

"You okay?"

Here it comes, thought Ethan. "Yup," he said.

Tom's face creased into a smile. "That good, was she?" he drawled. Ethan made no reply. Tom laughed. "Wait'll the boys hear this. You're not even going to be around to deny it this time."

Ethan's eyes narrowed. Outside he could hear the men, trucks running, ready to pull out. He didn't have the energy to put up a defense as, in point of fact, he hadn't slept a wink. Jerking his chin toward the door, he said, "Get out of here, Tom. You're going to be late." Pushing up from the chair, he stepped forward to hasten his friend's departure. Tom chuckled all the way across the parking lot. Ethan swung the door shut to silence it. After that, all he heard was the air conditioner's steady hum, the computer, and the oscillating fan circulating cool air around the office.

He couldn't figure out why the guys kept busting his ass about women. If they had a clue as to the scarcity of the 'hot dates' they hinted at, they'd likely be laughing all the harder. This morning was the first time in a long while Tom had come even close to the truth. If Tom or the others knew he'd turned Perry down, he'd never hear the end of it. Not that anything concerning Perry would be held up for scrutiny. He generally didn't say much about any woman he dated. Perry would definitely remain off limits.

Recalling her responsiveness the night before, he sucked in his breath. Recalling the possible reason for it, he strode over to his desk, lifted his cell phone from the scarred surface and flipped through his contacts to 'G'.

During college, Ethan had gotten to know his cohorts fairly well and had managed to keep in touch with a few over the years. With the exception of one, though, he couldn't recall the last time he'd exchanged more than a Christmas card or a congratulations on a marriage, a child's birth, another's graduation. A neglect fashioned from time and distance and, for one reason in particular, purpose. All those people from his past possessed an intimate knowledge regarding his earlier life. He'd rather not be reminded. Cowardly, he knew. Certain of them would be pretty darned pissed if they ever got a whiff of the carrot he was about to dangle. But he could think of only one man he felt comfortable enough to call about this now.

Lowering his frame into the chair behind the desk, he slid it on well-oiled wheels across the carpet. Leaning back, he put his feet up on the desk top, crossing his legs at the ankle. Ethan ran through the "G's" for John's new listing. John Gooden promised the most success for Perry's situation. The professor possessed a lengthy, though unofficial, resume relating to experience in similar matters. Even so, Ethan doubted John had encountered something like this before.

Finger hovering above the cell phone's surface, Ethan chewed his lip, hesitating. It had been a while since he and John had spoken. Too long. What would he think, receiving a call such as this from Ethan with so little contact over the past year or so? For Perry's sake, he had to, though. He tapped the contact, put the phone on speaker and waited.

"Hello?"

Ethan smiled. "Is this the Gooden residence?"

"Yes."

"Is this Janie?"

His smile broadened as she hesitated. She either recognized his voice or had learned to be cautious about giving information over the phone.

"Who's calling?" Caution. Good to hear.

"This is Ethan Taylor. Has your father left for work yet?"

Janie Gooden refrained from shrieking until after the phone had been covered on her end to muffle the noise. A moment later a gruff male voice spoke.

"Ethan? Can you hear her?" John's familiar laughter filled Ethan's ears. "All this time and I think she still has a crush on you. Ow. She just smacked me in the arm. Daughters!"

"John," Ethan said warmly. "How have you been?"

Just hearing his friend's voice made Ethan feel better. Not only about Perry's situation. About many things. He'd isolated himself too much these past few years.

"I'm fine, Ethan. Fine. What about you?  It's been...how long has it been?  I've probably only spoken to you once since we moved."

"I know, and I apologize for that. It's stupid, letting work and—other things get in the way of what you want and need to be doing."

"Well," said John, in dismissal. "So how are you, anyway?  To what do I owe the pleasure of this call?  Have you finally decided to visit us here in our peachy new house in peachy Georgia?"

Ethan leaned back further in his chair, grinning as he answered John's questions in rapid order. "I'm fine; I'll get to that in a moment, and—let's see—no."

On the opposite end of the connection John Gooden's laughter boomed again. "Have you no reverence for your mentor?" he demanded.

"Not really," Ethan retorted, continuing to smile fondly at the phone's mouthpiece.  He picked up a pen and began rolling it back and forth between thumb and forefinger, leaning the chair at a precarious angle.

"Well," said John, "I'm glad to see your success hasn't changed you. Neither has mine, which is a good thing. Do you want to get to the heart of the matter first, before we go off on a tangent of small talk?  Because I don't believe I'm wrong in assuming you've called for a reason."

Dropping his booted feet to the floor, Ethan sat

up, leaning his arm over the desk blotter. With the pen point, he began to scribe small, linked circles across the scribbled surface.

"You're not wrong, John," he said. "I've run into something I think may be of interest to you."

"Professionally, you mean? In one of those old houses you're constantly disturbing?"

"Yes," Ethan answered, "you could say that."

"Honey, go inside and get Daddy a glass of water. I'm probably going to be out here a while. Oh, and my sunglasses, too. Thanks. It's quite a bright morning. I'm glad I have the day off. Is it raining where you are?" he asked, addressing Ethan with the last three remarks.

Ethan glanced toward the window. Still too early to tell, but the day remained gray. "Not at the moment," he advised, scribbling over the circles he had created. "Wouldn't surprise me if we got more, though."

"I heard there's been an unusual amount of rain your way."

"A lot of mud. Not good for business."

"Uh-huh. So, go ahead," John said. Ethan heard him taking a sip from his glass. "What's up?"

Now that they'd come to it, Ethan felt uncertain where to begin. Tossing down the pen, he reached for the coffee that had been cold an hour ago. Nevertheless, he took a swallow, grimacing at the taste.

"Quite recently I met a woman—"

"Good Lord, you're not going to tell me you're getting married again, are you?"

Ethan exhaled abruptly. It wasn't often someone brought up his marriage, least of all someone who knew exactly how it had ended.

"Not yet," he said.

Gooden remained momentarily silent, probably trying to decipher exactly what Ethan meant with his reply. Ethan used the time to regain his equilibrium.

"She's a client," he went on and instantly felt regretful, perhaps a little superstitious, describing her in that fashion. "Actually, she's something more than a client at this point. What she is to me I can't really say, exactly. In all honesty, we just met a few days ago," he added, with emphasis.

"I see," said John after a moment's hesitation. "What's her name and what's she like?"

Ethan considered a moment, drumming his fingers on the blotter. Perry defied an easy description. He truly didn't know her well enough to offer specifics, although he felt as if he did. Beautiful and sexy? Without a doubt. Intelligent? Yes. That could be attested to by the quality of her work. Kind? Sure. Foolishly, she worried more about him than herself. Felt incredible in his arms while dancing? Oh, yes, soft and strong and possessing the most delightful way of moving. Funny? Uh-huh. Complex? Quite. Great smile? His mouth curved picturing it. Fantastic kisser?

Another part of his anatomy stirred as his thoughts went there. And possibly possessed? Yeah, not something he'd list on the pro side.

"Her name's Perry," he murmured at last. "And she's...something else. Another sort of woman entirely. You'll understand what I mean when you meet her."

"When I meet her?" John echoed. "So you do intend to finally grace us with your presence?"

Ethan shook his head at his friend's persistence. "I'd like to come down. I really need to make the effort, I know. I haven't taken a vacation in...well, a few years at least. I might even get Perry to come with me, if the two of us move in the direction I'd like us to go."

As he spoke those words, he realized how true they were. Only a few days knowing her and he already felt he wanted something with her that wasn't short-lived.

"But what I had in mind," he went on, "was a little trip for you, John. You and some of your equipment and all of your expertise. I don't know if you're available right now, but I'll foot the bill."

John's breath whooshed through the phone. "You're serious."

"Absolutely," Ethan responded. "Can you get a flight? Preferably today?"

"Shit. Sorry, Janie. Ethan, tell me what's going on."

## *Chapter Sixteen*

Chin wedged against her palm, Perry stared at the computer monitor. Ethan had said to make herself at home while he was gone, assuring her his offer included use of his computer. Ethan Taylor was a generous, trusting man. Maybe a little too trusting. For all he knew, she could be a lunatic. Considering what he did know about her, she couldn't understand why he didn't absolutely believe her a lunatic already.

Except Ethan had seen *him*, too. Or something.

Perry continued to stare at the monitor, a long breath escaping through her nostrils. She had been trying with less than notable success to work, starting a blank page with what she remembered as the last sentence she'd written. She needed her files, her notes, everything she had back at her house, which made her remember once again the cause for being at Ethan's. He had experienced something which quite obviously unnerved him. She didn't believe him a man easily disturbed. Recognition that she had brought him such a point effectively put an end to further attempts at working.

Continuing to stare at the blank page, she wondered at the events leading up to the last episode in the creek. She'd really thought she'd been imagining things, indulging herself in strange daydreams, her loneliness at this stage of her life making her...what? Wickedly horny, to be blunt? Had she really been so blind as to not recognize the abnormality of the occurrences? After losing three days, hearing the voice in the house telling her what it could make Ethan do, she'd finally understood, but even then the full impact regarding the supernatural, her part in it, didn't sink in. Not until she'd discussed what was happening with Ethan.

A chill danced up her spine with a centipede's running feet, making her wrap her arms around her body. She lifted her gaze to the double doors, the deck beyond warming in the sun. It wasn't just her part in it. Knowing something—spirits?—existed solidified belief. And frightened her. Was this a soul anchored to the world, or a being more evil? Religion spoke of demons and the like. She didn't even want to consider that.

Whispering a vaguely worded prayer, Perry

logged on to the internet, considering her phrasing for a search on the supernatural. How much did she really want to know, sitting here alone? If, as Ethan had suggested, he could get a friend to talk to her, someone with experience or knowledge or at least some comforting or hopeful advice, maybe she should just wait and not go off half-cocked on a trip into the unknown.

But she'd already done that very thing, hadn't she? Biting her lip, she started typing, deleted the phrase, typed again, then deleted the single word and typed another subject into the search box instead.

Ethan Taylor.

Her brows lifted at the numerous results. The first page pertained to his business. She scanned a few of these quickly. She'd been apprised of Ethan's professionalism and the quality he maintained in his work, but she'd really been unaware how far Ethan's expertise extended.

He'd received numerous awards, accolades from his peers, as well as the praise of local businessmen who raved about the care and pride he took in performing restorations. He'd done work for the county historical society and been presented a plaque for his contribution at a formal ceremony.

She spent a few minutes lingering over the newspaper photo in which he stood beside an older woman as he accepted the plaque, his grin a little sheepish, but pleased. The woman, on the other hand, looked as if she would like to eat him alive.

And why not? Perry thought. Ethan was a charismatic man, ruggedly handsome, tall and strong and definitely in control of himself. The latter he had proven beyond doubt last night.

Despite the fact she sat alone in Ethan's house with no witness to her thoughts but her own conscience, a blush warmed her cheeks. Definitely a gentleman of high caliber to turn down a woman's crazy willingness to sleep with a man she'd only known a few days.

Her flaming cheeks blazed hotter. She understood men and women did that, went out, met someone in a bar or elsewhere, then went home or to the nearest motel with one understanding, one intent. She'd never been one of those people.

Apparently, though, she'd become one. Or almost had. If not for Ethan's remarkable common sense and self-control, she'd be thinking less of herself this fine morning.

She brought her reflections up short. God, what must Ethan think of her?

The fact he held enough concern to want her safe said a lot for what he thought about her. She was touched by the knowledge, more than she cared to admit. She also knew that knowledge made her vulnerable. Worse, it made the situation for Ethan very volatile indeed.

Getting up from the chair, Perry went to the kitchen to fix herself some tea. While waiting for the water to boil, she stood with her back against the island counter, arms crossed, protractedly studying the configuration of Ethan's kitchen cabinets, trying to empty troubling thoughts from her mind. In the midst of her thought diversion, she found her gaze drawn to the hallway, remembering the fleeting, fevered moments against the wall. A pleasurable shiver coursed over her skin, followed by a determination not to think about it. Fortunately, the pot began to whistle. With a sigh, she poured water into a mug she found in the cabinet and returned to the computer.

"Right. And I ought to feel a bit more ashamed than I do," she reminded herself in a mumble as she sat down. But if shame hadn't prevented her from spending three days in a place and state that would have anyone else screaming in fear, why should she be troubled by her behavior with a flesh and blood fella?

Ethan Taylor's physical presence had brought reality to her situation. He'd grounded her. And she liked him. She didn't want him thinking the worst about her.

Sipping her tea, Perry resumed reviewing the links to information about Ethan. Setting her mug down, she pulled the chair closer to better view what appeared to be a dated photograph. Given the clothing and hair, the picture had likely been taken when Ethan was in college or recently graduated, by someone not a professional photographer. The picture had been scanned at some point for inclusion on an old reunion site from a university in Atlanta. The photo had not been digitally retouched and showed the scars from age and poor handling. Ethan stood beside a pretty young woman, their arms linked, smiling not for the photographer, but for each other. The caption entered beneath cleared up any doubts Perry might have had regarding the relationship in the photo.

Our buddy Ethan and his new bride, Cindy.

Perry continued to study the image on the screen, biting her lip. She wasn't sure why coming across a fifteen-year-old photograph bothered her so much, why she felt a little jealous twinge. Obviously this Cindy was no longer in his life, as the house held no evidence whatsoever of a woman's possessions, let alone a woman's touch.

Perry drummed the desk top, lips compressing. They looked so damned happy simply being together. Had she ever looked at Jack like that? Quite possibly. More than possible. It made one wonder what happened over time to tear a couple apart.

Taking another sip from the mug, Perry tapped the monitor with her fingernail.

"Where are you now, Cindy?" she asked it. Gone the way of Jack, or was it something more spectacular and less inevitable? Nastily bitter, or a common agreement? Did she and Ethan talk over the phone on occasion? Did he miss her?

Setting the cup down, Perry decided she had wasted enough time in dalliance. She really did have work to be completed, and on schedule. She needed to go home.

Pushing back the chair, she stood up, deleting her browser history before doing so. She carried her cup into the kitchen, washed it, set it in the drain board to dry. Walking to the landline, she lifted the phone from the wall, then carried it to the door to the deck where she stood a moment staring out at a neatly trimmed yard. Ride share in this area was notoriously expensive, but she was too far from home to consider walking.

Rolling her eyes at her own folly at not insisting on taking her car, her own phone, anything, and wondering if a regular taxi service existed, Perry hesitated. Ethan wouldn't be happy to find she'd returned to a place he felt unsafe for her. She understood his reasoning, but in daylight she felt far less vulnerable. She hadn't been afraid before, she saw no reason to allow her behavior to be influenced by fear now. It was her house. She belonged there.

Glancing at the wall clock, Perry was shocked by the hour. She dialed the phone, pleased at her ability to recall Ethan's business number. A woman answered.

"Hi. Is Ethan there?" Perry asked.

"Mr. Taylor is not in the office at the moment. May I take a message for him?"

"Do you know if he's headed home?"

"I...no, I believe he's at a job site. If this is an emergency I can reach him on his cell."

Of course you can, thought Perry, but I can't. Perry had no idea what his cell number was and she couldn't ask this woman for it without divulging more information about herself and Ethan than she cared to.

"When you hear from him will you tell him Perry Madison phoned?"

"Why, of course, Ms. Madison. I understand you've hired him to restore your home. You'll be very delighted with him, I assure you."

The woman couldn't have uttered a more correct statement. "Thank you," Perry said. "Just kindly give him that message."

"Naturally," responded Ethan's assistant, and hung up.

Perry crossed to set the phone in the wall cradle. She blew a long breath out over her lips. With any luck, Ethan would call soon to check for messages and ring her here at the house. She wondered if he'd had any luck attempting to contact those friends he said might be helpful. College mates, weren't they?

Her eyes strayed back to the blank computer monitor. Had Cindy been a college friend before they'd begun dating, got married, built a life together? Perhaps they kept in touch and this was the person Ethan intended to call. And perhaps she'd even misread both his passion and compassion. After all, she'd thrown herself at him, first by fainting and then by...well. Yeah.

Not for the first time it occurred to her just how little she knew about Ethan Taylor and his life. They were, in fact, little more than strangers and she, a very short time ago, had fallen into his bed with every intention of having sex with him. If he hadn't come to his senses she would have followed through with enthusiasm. She reminded herself she should be grateful for his conscience. In the wee hours this very morning, she had been. Now she wondered if there might be some other reason, some very female reason, why he had pulled away.

She needed to get home.

## *Chapter Seventeen*

Tipping his wrist, Ethan glanced at his watch, then returned his eyes to the road. Through the truck's radio, he listened to Ruth's voice listing his calls. He stopped her when she reached Perry's name.

"When did you say she called?" Ethan asked, wondering why she hadn't mentioned the call first and realizing she had no reason to know she should. Beside him, his passenger looked over with a questioning frown.

"I'm sorry, Mr. Taylor, I—"

"Ethan, Ruth," he corrected her irritably. "You've been working for me for three years, for cryin' out loud."

His contentious words were met with responsive silence at the other end. "Of course," Ruth replied woodenly after a moment.

"I'm sorry, Ruth," Ethan apologized. "It's been a long day and I'm cranky, although I realize that's no excuse. What time did you say Perry called?"

"I didn't. However, Ms. Madison phoned at around 11:45. She just asked if I would tell you that when you called in."

Ethan let his breath out. "Thank you. If I don't see you before you leave, just lock the door and have a good night. Once again, I'm sorry for snapping at you."

"That's all right, Mr. Taylor," Ruth said before hanging up, managing politely to get the last word.

Gritting his teeth, Ethan lifted the cell phone from the cup holder, scanning it quickly for missed calls from Perry and finding none.

Eleven forty-five. He had assumed Perry would be so tired she'd sleep most of the day away, or at least until a good deal past noon. He'd avoided calling the house because he hadn't wanted to disturb her. The hour was now a quarter after three and he was still on Route 95, heading up out of the city from the airport.

"Everything all right?"

Ethan glanced aside at John Gooden.

"I'll let you know in a minute," said Ethan. He pressed the button on the steering wheel to dial home. After seven rings, voice mail picked up. He tried again for good measure and swore beneath his breath when the call went to voice mail again. The woman was damnable stubborn.

"Ethan?"

"One second," he said, and dialed Perry's number. No answer there either.

"Damn it," he muttered. Why the hell hadn't she called him directly? Only then did he remember she didn't have his cell number. He swore again, his hand tightening on the wheel.

He supposed she might have gone back to sleep. Unfortunately, he didn't believe that for a minute. He knew she'd left and gone home. She was just stubborn enough to do it. Yet if that was so, why hadn't she picked up her own phone?

"Fuck," he said, resorting to an expletive he had utilized far too frequently in the past twenty-four hours. He repeated the word, smacking his open palm on the steering wheel.

"Ethan?"

"She's gone home, John," he said.

"Probably not a prudent move," John Gooden remarked, nodding his head as if in agreement to Ethan's unspoken thought.

"See any cops?" Ethan asked.

John glanced around. "Not at the moment."

"Good," said Ethan and pressed his right foot down on the accelerator.

## *Chapter Eighteen*

Coming home had done little to alleviate Perry's confusion about Ethan and had certainly not lessened the racing speculation on her more immediate quandary. She found herself looking over her shoulder repeatedly, remembering Ethan's words about seeing something, but nothing made an appearance. Even the voice kept silent.

Nevertheless, she had expended more energy researching such topics as hauntings and possession in the past two hours or so than she had on her work. Her files lay open at her elbow, but she had not so much as looked at their contents. Certain information on the supernatural she'd come across seemed ludicrous, while other details made the hair stand up along her arms.

Were all these paranormal experiences really as commonplace as they appeared to be? Given the vast and varying array of articles her search had revealed on-line, it seemed so. However, the one element lacking in all of them she had read thus far was definitive proof.

Bowing her head into her hands, she pushed her fingers through her hair, surprised to find it damp with perspiration. She shivered suddenly in the oppressive afternoon heat. Glancing out the window she noted another storm had begun brewing, the air close and humid, barely breathable. Shivering again, she touched her forehead in a futile check for fever. She wouldn't be able to feel an elevation in temperature with her own hands, would she?

Nevertheless, she had begun to experience muddled thought like a cloudiness in her head, sore throat, aching back, limbs extraordinarily heavy. Lack of sleep, she told herself. Three days without it, and then last night's few hours. Unless she really had caught something. A dip into the chilly creek certainly hadn't helped.

Sliding her chair back, Perry rose. Pressing her fingers into her lower back just below her waist, she leaned into the pressure. Her thoughts, gauzy and disjointed, drifted around Ethan and the events from the previous night. She hadn't been looking for a man in gilded armor, but she seemed to have found one.

Perry walked heavily into the living room, pausing at the window to peer out at the sullen sky. Just outside the glass panes the leaves hung limply from their branches while those in the distance had turned, silvered backs soft-edged in the haze. No air moved over the sill. A tiny, shining spider's web in the casement's outer corner dangled like a gossamer construction.

During the three generations Madison women had been living in the house, as well as who knew how many other women before them, why had the spirit, or whatever it was, chosen her to haunt? If anyone else had ever been aware, they'd never made mention. As closely knit as they'd been as a family, Perry, her mother and grandmother, it seemed unlikely a topic like that would have gone undiscussed. They were basically a unit, the three of them, freely talking over the most uncomfortable subjects if found necessary. As protective as those two ladies could be, a ghost in residence would not have been something they would have avoided mentioning to her.

An abrupt chill tripped along Perry's spine. Slowly she turned to look over her shoulder. Nothing. The air had become thick and nearly fetid and, quite suddenly, she felt as if she couldn't breathe. She needed to walk, get out in the open where the air, though humid, was still vast. Struggling to draw breath, Perry moved through the kitchen and out the back door, pulling it closed behind. Outside wasn't much better, the atmosphere thick and cloying. Her sleeveless cotton blouse glued itself immediately to her damp shoulder blades and close between her breasts where perspiration pooled.

She wanted nothing more than to strip off her clothes and dive headfirst into the cool, rushing creek. Even as the thought occurred to her she tried to banish it, afraid the yearning' in her mind would somehow conjure the connection between herself and *him* and he would call to her. She had no desire to be tested. She wanted to believe she had the power to resist.

Breathing heavily, Perry headed toward the barn, always cool and shadowed. Once she felt a little better she would get in her car and perhaps drive back to Ethan's. She wondered, fleetingly, why he had not yet called her back, and even said as much aloud. Her words sounded muffled in her ears.

Pausing in her lagging stride, she looked around, startled to find herself under the trees. She could hear the creek, but not see it, unable to recall any conscious decision to take this path.

Shaken, Perry turned around on the path to return the way she'd come, but she stopped short. She stared along the pathway, unnerved by the visible light, its strange color. The day seemed to have taken on the hue of the leaves hanging languorously from the boughs overhead. A sluggish mist, thickest beneath the trees, hovered at an indeterminate distance between herself and the bend in the trail that would take her home. The hair on her arms lifted at the sight, at the mist swirling without apparent cause in the windless air, seeming to take on shape, then spread, then form again.

An overwhelming sense of animosity took hold, directed at her, not from her. She felt anger, loathing, desperation like a palpable threat. Without further consideration as to the consequences, Perry turned on her heel and ran for the creek and the falls. Whatever had formed on the path, she knew it was not *him*. *He* would not hurt her. She had always known that. But this, this was something else entirely.

Breath rasping from her throat, Perry clambered down the rocky face to the creek bank. Sweat streamed from her brow, plastered her shirt to her back. She leapt into the water, shocked by the chill against her heated skin. Stumbling over slippery rock, she swung her arms for momentum, splashing into the churning falls. Water tumbled out from the hillside with unrecognizable force, the creek deeper than it had been, swollen from the torrential rains the night before. She could scarcely stay upright.

Pushing her sodden hair from her eyes, Perry peered up at the hillside. The mist had congealed on the ridge.

"Help me," she whispered, not caring to whom

she spoke, not even certain she had physically uttered the words..

The rushing creek sucked at her legs, pulling her off her feet. Perry scrabbled at the rock. Her fingernails bent back as she slipped under the surface. Water ran into her throat. She choked, fighting for air, spraying liquid from her mouth.

Opening her eyes, she saw *him* through the glaze caught in her saturated lashes. She reached out her hand, felt his fingers' cold caress, felt the digits unable to take hold of her own.

"Help me," she said again, sound lost in the crashing falls. She saw his face clearly, saw a dawning in some vague understanding, and then he was gone. Behind her the mist came down the hillside, spreading out over the water's churning surface. Something hit her leg with brute force. A log rolling in the torrent—yes, that was it, wasn't it?—the broken branches snagging at her pants and dragging her down. She went under again, fighting to resurface. Weight pressed on her chest, forcing her to release the remaining oxygen from her lungs. As Perry recognized her own pending death, a black, sweeping shadow appeared over the water to scatter the mist.

*Chapter Nineteen*

Ethan threw himself into the creek and almost went down as he slipped on the rocks. He had seen Perry go under while he still stood on the hillside. He prayed she hadn't washed downstream beyond his reach. Behind him he heard John calling encouragement, direction, telling him he could see her clinging to a rock by the falls. Ethan struggled in that direction, plunging beneath the roiling surface. Feeling sodden fabric, he held on and pulled, dragging her up with him. She came, sputtering and alive, flailing out at him as if she didn't know him.

"Perry, it's me!  It's Ethan!" He stumbled in the stream's force, holding her against his chest with all his might. Perry shook the hair from her eyes, then turned and coughed out  muddy creek water. Gripping her firmly by the arm, Ethan struggled with her toward the bank, heaving her out to John, who waited with arms outstretched.

"For the love of God," cried Ethan through clenched teeth as he dragged himself out beside the them on the bank, "what were you doing in there? Why did you come back?  I thought you understood—"

Her hand gripping his sleeve silenced him. "How did you find me?" she asked, her voice a rasping croak.

"I—" Ethan began, then stopped.

"He jumped from the truck and ran straight here," John explained. "I was hard put to keep up with him. He seemed to know where you would be."

Perry's gaze turned toward John's voice. She stared without comprehension.

"This is John Gooden, the friend I mentioned," Ethan stated in hasty introduction. "He flew up here today from Georgia to assist you."

"To assist both of you," said John quietly.

Ethan glanced at his former professor, alerted by the man's voice. Their eyes met and held. He nodded, a barely perceptible motion in John's direction. Then he stood, helping Perry to her feet.

Last time he had carried her through the creek bed until he had reached a place where he could climb out with her unconscious weight in his arms. The creek's raging was too strong to attempt such gallantry now. She was going to have to climb back up to the path above under her own volition. He urged her in that direction. With determination she began the assent, stopping every so often to cough or brush damp hair from her eyes. Ethan stayed close behind, ready to catch her if she stumbled. Gooden brought up the rear.

At the top she halted, staring back toward the water. She appeared pale and shaken, but essentially unharmed. Ethan thanked God in a silent prayer for that.

"He brought you, didn't he?" Perry asked suddenly.

"No," Ethan responded, not asking who she meant. He didn't need to. He knew.

"Are you certain?"

Drawing a long breath in through his nose, Ethan released it slowly. "I followed a hunch," he said, "nothing more. When you didn't answer the phone I figured you were in trouble. And subsequent to our conversation last night, I knew you might be here."

Perry hesitated. No doubt she detected the anger in his tone, perhaps even understood the reason for it.

"You didn't check the house first?" she persisted.

Ethan shook his head. She was being particularly argumentative for someone he had just rescued from near-drowning. He took her arm and steered her toward the path.

"No," he said, "and you should be glad I didn't. Now let's get going. Dry clothes all around. Oh, except for me once again."

Perry started to apologize. Ethan forestalled her, his sarcasm in direct response to his own emotional distress. If he'd been a minute or two longer he suspected she would be, if not dead, at least on her way to the hospital. Perry couldn't stay here any longer, or come back for any reason, until something had been done. He'd been right about that. If she wasn't going to take his word regarding the danger, however, he hoped she'd take that of someone considered an unofficial expert in the field.

"John," he said, "talk some sense into her, would you?"

John glanced at him over Perry's head. Concern darkened the man's gaze. "What happened here?  Would you care to explain it to me?" he questioned her in a soft, non-threatening manner, taking her other arm. Ethan recognized the tactic.

Perry turned her head toward John, her hair tangled about her shoulders, littered with debris from the water. Her shirt was torn. Ethan didn't recall ripping it when he dragged her out. Her shoulder was bruised, also. Lifting the torn edge with his finger, Ethan peered in for further wounding. She glanced back for a split second, then returned her attention to Gooden. Ethan dropped his hand.

As Perry spoke, Ethan heard her strength returning. Not one for hysterics, Ethan realized with an odd, proprietary pride. Good. From what John had been saying on the trip up from the airport, the situation might easily grow worse before changing.

"I'd been inside working. I came home because I needed my files and things. I know Ethan is worried, but I thought everything would be all right. I really did. I went outside for some air, and then suddenly I found myself here in the woods."

"You don't recall how you got here?"

Perry shook her head. "I'd gotten confused. I couldn't remember how I came to be here, or even when. Still, I decided it was a wiser course to head back to the house and not the creek."

Beside her Ethan growled in agreement. She glanced at him again and away, but not before he witnessed a disturbing expression in her pale eyes.

"When I turned around everything looked strange, altered somehow. I felt ill and disoriented. And then..." Her voice trailed off. Her shoulders jerk in a shudder.

"Go on," urged John quietly.

"Did either of you notice a mist on the water?" She looked from one to the other, seeking confirmation . Ethan exchanged a glance with John, shook his head.

"Why did you go down to the creek, though?" John continued. "I don't understand."

Perry blinked in consideration, pace slowing, trying, he supposed, to work it out. "To be safe," she said. "I thought he could protect me."

To his credit, John didn't ask who "he" was either. As Ethan had told him the story, he could only assume John had drawn his own conclusions. Ethan, however, felt stinging rejection. Apparently, Perry had not enough faith in him to keep her safe from harm.

"Protect you from what?" John persisted.

"I don't know," she whispered. John leaned closer to hear better. "I don't know what it was. It was in the mist, I think. Or was the mist. Something felt very...wrong somehow."

John pursed his lips, choosing silence. Ethan spoke instead.

"And did he?" he asked.

"Did he what?" countered Perry, pivoting her head to look up at him.

"Protect you."

His voice sounded strange to his own ears, strained by the interrogation perhaps, but he seemed unable to control his delivery. Perry stared back at him, something he could not name still evident in her gaze.

"I suppose he did," she answered, turning away. "He brought you."

## Chapter Twenty

Ethan watched John stroll slowly around the living room, picking up an object here and there for casual examination before setting it back in the exact place he'd gotten it. Ethan's wet clothes were slightly less so since vigorously  applying the towel unofficially designated as his. Still, whenever he shifted his weight the water in his boots careened around his toes. Upstairs, Perry packed some necessary items for a few days away from home. She had already gathered her laptop, folders and notes, and set them on the kitchen table.

"What do you think?" Ethan asked.

"She's an attractive woman," said John,

pausing to glance his way. "Stubborn, too."

"I didn't mean that, exactly."

"I like her."

"So do I. But I didn't mean that either. What about this?" he persisted, indicating their general surroundings with a wave.

John halted, pulling a book off a shelf. He flipped through the pages, returned it to the case, tapped the binding with his fingers. Tipping his sandy blond head back. he looked up at the ceiling, then into each corner.

"The light in here is nice," he said.

Ethan waited.

John lowered his head. "I can give you four or five days. That's about all the time I have right now, although I can always come back. However, for tonight I suggest dinner, and then you two need to get some sleep. Neither of you looks particularly well rested. Tomorrow we'll return and set up the equipment and see if we can get any readings here. If you don't think Perry would be adverse to it, I'd like to try a little hypnosis first just to get a feel for what's going on, when she's in a relaxed state. Does that sound like a plan to you?"

"Yes. Fine," Ethan answered, frustrated, worried. "Thank you. Did I say that yet? Thank you very much for dropping everything to come up. You're a lifesaver."

John's face crinkled into a smile. "You're more than welcome, Ethan. Besides, if this case promises to be even half what you say it is, I should be thanking you. As for the lifesaving, that appears to be your job here."

Ethan knew Gooden referred to the escapade in the creek, but for a full ten seconds, enough time to be noticeable, he couldn't muster a reply. John's expression altered as he realized what he had said. He ran his fingers through his sparse hair in discomfort.

"It's all right," Ethan hastened, shaking his head. "Perhaps it's Karma."

Smiling to soften his statement, Ethan turned and walked to the kitchen. He opened the cabinet, removed two boxes of tea and set them beside the computer case. At John's questioning glance from the doorway, he said:

"She likes tea. The selection at my place is rather limited."

John smiled again, softer this time, more reserved. "So Perry has agreed to stay with you."

"As opposed to a hotel? Yes. Besides, I'd like her to be where I can keep an eye on her to ensure there's no repeat of today's little adventure."

"Is that your responsibility?"

Ethan said nothing.

"Do you even think it's advisable, Ethan?"

Ethan paused in his search for a container for the tea and honey jar. He knew why John asked the question, perhaps would have appreciated the concern in another circumstance.

"It may not be advisable, John, but it's best," he said, and went back to his hunt.

John stayed a moment longer in the doorway before he, too, turned away. He strode to the staircase, calling up to Perry to ask if she needed assistance carrying anything.

Locating a paper lunch bag, Ethan slipped the tea items inside. John had always been a good friend, a wise one. Ethan knew John wouldn't question his actions without feeling just cause. He also knew John would likely not bring the matter up again. Once was enough to serve as a reminder. Nothing further necessary.

A few minutes later Perry appeared carrying a single, sensibly-sized suitcase. John, who had gone up, followed empty-handed and bemused. "I hope you have an iron," she said to Ethan as she entered. "I rolled up a few things to make them fit and they won't be wearable if I don't take the flat of an iron to them." She seemed a bit irritated at the inconvenience, but when she smiled he recognized her annoyance had not been not directed at him.

"I have an iron," he assured her.

She crossed the floor to grab keys from a peg by the door, dressed in dry clothes following a record-breaking shower. Even so, leaves fragments clung in her damp hair. When it was wet like this her hair took on the color of iron-oxide, a rich earthy red. He decided he liked red hair. He had never particularly cared for it before, but he didn't think he'd feel the same about it again, even if...well, no point in the 'even ifs'. They'd only known each other a few days.

"I'll follow you in my own car," she said, spinning on her heel, tossing the keys once in her hand. "This way, if there are any problems with the arrangements, I can find another place to stay for the next few days without troubling you."

"I don't anticipate any difficulties," Ethan rejoined. "You get the couch. I get the bed."

Behind him, John suppressed an amused snort.

## Chapter Twenty-One

Perry sat at an angle on the couch with her knees drawn up and her bare feet tucked up under her. In the kitchen Ethan moved about on some furtive mission. She heard the refrigerator door open and close, then dishes rattling in the cabinet before being quickly subdued. Glancing at the clock, Perry noted it was still early enough to expect a reasonable amount of sleep. Following dinner and the storage in the locked garage of the pickup truck with its load of sturdy cases filled with expensive equipment, John had retired to the spare room. Apparently there had been some prior agreement. A pillow and a set of sheets now sat on the chair for her use when the time came. Ethan had thus far shown no inclination to duplicate last night's heated episode.

Steering her thoughts from the memory of those fifteen ardent minutes, Perry's contemplation returned to the incident in the creek. She had gone through it several more times with John over their meal, the man's professional yet easy manner helping to allay her lingering fear. After explaining why he wanted her to submit, she had agreed to hypnosis in the morning. Ethan requested to be present. To her relief, John advised against it. He would, John said, be more a distraction and deterrent to her relaxation than an aid. His statement made Perry wonder just how much Ethan had told him, or how much he was able to discern through his own shrewd observation.

"Here you go. I hope you don't mind, but I seem to remember you are a chocolate kind of girl."

Perry turned her head, eyes alighting on a dish nearly overflowing with chocolate ice cream liberally doused with chocolate syrup. Taking the offering into her lap, Perry laughed.

"Thank you," she said. "Comfort food. Yum. Where's yours?"

"Don't need any," he answered. "My dessert will be watching you eat your own."

At his words, warmth rushed straight to Perry's groin. She blushed, ducking her head to keep him from seeing it, and toyed with the spoon, hesitant to eat now he had presented such a stimulating mental picture. He sat down beside her at a small distance, reaching out to tuck her hair behind her ear before laying his arm along the couch back.

"Go ahead," he said. "I didn't mean to make you feel self-conscious."

"Good job with that one, then," she muttered, jabbing at the ice cream.

"Sorry. Just eat it, will you?" As if to add weight to his words, he reached for the remote and turned the television on at low volume. Placing his legs one at a time across the coffee table, he crossed his ankles and leaned back into the cushions. Satisfied as to his momentary preoccupation, Perry lifted a spoon filled with ice cream to her mouth. Syrup dripped down her chin.

"Crap," she said.

His chuckle tickled rushing heat across her skin yet again. Without turning his head he handed her the napkin tucked into his pocket. Perry scrubbed the chocolate from her chin and resumed eating, her eyes drawn to the flickering image on the television. Ethan had turned on the early news. The weatherman gesticulated before a weather map.

"More storms?"

"Looks like it. Not tonight, though."

"Good. I don't know how much more water the soil can take."

"My clothes aren't exactly waterproof either."

He hadn't turned. Perry glanced at him. His tone gave no indication what emotion lay behind his statement. Lamplight and the illumination from the television set highlighted his profile, the bunched muscles in the arms folded over his chest.

"I'm sorry." Perry stabbed the spoon down into soupy melting ice cream and dark, chocolate syrup. "I don't plan on letting that happen again."

Beside her he nodded, apparently appeased, attention focused on the weather report, volume low. Perry turned her spoon once through the bowl.

"I just want you to know that I appreciate everything," she said.

He nodded again. Perry sucked her lower lip between her teeth, sensing a brief awkwardness before resuming her dessert.

"Thanks for the ice cream."

Ethan responded with a barely audible comment. Perry continued to eat, relishing the sweet taste all the more for Ethan's thoughtfulness. His consideration touched her.

Normally she would have been disinclined to accept any overture toward friendship, let alone more. But with Ethan, the interest, the chemistry, the liking, had been instantaneous and not just because of the other being. Those chaotic incidences in the creek were something altogether different. No companionship, no interaction except a certain type, in itself unsettling in the extreme now that she viewed it from a perspective geared toward normal behavior. But Ethan...Ethan made her feel comfortable with herself, and that wasn't a bad thing at all.

After scraping the residue at the bowl's bottom

for good measure, Perry licked the chocolate gloss from the curved spoon. The television clicked off.

"Tell me it was me."

Turning her head, she found Ethan still staring at the dark television screen, Perry removed the spoon from her tongue, setting the utensil into the dish and leaning forward to place both on the table.

"What?"

"Tell me it was me," he repeated quietly. He pivoted his head to face her, his gaze steady and intent, the dark iris glittering behind his long, slanted lashes.

"Last night," he stated as though clarification could possibly be needed. "Or perhaps I should say this morning. I need to know it was me you wanted, that it was me who made you that wet, that it was me who made you tremble like the earth had just undergone a major shift in its axis."

Perry's skin warmed as her eyes widened. "As opposed to?" she asked.

"You know as opposed to what," he answered with a flat, nearly emotionless delivery that belied what she could see in his eyes. Perry brought her knees up again, wrapping her arms around them. She suddenly felt the need to keep herself covered and as small a target as possible.

"Do you want an honest reply?" she asked him.

"I do," he said.

"You do," she echoed, hedging as she contemplated the best way to word her response. So many things to be said. That needed to be said. But it was too soon for that conversation.

"I don't know," she admitted with a small sigh. "I would love to say yes, unequivocally, but I can't. You know I can't. However, before you start thinking there's nothing real between us, let me assure you that you would be wrong in such an assumption. I find you attractive. Me. The real me finds you immensely attractive. And I like you. I enjoy your company. Not to mention you've rescued me from some pretty hair-raising situations. Despite what happened earlier in the creek, I felt nothing overwhelming me in that way. Nothing that would mislead me. Okay?"

He made a sound in his nose, somewhere between a laugh and affirmation. "No shade between us?"

"Not even the tiniest ghost."

He shifted his hips on the sofa cushion. She glanced at the shoeless feet crossed at the opposite side of the coffee table. "This conversation is pretty crazy," he stated.

Perry nodded. "I agree. I can't imagine you having it with anyone else."

"Me either. But you understand it's important to me, right? Because of the circumstances."

Perry dropped her chin onto her knees, tipping her head to study Ethan's posture, his expression. She didn't think she had ever seen a man look so earnest in her life. He sat unnaturally still, his respiration barely visible, his gaze so intense it could have burned a hole through glass.

"You have to admit, Perry," he went on, "that we've been thrown together rather abruptly. And last night—"

"This morning," she corrected.

"This morning," he echoed her. "This morning was premature. And yet, getting out of that bed and into the shower was one of the hardest things I've had to do in quite a long time."

She understood well enough what he meant. Still she had to ask, "Then why did you?" Although he had explained it to her at the time, she needed to hear him state his reasons with a clear head. Needed to know it wasn't Cindy.

Unfolding his arms, he smoothed his jeans along his thighs. "Because I like you, too. I like you more than I would have expected given the duration of our acquaintance. And I was afraid by the light of day it would seem to you I'd taken advantage of your state of...mind."

His eyes closed. He leaned his dark head against the sofa. Perry wondered if he was trying to shut out the image. She waited.

"I want whatever happens between us to be mutual."

Perry shoulders relaxed. "Understood."

"And," he added, slowly, quieter, as if hesitant but compelled to say everything he had to say, "I need some assurance you'll be able to recognize the difference."

Air rushed from Perry's nose. Her stomach muscles tightened as if they'd just received a blow. She curbed her angered shame. "There's no reason to be insulting."

Ethan sat up, swinging himself around to face her, cocking a bent knee across the cushion between them. He leaned toward her. "I don't mean to be," he said. "Please don't take it that way. I just want— never mind. I don't know why I'm getting into all this now. John is in the other room and I'll shortly be retiring to my own bed. It's not like something's going to happen tonight."

Still piqued by what she viewed as censure, she murmured in a flippant attempt to get under his skin, "Hmm, yes, I agree, as I tend to get a little noisy. We wouldn't want to be disturbing your friend."

He had been reaching for the empty ice cream dish, but he stopped short. "I'm quite aware of how vocal you can be," he stated, eyes on hers. "Odd thing about that, though. We'd barely gotten started."

Flushing with heat, Perry shot up from the couch, bringing the bowl to the kitchen herself. She stood before the sink washing it, listening to sheets flapping open in the living room as Ethan prepared her bed on the couch. A minute later he came into the kitchen while she dried the dish. Taking it from her, he returned it to its place in the cabinet above her head. She stood pressed to the sink's edge with every square inch aware of his body, his height and breadth and the warmth he gave off behind her. If she had moved at all she would have backed right into him. And that, she knew, would have been trouble.

"Perry."

The breath she'd been drawing caught mid-inhalation at his tone. His respiration drifted across her nape, disturbing the tendrils loosened from her braid, causing her to shiver as if he'd touched her. A second later he did, pressing his mouth lightly just behind the place where her neck curved into her shoulder's slope. Breath rushed from her lungs with a low sound, a whispered, pleasured sigh. Her heart rate raced to a gallop.

"Tell me that was me," he whispered.

"It was," she said. "I promise."

He straightened. Placing his hands to either side of her jaw he tipped her head back, kissing her in tenderness on the crown.

"Good to know." He dropped his hands and walked away. Two seconds later she heard his door close.

Clutching the counter, Perry waited for her pulse to slow, her respiration to even out. "Bastard," she murmured as she shut out the kitchen light, heading into the living room. "There's a name for men like you."

But actually, she realized as she slid beneath

the cool sheets he'd tucked thoughtfully around the couch cushions, there wasn't. There wasn't any sort of name for a man like Ethan, a man who'd just done something like that to her and then walked away. She figured she would have at least a sleepless hour to come up with one, though, thanks to him.

## *Chapter Twenty-Two*

When John took Perry upstairs to conduct the therapeutic interview, Ethan started setting up the equipment Gooden had brought with him. Some appeared unfamiliar, but the majority he recognized as the same type they'd used more than fifteen years earlier in their experiments. Infrared cameras, devices sensitive to sounds not detectable to the human ear, machines to detect changes in temperature and in electromagnetic fields. John had decided all should remain in the house at least through the weekend, in the hope the equipment might pick up some activity they could determine not explainable through natural events. At some point after that, other equipment would be moved outside to the creek, but not yet. John still needed to calculate the necessary settings to eliminate the disturbances which would be in evidence from nocturnal creatures, bats in particular.

Coming from a room at the stair top, Ethan heard the drone he recognized as question and answer, with John's gravel tones and Perry's fragile-seeming, sleepy responses. What they said remained unclear through the shut door. Ethan managed to place himself in the area on one excuse or another several times now, blatantly and admittedly eavesdropping, but he couldn't discern the conversation's drift or content.

Frustrated, curious, worried, he continued to work as the morning wore on. Finally, he heard a heavy tread on the stair and turned to find John descending. He didn't care at all for the expression on his friend's face.

"What happened?" he asked, setting his foot on the lowest tread, ready to race upstairs. "Is Perry all right?"

John nodded, continuing down the steps. Ethan moved aside. "She's sleeping. She drifted off at the conclusion. You can wake her shortly, but for the moment let her rest."

"And?" Ethan prodded. "Is she imagining all of this?"

"You of all people should know she's not. You saw something yourself while you were here. What's happening to her may not be real in the sense of physically evident interaction, but it's not something she's made up in her mind, I assure you."

Wearily, John entered the living room and lowered himself into the overstuffed chair where Ethan had spent his sleepless hours two nights past. Ethan strode to the window, standing before it with his hands at his sides. Outside the sun shone brightly, the threatening weather from last evening's news blown out to sea before it could strike. Observing the morning's beauty, Ethan found it hard to believe another potentially heavy storm was forecast to hit the area sometime in the next day or so. Weather prediction was an ambiguous science. Despite all the technological advances a good deal of the art remained in the guesswork. Mother Nature had the last say in it, after all.

"I know this is going to sound ridiculous, John," Ethan spoke to the glass pane, not turning his head, "especially considering our early relationship, Perry's and mine. But I almost feel like she's cheating on me. How stupid is that?"

"It's not an altogether surprising reaction," John said behind him. "If it makes you feel any better, though, I don't believe there's been any contact of that nature since you entered the picture."

Ethan lifted his chin a little higher, feeling a tension spread from his shoulders into his neck. "So she told you everything," he said.

"She did. Perry's a good patient for hypnosis. Most psychically sensitive people are, which, as you know, leads many skeptics to question the authenticity to be found in the incidences they report."

"Yes," murmured Ethan, "I remember."

"I figured you would. Look, Ethan, you're too personally involved in this. Your judgment is being clouded."

Snorting, Ethan glanced back over his shoulder. "You think so?"

John smiled. "Just a wee bit. I'm glad you called me."

Wordlessly Ethan nodded, turning back to the window. Contemplating the events he knew about and the others he suspected, he watched a robin engaged in a hunt for food on the lawn.

"Wait a minute," he said, pivoting on his heel. Striding over to the couch, he lowered his frame onto a cushion, dangling his hands between his knees as he leaned forward in earnest. "She told me this spirit spoke to her, here in this house, the first day we met. She said it hadn't done that prior, that she only had awareness at the creek. And then later, when I returned, she told me it was trying to control my actions, that it was here in the house with us. There was contact then. She was obviously being influenced by something at that point. All you needed to do was look at her. And her skin felt like it was on fire."

John inclined his head. "I don't think it's the same entity. I believe there are two."

"What?" Ethan stood up quickly, pacing back to the window and returning. "There are two entities who are...who are..." He stopped, at a loss for words.

"No," John clarified. "I think they seek entirely different things from her. But I'm fairly certain they are, or were, both male."

Ethan swore softly. "Does Perry know?"

In the cushioned chair depths, John sat forward, cupping his hands over his knees. His sandy hair stood out in multiple directions. He'd obviously been running his fingers through the thinning, unruly mass. Ethan understood John's disturbance.

"Does she?" he asked again.

"She will," John answered. "Sometime after she awakens. An idea of it was already in her subconscious and will probably work its way to the fore over the course of the day."

Sitting down again on the sofa edge, Ethan leaned his elbows on his thighs. "How do you think she'll take it?"

"She's a fairly strong, resourceful woman, when all is said and done. Considering the length of your relationship, she spends an inordinate amount of time worrying about you, though."

"Yeah," said Ethan gruffly, "I know."

"The same can be said for you."

"Yeah," Ethan repeated. "I know."

John drew and released a ragged breath. "Be careful, Ethan."

Right. Careful. Ethan shouldn't need reminding. He nodded. "Your concern is duly noted. Let's move on. What makes you think Perry is aware there are possibly two entities rather than one?"

John sat back again, interlacing his fingers across his stomach. "She recognized some animosity being directed at her in the woods. And that feeling certainly isn't what she's been used to. That's why she went to the creek. Although she didn't say as much yesterday, she knew when she sought help from the first entity that something different was pursuing her through the woods. She saw them then as distinctly separate, a fact her conscious mind skirted after the incident. Not so her subconscious. She knows, Ethan. It'll come to her sooner rather than later."

Ethan closed his eyes, reliving in his mind's eye the frightening moments in the creek when he feared Perry would drown. He remembered yanking her from the water, the sensation she fought his efforts to save her. Or something did.

"You've said over and over again that a supernatural entity cannot do harm to a living being," Ethan said, hoping for reassurance.

"And I stand by that. For now. That doesn't mean Perry isn't sensitive to the ill feelings directed at her, which caused her panic yesterday, and perhaps even her inability to save herself when she went under the water. You were right to get her away from the house. She ultimately could be hurt because of these experiences."

Ethan stood and walked away again, pausing with his hand on the window frame. He leaned his weight into his arm, staring through the glass, jaw set, muscles tight from emotional restraint.

"What do we do?" he asked at length.

"I don't know yet. It would help if we knew why she was chosen for these hauntings. Or even who these people were in life. Have you made any headway in that area?"

"No. It's only been a couple of days and it wasn't something I was looking for in the beginning. I've done a rough research back to the late nineteenth century and haven't located anything that would suggest a cause."

"Is there anything in the house?" John continued, following the train of his thoughts. "What's in the attic? Could there be any journals, diaries, something of that nature?"

Ethan laughed, a short, humorless noise. "That attic is loaded with stuff," he said. "There are objects up there I couldn't begin to date without closer examination, some of them probably quite valuable. Perry hasn't touched any of it since her grandmother died."

"She probably can't," said John. "Whether she recognizes it or not, she's in all likelihood hypersensitive to any aura that might be given off. But I would take her with you when you go to look around. It might be helpful. I'll finish setting up here."

Summarily dismissed, Ethan reminded himself John was working within a limited time frame. He started to walk away, pausing halfway across the room.

"One other thing," he said.

"Yes?"

"The first day I came here, for the estimate, I followed Perry into the woods. I should say, I thought I followed Perry into the woods. After subsequent discussion, I don't think it was her."

"Because of how long she believes she was behind the falls," John said.

Ethan's jaw tightened. "You mean it might not have been three days?"

"It could have been, but I'm not sure. Even in her subconscious there's some disorientation. However, for the sake of argument, if it wasn't her, who do you think it might have been?"

"I don't know. A trick of the light? A neighbor who disappeared awfully damned fast?"

"Or another entity? A female one? Is that what you think?"

Sighing, Ethan crossed his arms. "I don't know. What I saw seemed too substantial. The other night—last night, here in this room, I witnessed something, but that day what I saw seemed very clear to me."

"It can be," John reminded him. "People swear to it."

"Yes, but we've never caught anything like that. Or have you?"

John shook his head. "No."

Ethan shrugged, lowering his arms. "I don't know," he said again. "That would be just too much. There's enough going on here without a third spirit."

"Some places are magnets for activity. There's water nearby, a lot of limestone in the geological makeup. Some past event we're missing still."

"Right," said Ethan, not reassured by any means. "But I think what you said makes sense. There is disorientation, and you know when you dream how much mental time passes in a twinkling. Couldn't an experience like Perry's follow the same guidelines?  She might have only been behind the falls a few minutes, and it seemed like days to her."

John was a long time in answering. "Could be. Why is this so important to you? Compared with the rest of it, I mean."

"I'm trying to wrap my head around what Perry said, about me being lead to find her yesterday. Maybe that's what happened the first day, too, although I don't like to think anything has that control. I'm grateful, in both instances, yes, but I'm just not comfortable with the idea of being influenced. Not comfortable?  Hell, I refuse to believe it's possible. Still, if she'd been ahead of me that day, I don't think there was enough time for her to have been back in that cave for more than a minute or two."

"Uh-huh."

At his friend's tone, Ethan glanced John's way. "What?"

John shook his head. "Nothing. I'm just listening. But I repeat, Ethan: Be careful."

"Got it." Ethan turned away, mounting the stairs. He strode straight to the room where Perry lay sleeping on an old trundle bed. She looked quite angelic in sleep, definitely not like she had when in his bed. The hem of her sleeveless summer dress, a lavender cotton with buttons down the entire front, had tangled between her knees. He touched her lightly on the upper arm, calling her name.

She rolled over, slowly opened her eyes. "Ethan." He liked when she spoke his name in that sleepy manner. One day, he mused, she might greet him in that exact fashion from the pillow next to his.

"How are you feeling?" he asked.

"I feel like I've been sleeping for hours. Have I?"

"No. Just a little while." He sat down on the bed beside her. She scooted over to give him room.

"John wants us to have a look around the attic for anything which might give a clue to past residents in your house, particularly written journals and the like. Are you up for it?"

She struggled to sit up, leaning back on her hands. The fabric of her dress stretched tight across her breasts. Ethan looked away.

"I'm game," she said. "I really feel quite refreshed. Are you sure I haven't been sleeping longer?"

"Positive," he answered. He stood abruptly, extending his hand to help her. She slid toward the mattress edge, disentangling the dress as she moved to rise. As she leaned forward the neck of her garment hung slack, revealing a bruised discoloration on her breastbone above the "v" front of her bra. From where Ethan stood it looked exactly like the shape of four fingers from a hand. He jerked forward.

"Perry, stand up."

"What's wrong?"

"Unbutton your top two buttons, would you?"

She hesitated for a fraction of a second before doing as he asked. Taking the two sides, Ethan parted the garment, tracing the uppermost of the four bruises with his fingertip.

"What's this?" he asked. "How did this happen?"

Perry looked down, following his finger. "I must have slammed up against something in the creek. I remember feeling like I had, like there was a weight on my chest."

She didn't seem alarmed. Apparently, from her

perspective the bruises didn't look as ominous as they did from his. Without another word on the matter he re-buttoned her dress. Somehow he needed her to show them to John without frightening her. Hell, they were frightening him.

"Let's get this over with," he said.

Perry exited the room, heading for the attic stairs. Having no idea that he meant to take her down to John she had misunderstood his intent. Still not wanting to scare her, he followed her up, determined to get John's opinion on the marks as soon as they had finished.

## Chapter Twenty-Three

Centered in the attic floor, Perry thought about the first time she'd brought Ethan up here, to examine the roof and beams. It seemed impossible this had been less than a week ago. At that time he'd needed a flashlight to inspect for damage. Now he seemed content to search through the stored accumulation using only the sun through the windows set far apart in opposite walls. Perry found the task daunting. She couldn't imagine where to begin, but Ethan opted for the most direct approach, starting at the attic's northern end, suggesting she commence at the other and they would meet in the middle.

Perry opened the window on her side to let fresh air into the vast space beneath the slate roof. Though not exactly stifling, the atmosphere felt close and heavy with dust, and smelled slightly of age. The latter she didn't mind, as it had always given her a sense she could reach out and touch the past.

Yanking up her dress hem to tuck it between her knees, Perry crouched low over the floor to look through books stacked in a pile not far from the elongated rectangle where sunlight shone across the random width planks at her feet. They all appeared to be hardback novels from a fairly recent era, the oldest perhaps no more than twenty years and none the type thing they were looking for. She moved on.

Next she found an old Singer sewing machine in its cabinet. Lifting the lid off the bench she shuffled through old patterns, packs of needles and thread bobbins in many colors. At one time the machine had been downstairs, in the little room off the kitchen.

A vivid image appeared in her mind, her grandmother sewing a beautiful burgundy velvet dress for Perry's Christmas dance one year, while she and her mother looked on. That would have had to have been about two or three years before her mother died. On and off through her life—mostly on—she and Mom had lived here with Nana. Perry had never known her father. She didn't feel she had suffered unduly for his absence. They had been a closeknit family, the Madison women, for a long time. Until she moved away with Jack.

Biting her lip, Perry replaced the cushioned lid. Taped boxes clearly marked with dates and contents she bypassed with a glance. Opening an old armoire, she rifled through musty clothing, then yanked open the drawers beneath. Old photos in frames stared up at her, remembered faces in dated attire. She wanted to take them out and look at them, but she understood they hadn't the time. She pushed the drawers shut.

"Any luck?" Ethan called from his side.

"Not yet," Perry answered.

A dresser from the prior century yielded no results. Perry ran her hand over the crazed finish. She needed to get this furniture out of the attic before the seasonal temperature changes, exaggerated beneath the roof, ruined its value.

Perry relocated some stacked and dusty chairs, shoved aside a metal rack, repositioned old and moth-eaten coats. Several more marked boxes she pushed across the floor to clear a path. Ethan exclaimed softly over something he had found, although Perry figured it less important than personally interesting to him because he moved along without saying anything further. She continued to peer into cabinets and cases and the occasional open crate, locating clothing, blackened silver, frames and books and miscellaneous articles which had once been part and parcel of someone's past. She spent little time studying these objects, sensing immediately she wouldn't find what she needed there.

A half an hour or so had passed when she discovered a steamer trunk shoved close up under the eaves. She stopped, staring at it. The words Lincoln-Fairfield stenciled on the side of it meant nothing to her. However, she knew before opening the lid what lay inside held personal significance. A recollection from when she'd been too young to have been up in the attic alone suddenly materialized. She remembered her mother's voice above her head, and her slender arm reaching past Perry to lift out a dress folded on top. Dropping to her knees, Perry pulled the trunk toward her and raised the lid.

The dress was still there. A strapless gown with a high waist and a full taffeta skirt in a  shade of pink Perry would never consider wearing, but which her mother had proudly worn to her own senior prom. The very night Perry had been conceived. Yes, if there was one thing Sheila Madison had been, it was honest, and she had not covered up the story of Perry's creation with any glossy tale having to do with romance and tragedy. No, Sheila had gone to the prom with her boyfriend of six months and made a misguided decision later that night. The boy, Frank Harris, vanished into the service as soon as she told him she'd gotten pregnant. And though she might have had mixed emotions about raising a child on her own, Sheila Madison swore she never regretted the decision to keep the baby that would be her one and only.

Lifting out the dress, Perry sat back on the floor and laid it across her knees. She stroked the outdated, brittle fabric, touched the delicate stitches on the bodice, clearly Nana's handiwork. Bending her head, she raised the gown to her cheek and breathed in. The dress smelled musty, yes, but a perfume lingered in it as well. Perhaps the gown had been stored with a sachet to keep out the insects, but she preferred to think she scented the fragrance her mother had worn that night.

"Perry?"

Perry shot a glance over her shoulder, her cheeks wet from tears.

"What do you have there?" Ethan's voice held remarkable gentleness.

"My mother's prom dress," Perry answered, the tears coursing anew at his tender, considerate tone.

"She's no longer with you, then."

"No," said Perry. "She died when I was seventeen."

Ethan crouched down beside her, setting some large volume he had tucked under his arm onto the floor by his feet. He touched her shoulder, leaning close to view the dress in her lap.

"Not your color," he said.

"No," she smiled damply.

"You miss her."

"Yes," she said.

His fingers slipped around the back of her neck and he drew her head close to his own, pressing his mouth to her temple. "Do you want to take the dress downstairs with you? Or perhaps the whole trunk?"

She nodded mutely.

"Let's do that, then. We'll just drag it out here to the middle of the floor as a reminder."

He took the dress from her, laying it back in place with care. Perry rose from her knees, catching sight as she did so of a small, thick ledger tucked down against the chest's side. Before Ethan closed the lid, she reached to take the book out. Rising to walk into the sunshine with it, she left Ethan to carry the trunk over to the staircase. She flipped through the pages, recognizing her mother's feathery scrawl.

"It's her diary," she said to no one in particular.

Ethan, having returned to her side, bent to peer over her shoulder once again. She witnessed his slow smile.

"That's a find of inestimable value," he said.

She nodded agreement.

"I came across a very old Bible," he added. "I set it by the stairs, too. Someone has written on slips of parchment held loose inside. There's also a record of birth dates and deaths and the like. It appears to have belonged to a pastor or minister who once lived here, but I'm not certain. We'll look at it later."

Perry nodded again. Placing the diary carefully on the windowsill, she turned to face him.

"You're a very sweet man," she told him.

"I can't say I've ever heard that before," he answered. He smiled again, took her face into his hands and lowered his mouth onto her own. With a swift breath, Perry's lips parted to accept his tongue's caress across hers in a single stroke. He withdrew, kissing her nose.

"And you're a man who leaves a woman wanting more," she stated dryly.

"Am I now?" he drawled, spinning her back toward the window. Taking each of her hands into his own, he crossed her arms over her chest before drawing her back against his. Bending, he pressed his mouth to the top of her head. After, he propped his chin there.

"I thought we were supposed to be searching for information," she said.

"In a minute."

Perry relaxed into his embrace, her gaze on the barn outside the window. The breeze, though warm, felt pleasant across her arms and face in the sticky attic atmosphere. Her hem fluttered against her knees. Ethan's breath moved subtly through the loosened tendrils on her crown, his chest rising and falling along her spine.

"My wife died," he said.

Perry's head jerked. She would have turned around again but he held her fast.

"About seven years ago," he added.

So much for her stupid, jealous reaction to Cindy. "I'm sorry," she whispered. "What happened?"

He remained silent for so long she thought he hadn't heard her, and then he shook his head. "Not now. Some other time."

Perry nodded, her hair catching the stubble on his chin. Inhaling deeply, she loosened one hand from his own and reached back to touch his throat, feeling his drumbeat pulse beneath his jaw. He turned and kissed her wrist. With his free hand about her waist he pulled her closer still.

"Thank you," he said.

She nodded again, a little less forcefully, nestling closer against him. After a moment he bent his head to her nape. His breath passed over her skin. She shivered in his arms.

"I like that," he said.

"What? What do you like?"

"This," he said, and kissed her where his breath had been. She closed her eyes as the pleasant chill tripped along her spine and turned to heat where he had positioned his mouth.

"Uh-huh," she breathed. "I like that, too."

"I can tell," he answered, and she felt his smile stretch into a grin against her flesh. He kissed her again, harder, and her breath rushed from her lungs.

"Don't start what you're not going to finish," she warned in a low voice.

"I'm not."

He kissed her again on her nape, opening his mouth to graze his teeth lightly over her skin. She arched into the caress and he increased the pressure, just enough. The sound she made inflamed them both. She could tell by the way his arms tightened around her, almost convulsively, possessively, and he buried his face into the place where her shoulder curved upward, scrubbing his jaw back and forth gruffly over the tendon there. His heated breath rushed across her skin.

"Ethan."

It was neither the time nor the place, but she had no desire to refuse him. And hadn't she told him not to start if he had no intention of seeing them through to completion? She turned her head slightly, toward the stairs, thinking of John below, and then of the voice which had not come to haunt her. She closed her eyes again as Ethan's mouth opened once more upon her nape. Her knees nearly buckled. Sensing her lost balance, he tightened his grip.

"Ethan."

"Shhh," he murmured, the whispered syllable a caress in itself, the light and airy passage rippling over her ear and along her jaw. Releasing one hand, he moved it to her dress buttons, deftly unbuttoning them all to her waist one by one. The damp breeze through the window coursed along her stomach where the fabric parted. Wordlessly he slid the dress down her arms to her elbows, then ran his hands along her shoulders and up the sides of her throat, pressing his teeth again to the place that made her quiver. Her nipples tightened within her bra. His hands were suddenly there also, as if sensing her need, sliding without pressure over her undergarment, then pulling it down slowly to expose the taut flesh to his fingers.

"Oh, God," she breathed, "don't stop this time."

"Sweetheart," he whispered against her throat, "I don't think I could."

Something in his words chilled her, just for an instant, and then she responded again to his manipulation of her nipples with his fingertips. She knew she was wet already, could feel her body's moisture between her legs. He unbuttoned the remainder of her dress, sliding his right hand along her belly's subtle swell to linger just within the low band on her panties.

"You're trembling so hard I can't hold you still," he said.

"I know."

"And if I put my hand between your legs, it'll be over for you."

"No," she contradicted, "it'll be just beginning."

He groaned, possibly the only articulation he

could make, and followed through with his threat. All he did was cup his hand over her, but it was enough. With a cry she pushed herself against his curved palm and arched her back. His arm tightened across her rib cage to keep her from rocketing away from him. A string of words escaped him, mostly unintelligible and some doubtlessly profane, and then he stepped nearer to the wall beside the window, lifting her along with him. She put her hands up against the cool stone surface.

Breathing heavily, her head against the stone, the perspiration streamed between her shoulder blades. Behind her she heard his zipper drop and then he took her dress off. Her underwear slipped to the floor. He ran his hands along her buttocks to her thighs as he stepped forward, parting her legs with his knees. She rocked her hips toward him, her head dropping back on her shoulders. As she moaned a subtle syllable he slid into her from behind, his hands on her hips to steady her precarious balance.

"Oh my God," she whispered.

*This is what we wanted.*

Perry gasped in cold shock. "No."

If Ethan heard her, he made no sign. With his knees slightly bent he slid in and out with maddening leisure, almost making her forget *he* had spoken. Her heart raced as her breathing grew shallow and rapid. Ethan's hands were on her hips, then up her spine, curving around her shoulders. Her breasts yearned for his attention, but she knew if he reached forward she would topple off balance. She had to hold herself still, despite her inclination to move with him. The enforced immobility was agonizingly sweet to her senses.

"Perry," he whispered, "Perry, I'm going to pull out now. I have no protection. I don't think it would be wise to continue."

*This is what you wanted.*

"No," Perry said again, as a chill cat's paw crept along her heated flesh. *His* declaration held a vicious note, a frightening intonation. She perceived a touch across the nipple of her right breast and knew Ethan's hands were elsewhere. Even so, for a moment she reacted to the sensation with the mindless eagerness that had consumed her in the days she had lost, feeling her muscles contract spasmodically as Ethan drove forward again inside of her. Fighting the sensations, she pulled away. The phantom caress followed, without tenderness, without warmth. Not the same as it had been. No, not the same at all.

"Perry," Ethan, questioning her sudden movement, seeking a response to what he had said.

*You filthy harlot.*

Abruptly, Perry found herself shoved to the wall. She thudded up against it, her breasts pressed flat against the cold stone, her cheekbone bearing the brunt of the impact. She cried out.

"You fucking whore."

"Ethan!"

His voice spoke, and yet not his voice, the tonal qualities recognizable but the manifested animosity entirely alien.

"You don't deserve to be treated like a woman."

The menace was obvious. He grabbed her roughly between the legs.

"Ethan, stop it," she said, her mind cartwheeling in a dozen directions. She attempted to turn around, to look him in the eye, to recall him from wherever he had gone, but he planted his forearm between her shoulder blades, his hand locked around the back of her neck, her battered cheekbone lodged still against the cold, unyielding stone. With his next move his intent was clear to her, the pressure of his fingertips on her buttocks brutally implicit.

"Ethan, don't do that. Ethan!"

She cried out again in shock and pain as he thrust himself into resistant tissue, and with the impetus of both she managed to push off the wall and jerk away from the hand restraining her. He reached to grab her again.

"Damn your soul to hell, Lily, you shall take what I choose to give you. You deserve no respect from me. My brother? You are worse than a whore!"

Perry struck Ethan across the face. Hard. He staggered backward from the blow, but lunged at her again. She struck him with both fists in the chest, forcing him back. His hand came up, closing around her wrist. She lifted the other to strike him once more and he grabbed that one also.

"Ethan!" she cried. "Ethan stop!"

He already had. She could see the change in him, in his stance, his eyes. Mouth agape and breathing heavily, he dropped forward, one hand on his naked thigh, the other still clutching her upper arm.

"Perry, my God, Perry, what have I done? I've hurt you!"

"Oh, you were aware of that, were you?" Perry spat, yanking herself free. Bending, she grabbed her dress from the floor where he'd trampled it. Dazed, he pulled his pants up over his slim hips, fumbling with the zipper, his countenance blanched, white with shock in the unrelenting sun. Whatever ardor might have been present in his gaze when their lovemaking had begun had been stripped away by the intended savagery of an act uncompleted.

"Perry, I don't—I don't understand what happened. I swear to you." He reached out to her and she stumbled away from him, spinning with her dress clutched close to her body. His hand fell to his side. "Part of me was aware of what I was doing, and it seemed to make perfect sense in some warped manner. But I didn't want to do it. Hell, I would never hurt you. Never. You must know that."

Feeling sick, Perry struggled back into her clothing. She brushed the boot prints from her dress with an edged hand, a hand that ached from striking him. Raising her fingers to her bruised cheekbone she started to cry. When Ethan reached for her again she didn't fight him, but allowed him to envelop her in his arms. She buried her face in his shirt, breathing deeply.

"I'm sorry," he said in a voice like heartbreak. She shook her head against his chest, wanting him to be silent. No apologies. There could be no apologies. Whatever had just happened did not occur by his choosing, she knew. She'd heard the change in his voice, felt the malevolent impulse of another presence. Nevertheless, her body cringed from the remembered assault when he lifted his hand to stroke her hair over her head and down her back. His fingers trembled.

"This is not good, Perry," he said.

"I know."

A rapid, heavy tread sounded on the stairs and then the steamer trunk Ethan had set at its head slid back. John appeared, breathless and excited.

"I had an extraordinary reading. I don't know if it was an anomaly, because not all the equipment is interfaced. But I—good Lord, what happened here?"

John stared at Perry's battered, tear-streaked face, the manner in which she clung to Ethan. If John noted Ethan's haggard expression, he gave no sign as he slowly took in her clothing's filthy, rumpled condition. Swallowing hard, Perry could only stare back at him.

"I'm not certain what happened, John," Ethan said above her head. "But we need to find out who the hell Lily is."

## *Chapter Twenty-Four*

The spigot in Ethan's tub dripped. Perry observed it in some surprise. She decided there must be some truth to the adage regarding the shoemaker's children never having any shoes. Ethan's house certainly didn't suffer from neglect, but the small irony of a leaky faucet made her smile, although without much humor. She lifted her foot from the water, waiting for gravity to do its work. After several seconds a tiny drop slid down her toe. She lowered her foot back into the tepid liquid.

She had permitted John a cursory examination of the bruise to her cheek. Ethan had wanted him to see the blue-black ridges across her breastbone as well, but she hadn't been disposed to open her dress for anyone. Whatever concern Ethan had regarding that particular injury could wait until a better time. The discomfort she felt in other regions was more pertinent, though she had no intention to see a doctor for that either, even one at the hospital, which Ethan had suggested. The injury was not life threatening or even particularly painful, as she had managed to prevent further damage when she pulled away from him. What it had been, though, and continued to be, was violent, humiliating, and disturbing.

Ethan had driven her back to his house after a minor disagreement with John. It seemed Ethan had concerns about leaving his friend alone in the house. John successfully argued that any entity making itself known had no interest in him. Conceding, Ethan left him there with a promise to return in a few hours' time.

Solicitous, traumatized and guilt-ridden, Ethan had immediately filled the tub with hot water for her upon their arrival, then left her in privacy to soak her sore body. The water had neared room temperature as the heat dissipated, but Perry felt no inclination to rise from the tub. She eyed the clean, folded towel next to the sink, then returned her scrutiny to the next drip forming at the spout's edge.

Perry held no doubt Lily was someone or, to be more precise, had been someone very real. Lily was the name by which *he* called her—it seemed oddly forever ago now—and the name to which she had responded so readily. Until she heard the name from Ethan's mouth, memory had eluded her. In the silent ride back to Ethan's house she made no mention. She had a feeling he suspected the truth already. Through some ghastly logic it only made sense, after all.

A light knock sounded on the door and then it opened, only enough for Ethan to speak through, asking if she was all right. The defeated tone in his voice saddened her. She fought back tears.

"I'm fine," she said.

"That water has to be getting cold."

"It is cold," she answered.

A momentary silence followed her statement.

"I made you a cup of chamomile tea. You should drink it while it's still hot."

"Thanks."

The door started to close.

"Ethan?"

The door swung open again. His dark head appeared around the edge. God, he was a handsome man, even wearing an uncertain expression, sorrow and confusion moving through his eyes.

"Come in and sit down a minute, will you?"

He pushed the door all the way open, shutting it only partway behind him, and crossed the floor to perch on the lowered toilet lid. He forewent his usual stance, legs stretched before him, for one not quite as confident, knees and feet planted slightly apart at strange angles, his arms folded across his thighs and his hands clasped loosely together between. A frown marred his brow. Perry had a strong, oddly maternal urge to reach out and smooth the mark of worry, but it would have meant getting up from the tub. A draft through the open door rippled across her arms. With his innate sense of what she needed, Ethan extended his hand and pushed the door shut.

"Ethan, we must find out who Lily was," she told him, amazed at how calm she sounded. "We have to find out who might have wanted to...to do that to her. It seems to me," she said and paused, drawing a steadying breath. "It seems to me," she went on, "based on what you said at the time, the act was not consensual but meant to punish in some fashion." She witnessed him flinch, but he stoically nodded his head. "I am assuming you spoke through no context within your own past life," she went on, "so, I think we can safely say Lily slept with somebody's brother."

"I agree," he stated quietly.

"Lily is the name he called me by, the name I couldn't recall before. The spirit in the creek, I mean. I don't know who this was in the house. It wasn't him. And Ethan, it wasn't you either. You didn't intend to hurt me."

He lifted his hand, dropping his head into it, running his fingers through his hair. "But I did hurt you, Perry," he said, "and it could have been worse. What happened was fairly close to rape."

Perry clamped her mouth shut. Not close to. If the act had reached its conclusion, it would have been. The violent intent indeed was. No close about it. The muscle in her jaw tightened as her teeth ground together. She slid her hips along the tub bottom, dropping down into the water until her chin dipped below the surface. Once there, she held herself very still.

"It's tearing me up," he said, pivoting his head to look at her. "To realize that I'm not man enough to fight something like that. To abandon my own instinct to protect you, to keep you safe. I hurt you, Perry. Damn it, I hurt you. It makes me wonder just what kind of man I am inside, that I could give in to that urge without so much as a struggle."

Perry sank her teeth into her lower lip, nearly raising a welt. She had no desire to tell him she'd spent the past twenty minutes wondering the same thing. She'd been reminding herself of her own, uncharacteristic behavior. It was nothing compared to what he had done, but she believed, truly believed now, that they were both influenced, horrifyingly influenced, by something from beyond the grave.

It was like insanity.

Her gaze remained riveted to the drop still

quivering on the metal tap. Come on, she urged it silently, come on. When you fall, I'll get up. I'll get up from this tub and decide what next to do with my life. With mine and with his.

"Perry," Ethan went on, his voice resonating in the tiled enclosure, "you mean a great deal to me. I'm not going to go on about love at first sight or any of that. But I don't want to lose you, I really don't."

Plop.

Perry scrambled from the tub so fast she nearly fell, flying across the hazardously slick tile to throw herself into his lap, soaking wet. He grunted from the forceful landing. His arms went around her, pulling her close. He stroked her hair and kissed her brow tenderly, reaching over to the sink for the towel to wrap it around her naked, shivering body.

For a very long time they sat there, exactly like that, the only sound the steady dripping water from her skin and hair onto the floor at his feet. Eventually, even that stopped.

## Chapter Twenty-Five

"Where's Perry?"

Ethan closed the exterior kitchen door, crossing to where John stood on the threshold to Perry's living room holding a print-out from one of the machines in his hand. A frown creased the man's brow. Though he'd asked the question, his attention seemed concentrated on the paper in his fingers, as if deliberately avoiding eye contact with Ethan. Ethan stepped up beside him, glancing at the print-out.

"At my place curled up in bed with the television on," he said. "She took a couple over-the-counter sleep aids I've had in the medicine cabinet for God knows how long. I don't know what shelf life they have. They may not do her any good."

John nodded, glancing sidelong at Ethan before

returning his focus to the task. "And you? How are you doing?"

Ethan shrugged. "I've been better."

John nodded again, then wordlessly handed the lengthy paper strip to Ethan. Ethan slid the print-out through his fingers, tipping it to the light.

"I don't see any activity here," he said.

"There hasn't been any since you two left," John told him. "But this," he said, handing him another register, "is what appeared when you were in the attic."

Ethan let out a low whistle. "Crap," he said, unconsciously using Perry's favorite expletive. At mention of the attic, Ethan felt slowly rolling lust tinged with lingering rage, and then shame. A far away feeling, as if it didn't come from him, but it did, it had. He knew it had, and yet he was not that man who would use a woman so wrongly. Still, he experienced the emotion as if it were some echo of his own. Swearing a bit more potently, he handed the paper back to John.

"He calls her Lily."

At John's questioning glance, Ethan explained further.

"The entity at the creek. He—it calls her Lily. She hears him in her head, where I sure as hell can't go to drive him out. It out," he amended.

John arched his shaggy blond brows.

"And you called her Lily," he said.

"Yes," Ethan admitted, lifting his gaze to stare

across the living room to the window and beyond. The sunlight lay golden on the grass. In the deep shadow surrounding the casement, silhouetted leaves shivered in a short-lived breeze. "But it wasn't him in the attic. She said it was someone—I mean something different."

John nodded. "As I suspected."

"Yep."

John sighed, folding his arms across his chest. "You are in definite pain, my friend. This is a very dangerous situation for you as well as for Perry. You understand that, don't you?"

"I do," said Ethan. In the yellow-veiled sky beyond the treetops he watched a bird circle. A moment later another joined it, and then another, circling higher until they disappeared from sight.

"Well, what do you want to do about it?"

Ethan turned away from the window, blinking. "Whatever we can."

Lifting his hand, John scratched his nose. "This is a start," he said, indicating the monitoring equipment. "None of this needs our babysitting, however. I suggest we leave the equipment undisturbed overnight, then return in the morning to check any results."

Slowly, Ethan nodded agreement. "And if nothing shows up? You know that's the most likely scenario. What you showed me there," Ethan jerked his chin, indicating the readout, "is a rare detection."

John grunted. "Yeah, I'm only too aware of that. I wish I had more time to spend here, but I don't. Not this week. I hate to make this suggestion, but we might need Perry to return at some point. I don't want to put either of you at risk, but Perry is apparently the catalyst for what's been taking place at the creek, and you appear in some way responsible for the contact of this second entity. Or perhaps it's you and Perry together producing the necessary conduit. After all, there have been no tales of haunting associated with this house before. Have there?"

"Not that I'm aware," answered Ethan. "Who knows, though?  There aren't any published eyewitness accounts, to be sure. We couldn't be that lucky. But I don't like putting Perry in harm's way."

Nodding his agreement, John turned to make a minor adjustment to a camera position. "Between the two of us we'll guarantee she doesn't do herself any harm," he said.

Ethan eyed him sidelong. "That guarantee carries no weight with me," he stated, voice tight. "She didn't hurt herself due to some confused or entranced state. I hurt her, John. Me. For Perry's sake I wasn't too specific with you while she was withing earshot about what took place in the attic, but you have to know something of it."  His hand shook against his thigh and he curled his fingers into a fist to stop the spasmodic movement.

"I hurt her, John. For a moment it was as if my thoughts were in perfect sync with someone else, and that someone else did not have Perry's, or I should say Lily's, best interests at heart, believe me. She didn't fall against the wall. I shoved her there, and...and worse. And those bruises on her chest that she didn't want to show you? They look to me very much like a hand print. I didn't cause those. She said they appeared after something struck her in the chest while she was under the water yesterday. To be exact, she said she felt as if a weight was on her. I don't like this, John, not at all. This goes beyond anything I've ever experienced while working with you. To be honest, it's scaring the hell out of me."

For a full minute John remained silent, staring at the floor. He reached up, pulling at his chin with his thumb and forefinger. Ethan recognized the old habit and chose not to hasten his friend's thought processes. Give the man time, they all had been wont to say, and he'll come up with something new to try.

This time, however, he didn't. He blew his breath out through his nose and shook his head. "Hypnosis would probably aid in deciphering your actions."

Ethan felt a flicker of annoyance. "You want to put me under? Haven't we tried this before?"

John looked him in the eye. "For an altogether different reason, as you will recall. I'd like to make certain that what occurred wasn't the result of some repressed anger in you. The fact you used the name Lily and so did the entity by the creek, which I believe had not previously been revealed to you, bodes well. At least for your behavior. Not, though, for Perry's chances to live a normal life in this house of hers. What I want to know is what sparked this? Until we have some answers from the past, there's no telling what we're dealing with."

Ethan nodded, rubbing his hand wearily along his jaw, feeling the scratchy stubble from a day's growth of beard. He realized with a start he hadn't shaved that morning. Dead beat, he could barely remember what day it was.

"In the morning, before we return?" he suggested.

"Whenever you'd like."

Yawning, Ethan turned away into the kitchen. "Let's lock up then. I just want to make one stop on the way home."

John didn't question him, merely giving the machinery nearest to hand a cursory check before following him out the door. In the truck, Ethan remembered the equipment John had wanted to set by the creek, but his former professor waved away his concerns.

"Tomorrow," he said.

Complacent in his exhaustion, Ethan backed the truck in a half circle, nosing it toward the road along the deteriorated driveway as he suppressed another yawn. The late afternoon sun slanted through the trees, barring the dirty windshield in shadow and glare. Reaching for his sunglasses, Ethan slid them on single-handed, glancing in the rear view mirror as he did so. When he slammed on the brakes John hit the dashboard hard with a flat palm, the seatbelt he had not yet finished fastening falling from his right hand to clatter against the door.

"Look on the porch."

"What?" John asked, fumbling for the fallen belt.

"Look on the porch, now."

Beside him John spun in his seat, narrowing his eyes against the sun's brilliance.

"Take these," said Ethan, handing him his polarized sunglasses. John slipped them up his nose, tilting his head to look through them.

"I don't see—"

"Third post from the right. Your right. Near the rocker," Ethan explained rapidly as he rummaged in the narrow space behind the seat for the 35 mm camera he used to photograph houses before he began work on them. With any luck, the polarizing filter was in place. He had used the camera last to take pictures on a day such as this.

"Son of an f'ing bitch," John murmured, focusing on the place where Ethan had directed him. "What is that, do you think?"

"I know what I think it is," Ethan said through his teeth, excitement and dread surging through him despite his efforts to stay calm. "Your opinion is what I want right now."

Opening the driver's door Ethan stepped from the cab, camera in hand. He made a quick adjustment and raised the viewfinder to his eye, hoping for the best.

In the truck, John leaned across the seat. "Want these back?" he asked, preparing to remove the sunglasses.

"No time," Ethan said brusquely. "Just tell me if it's still there."

"I–no. Yes!  A little more to the left of where you said it was. Can you see it at all?"

"I can't see it," Ethan answered, "but I sure as hell can feel it."

A rill of hair stood up along each arm together with every follicle on the back of his neck. As he repeatedly shot and wound the film forward, varying the focus point only slightly each time, he could hear John talking rapid-fire from inside the cab.

"I'm half tempted to go back in the house and check those read-outs now. Left, left, again!  It's half-formed. I can't make out the shape. It's definitely not a trick of the light. There, again! Left again, towards the far corner. Yee-hah!"

A grin broke out across Ethan's face at John's well-remembered enthusiasm. John Gooden had grafted well in his southern home, combining New York cynicism with rebel exuberance into a heartfelt, endearing symmetry. Still smiling, Ethan moved along the truck bed, nearer the house. As he did, he stepped away from the sun and into the shadow cast by the trees.

The substance on the porch turned, drifting like a mist and coalescing again, quite as if it had seen him, detected him, made him the focus of its attention. Ethan stopped shooting. What had Perry asked? Did either of them see a mist on the water?

Setting one foot behind the other, Ethan began backing away.

"John?"

"I see it."

Ethan nodded. He shot two more exposures as he walked backwards, and then lowered the camera to his side. The mist drifted off the porch into the ragged grass at the structure's edge.

"What are you feeling, Ethan?"

John had gotten out of the truck. Ethan could tell by the way John's voice traveled to him, but he didn't turn his head to check.

"A little alarmed," he answered. "Curious. Angry."

"Angry?"

Ethan gave brief examination to his feelings. "Yes. Like there's this rage beating against me, wanting in. I'm not going to let it. I know better now. I didn't expect it before and got caught off guard."

John sucked in his breath, audible to Ethan on

the vehicle's opposite side. "Get inside the truck, Ethan."

"I'm coming."

"No. A little faster, please."

Ethan couldn't remember hearing the unique note to John's voice in all the years he'd known him. In response he backed up more quickly still, until he found himself in the sun and temporarily blinded. Fighting down panic and fury, Ethan made his way along the truck, one hand trailing over the body to guide his steps. He tossed the camera to John even as he slid behind the wheel. Gravel spurted from the tires as he gassed the truck, shooting it out into the driveway, jolting John from his seat yet again in the ruts.

Ethan drove in silence until they were out on the roadway and he had looked back too many times for comfort. John had silently and calmly belted himself in and checked the camera, for what Ethan couldn't tell, except possibly to be certain he'd had it turned on.

"I've never known you to be afraid," Ethan said after a moment.

"I wasn't," countered John. "I'm not. Well, I was. For you. How are you feeling now?"

Ethan tested his emotions before replying. "Unnerved," he answered, "but myself."

"Good man."

Laughing in grim humor, Ethan leaned closer over the wheel. Drenched with reeking sweat, his shirt stuck to his back. The first thing he planned to do when he got home was take a shower. The second, well, the second depended on Perry. If she was sleeping, so be it, but if not, then, God help him, he needed her to make him feel normal again. To show him he wasn't this raging creature, the residuum of which seemed to be clinging to his clothes, his skin, his very soul.

Rolling down the window, he turned his head and spat. Even his mouth tasted foul.

"You all right?"

"I will be," Ethan said.

With abrupt recognition of where he was, Ethan veered off the road. He didn't bother using the signal.

"What's wrong?"

"I passed the church. We've got to stop there."

"Feeling a sudden need for redemption?" drawled John. "Not that I would blame you in the slightest," he added.

"No," said Ethan, glancing up and down the road for traffic before swinging the truck back in the direction they had come. "I want a quick look at the graveyard."

"Ah." John refrained from further comment even after they had pulled into the narrow, graveled lane and parked in the lot. Ethan sat behind the wheel a moment longer, studying the church's facade. A small building, more the size of a one-room schoolhouse than anything else, except for the different height and steeply pitched roof. Nearly two hundred years earlier the building had been constructed of brick and stone, then plastered for insulation, and would have accommodated a minimal congregation. No longer in religious use, fifteen years ago the church had been closed due to some damage to the floor yet to be corrected, and now fell  under the historical society's jurisdiction. Ethan knew some very old records were housed there in proprietorial insistence and regularly maintained, though not available to the general public. Beside the structure stood the graveyard, shaded by a gnarled canopy formed by an ancient white oak in heavy leaf. Its moss-covered markers leaned with age over the unevenly humped earth. Beyond, corn in a farmer's field stood tall in rustling green contrast, a breeze fingering through the stalks.

Ethan shoved open the door and got out, advancing toward the narrow gravestones. The other door closed as John followed. Striding across the roughly shorn grass, Ethan scanned engraved names and dates discolored by pale, gray-green lichen.

"Here's a Lily," John announced. Ethan moved to his side, gazing at the inscription.

"1902?  I don't know. If you've got a pen and paper, would you write that one down? Thanks." Ethan continued on, finding another Lily a short distance away. This grave was some thirty years older than the first which had, by its date, appeared to be one of the last dug. The cemetery had not been used since the beginning of the twentieth century.

"Popular name," commented John dryly, jotting down the information. "There can't be more than sixty stones here, and at least two of them bear the name Lily. This isn't going to be easy, if she's even buried here."

"I know," said Ethan. "It's just a hunch, a hope, given the proximity of the church to the property. Besides, I think there's some connection between the house and the church building. The Bible I found in the attic belonged to a Reverend Edward Nicholson. If I thought someone was inside on a Saturday, I'd go and ask to see the old records."

"How do you know there's not?"

"Do you see a car?" Ethan asked, looking around.

"Behind the building," answered John, indicating the back end of a late model Dodge with his chin. The strengthening breeze tugged the frizzed ends of his thinning blond hair. "Let's give the door a try."

Ethan heard the last about two seconds after he was already in motion and the door in question opening at his approach. A pretty, middle-aged woman stepped out onto the shallow marble steps.

"Ethan?" she said.

Ethan faltered before continuing forward, leaping the stairs to stand at the woman's side. After a minute hesitation he bent and kissed her on the cheek. She made little, flustered noises as she smiled up at him.

"John," he called over his shoulder, "this is Maggie Barnes, an old friend of mine. She's on the Board of Directors for County Historical Preservation. Maggie, this is John Gooden."

John mounted the stairs to shake Maggie's hand. She seemed startled by the gesture, quickly snatching her fingers back to her side.

"What brings you and your friend here?" she asked. "I didn't hear you pull up, but I heard voices."

Ethan exchanged a quick glance with John over Maggie's head. "I'm doing some research," he said. "Before I start work on the Madison property. Water on Stone? Perhaps you're familiar with it."

"Goodness, yes," she said with a tittering laugh, her green eyes looking him up and down in quick appraisal, hesitating at the sweat stains causing his shirt to cling across his chest and abdomen. "How not," she went on, her cadence measured, "considering my work here? A great many inhabitants of this graveyard made their home there at some point. Our most infamous is the Reverend, however. But you must know that."

"Must I?" Ethan responded, exchanging a second glance with John. "I'm not familiar with his history at all."

"No? Then come in. I'm sure you have a few

minutes to catch up on old times and then I'll show you what we have." She tucked her hand into Ethan's elbow, leaning around him to smile sweetly at John. "You're welcome to come in, as well," she advised.

The third glance exchanged between Ethan and John was prompted by his friend and embodied an entirely different message than the first two. Away from Maggie's direct gaze, Ethan rolled his eyes and shook his head. Don't ask, he mouthed.

Grateful for John's restraint despite the man's suppressed mirth, Ethan allowed himself to be led into the former church by the woman he had, on more than one occasion, been forced to physically fend off. Though he'd been careful not to hurt her feelings, he had certainly gained a better understanding of what women went through when confronted by unwanted attention.

The building's interior still contained what appeared to be its earliest seating, dark wood glistening beneath a silt-like dust layer. Two saw horses blocked the floor's center. As they traversed the worn planks, a finer dust rose into the air, shimmering in the sun.

"Careful," said Maggie. "One of these years we'll get that fixed. There's a small problem with the allocation of money. I don't suppose you'd be interested in performing the job for, say, some other type of compensation?"

Behind them John coughed, cleared his throat,

then apologized, attributing the outburst to the floating dust.

"I'm very busy at the moment, Maggie," said Ethan. "I haven't time for much of anything these days."

She made an extremely unfeminine sound, but dropped the subject, tossing her head. "Through this door," she directed. "What fortunate timing. I stopped by to gather some paperwork and in another couple of minutes would have been gone."

"Yes, quite fortunate." This from John, bringing up the rear. Maggie cut her eyes in John's direction as if just recalling some annoyance.

"Sit down," she said, indicating a single chair. Which one of them she meant to remain standing was anybody's guess. "Tell me how you've been."

"I've been well," Ethan said, remaining on his feet. "Busy, as I've said. In fact, I'm pressed for time, so if you could just share that information with me?"

She pivoted on her heel, patently disappointed. Then she shrugged. "As you will," she murmured, crossing the floor with an exaggerated swing to her stride. A good-sized floor safe held court against the wall, too heavy to be moved by someone intent on mischief. Ethan watched discreetly as she spun through the combination, then yanked open the door. She pulled an old registry from the interior. Other documents were visible within.

"Why aren't those things kept someplace better suited?" John ventured to ask from his post by the doorway.

Maggie lowered the register onto the table at Ethan's elbow. "Part of the stipulation," she said, all sign of sweetness and patience gone.

"Stipulation?"

"Neither the building nor the land on which it stands were ever donated to the cause of religion. They have been privately owned through the years by the original founders and the heirs of the estate you're going to be working on," she said to Ethan, rather than John. "Both remained in the family for generations until the early 1920's. At that time, when the last Nicholson died—although by that time, marriage had changed the name to something else, Smith, I think," she added in a flippant aside, "there was some legal clause in his will that this portion of the property, albeit part of the estate in its entirety, would go to use by the State in preservation with each successor. Nothing inside can be removed. There was, of course, no money willed to that end, but the State has continued its guardianship. I can't imagine what sort of contract could legally bind any new owner to continue the agreement. I suppose it might have been a condition of sale. I believe the Madisons bought the place in the 1950's, didn't they?" Once again, she directed her remarks to Ethan, ignoring the fact John had asked the initial question.

"They did," Ethan answered. The other information surprised him, as he hadn't yet come across any of it in the course of his own research. Neither had Perry made mention of owning this property, nor the stipulation that it remain in preservation. Of course, questions of ownership had not come up in a natural conversational course. Not knowing the Reverend's connection to Perry's home until he had stumbled across it in the Reverend's Bible, the matter hadn't been brought up. He saw no reason Perry would have gone out of her way to tell him.

"I hear the new owner is...a little standoffish, shall we say?" Maggie volunteered. "An old-fashioned term, but I've heard it's an accurate description."

At Maggie's tone, Ethan's hackles rose, the protectiveness he felt in regard to Perry unsettling.

"Funny," declared Ethan, "but I didn't receive that impression at all. In fact, I'm getting on quite well with her."

Maggie faltered fractionally as she opened the leather-bound register, the only sign of her vexation besides her lashes rapidly blinking three times in succession.

"Here," she said, pointing with her blood-red fingernail. "All the births and deaths in the Nicholson family from the time the church first opened its doors for worship. And this, this is the family of Edward Nicholson, the Reverend I spoke of. The eldest of eight sons he was, not a female among the brood. Prolific family in their own right as well, as you will note by the number of births, christenings, and infant deaths. No lack of libido there."

Ethan ignored the jibe, tilting his head to look where she pointed. If Maggie wanted to believe some sexual deficiency explain his disinterest in her, he would leave her to it, and gladly.

"Except for our friend Edward, perhaps. He married late in life, and not until he had been goaded into it by members of the community. There are numerous letters which have survived the passage of years attesting to that fact. For some reason, he felt disinclined to take a wife."

"Homosexual?" asked John. Maggie glanced at him briefly, and away.

"Possibly. Or marriage just didn't hold any appeal for him. At any rate," Maggie went on, warming to her subject, "he married when he was forty-three, a venerable age for that period. Married a girl some twenty years his junior, a spinster who had been waiting, apparently, for his youngest brother to ask for her hand in marriage. There's some vague communication about that, too, between the Reverend and one of the other brothers."

Ethan's heart seemed to falter a beat. John

abandoned his position supporting the doorframe to step closer.

"What was the wife's name?" John queried, staring hard at Ethan.

Maggie leaned over the page, moving her fingernail to another point and tapping, once.

"Lily," she said. "Lily Madson. Now there's a coincidence for you. One letter short of Madison. I've wondered if it might be the same family, generations later. You know how sometimes the spelling of a surname is changed over the years, due to the miscopying of official documents. Wouldn't that be a strange happenstance?"

A chill settled into Ethan's stomach. For several seconds he couldn't breathe. Lily. Lily Madson. Waiting for the younger brother to claim her, settling instead for the eldest. Had the youngest one day come home?

"When did Lily die?" he asked. At his tone, Maggie stared at him, then turned back to the tome beneath her hand.

"There's no reference to a date in the registry. That's where the infamy comes in. Apparently it was quite the scandal. Lily disappeared with her husband's brother Daniel sometime in 1824. The relationship between a brother-in-law and sister-in-law was viewed, in the morals of the day, to be nigh on incestuous. You know, accepting the spouse's family as your own and all that. Edward personally survived that embarrassment, I suppose, but his reputation suffered tremendously. His congregation began to seriously doubt his ability to lead them. There were some episodes of bizarre behavior recorded. Edward retired from the ministry in 1829 and became a recluse. He died in 1831 and is buried at the upper end of the graveyard behind the wrought iron fence. Where once," she added, "he had been expected to lie beside his bride."

Ethan closed his eyes, willing himself to breath normally. But the words that had exited his mouth in the attic came back to him with thudding force.

*Damn your soul to hell, Lily, you shall take what I choose to give you. You deserve no respect from me. My brother? You are worse than a whore...*

Commanding his lids to lift, he turned to John with a stifled word and headed for the door, not caring what Maggie thought regarding his behavior. He needed air, fresh air. And light. The dusty confines in the church were choking him.

Behind him, John extended a hasty thank you for them both before following him outside. Ethan didn't lessen his stride until he'd returned to the driver's side door and slid into the pickup's seat once more. He leaned his forehead against the wheel. John climbed into the passenger's side, hastily donning his seatbelt before Ethan had a chance to put the vehicle in gear. Respiring heavily, Ethan turned his head on his knuckles to look at John.

"I believe we may safely assume the entity in the house is the shade of the dearly departed Reverend Nicholson," he said.

"And the other by the creek? Daniel?"

"I would think so," agreed Ethan, raising his head and putting the truck into reverse. "The question is: Why?"

## Chapter Twenty-Six

*The noise the water made falling onto stone sounded hollow and echoing and limitless, seeming to repeat the same expanded pattern, like music, like a symphony with the hand of God in it somehow. He felt uplifted by it and at the same time cast down and made humble. Sad. Hopeless. If he thought he might ever come to the symphony's end he might have felt differently, but it seemed to him he had been listening to it forever and would go on listening to it forevermore without the promise of completion. Alone.*

*Prone on the water-smoothed surface, he turned his cheek against the stone, remembering her skin's smoothness, the tiny droplets of liquid spray from the falls glistening across her breasts, and how he had taken the time to lick them off, one by one, only to find they had been replaced by others in due course. He had spent more time than they had available committed to that service, bidding her be patient as she arched against him pleading for more, her flesh taut and heated beneath the cooling sheath of water, and then he had slipped his hand between her legs. The cries she made echoed in his head. He moaned with the memory.*

*Lily, Lily, the child in your womb is ours. Do not let my brother lay claim to it. You promised me. You swore on the blood in your veins.*

*But it was too late. He knew that now.*

## Chapter Twenty-Seven

Standing in the open doorway, Ethan watched John pull away from the end of the driveway in Ethan's truck, headed for a hotel. Ethan had given him directions, a less than complex process as there were only three turns to make, and the Bible. John had promised to look through the aged volume overnight. As for processing the film, that would have to wait. It needed to be done by hand, not run through a machine. Tomorrow they would have to take the film into town, to a camera shop where

Ethan knew they still performed their own developing. John never trusted digital and Ethan had found himself with the same mindset, to the point he even continued to use his old 35mm camera for many photos he took for business.

Sunlight's last reflected in the side view mirror, flashing like a beacon as John swung left onto the main roadway. He waved his hand out the window in a brief salute. Ethan waved back and closed the door.

Turning, Ethan stripped off his sweat-soaked shirt, rolling it into a ball in his hand. He clicked off the foyer light. His diaphragm collapsed, rushing air from his lungs as he recalled the  first night he had brought Perry into his home, how he had lifted her in the darkness and she  wrapped her legs about his waist as he carried her to the wall. He would give one hell of a lot to believe lust alone had been the impetus, but with each passing minute he grew more fearful another influence had been the only reason.

Still, he just needed to remind himself the feelings he had for her to stave off uncertainty. Edward, if the entity was indeed Edward Nicholson, had no such tender sentiment in reserve. That emotion was Ethan's and Ethan's alone. Yes, he simply needed to remind himself of that difference. Unfortunately, the necessity was coming with increasing frequency.

Wiping his forearm across his brow, he went to the bedroom door, listening as he had a short time earlier when he arrived home. Hearing nothing within he carefully rotated the knob, easing the door open to peer inside.

A break in the drawn curtain permitted enough light into the room for him to see Perry. She was as usual sleeping on her back, one arm thrown up on the pillow above her angled head. Beneath her other hand on her abdomen was her mother's bound diary. She had one finger in between the pages as if to mark the place she had left off when she decided to close her eyes. The other fingers curled in relaxation. Requiring clean clothing, Ethan entered the room, tossing his soiled shirt into the hamper in the corner. Quietly pulling open the various drawers in the dresser, he took what he needed and turned to depart. On the bed Perry rolled in her sleep, the diary slipping from her grasp.

Ethan reacted nimbly, grabbing the diary before the volume fell to the floor. His clothing tumbled across the comforter, the clean shirt coming to rest on Perry's outstretched leg. Her hand moved to brush it aside, closing around the fabric. Her eyes opened.

"Hi," said Ethan.

"Hi," she greeted him sleepily. "What time is it?"

Retrieving his clothes, Ethan sat down on the bed. "A little after seven-thirty. Hungry?"

"Not really. I don't know," she said. After a moment, her gaze trailed over his naked chest in a manner that made him adjust his hips on the mattress. Her gaze shifted to the clothing lying rumpled across his thigh.

"Did you eat yet?" she asked.

"I'm not all that hungry, either. I think I might just grab a bowl of cereal."

"I'll get it for you," she offered, starting to rise.

"Not necessary," he said, forestalling her movement. "I'm taking a quick shower first."

She subsided onto the pillow, her head cradled on her arm. "Where's John?"

"Gone to a hotel for the night."

To that, she said nothing. Lifting his hand, Ethan held out the diary.

"You were reading this when you fell asleep."

She took the book, cradling it against her stomach. "Thanks. I just started to read when I dozed off. It's amazing," she elaborated with her sleepy smile. "My mother was so young when she began the journal. There are thoughts of hers in here I would never have recognized as hers, if not for the fact she wrote them down. By the time I was old enough for her to share her life with me, she probably didn't recall any of this. At least not with the clarity revealed on these pages."

Ethan smiled, too, a slow turn, feeling sadness and regret. Too bad everyone didn't take the time to document their experiences and emotions in such a manner. So many times during one's life that revelation could be of immeasurable value. He knew it would have helped in his.

"Are you all right?"

"Yeah," he said. "I'm jumping in the shower."

Perry nodded as she sat up, pushing her hair off her brow. "Okay. Are you sure you're all right?"

"Yep." She looked more than a little dubious. Explanations would have been unnerving in the best case scenario, and downright frightening in the worst. For both of them. He chose to remain silent.

"Do you mind if I scrounge around for something for dinner?"

Ethan's eyebrows lifted with effort, as if a weight sat on his brow. "I thought you weren't hungry."

"I'm not. I just want to do it for you." She made a small movement toward him, stopping herself short of touching him. "You've been very kind, Ethan."

Have I? Ethan thought, but left his doubts unspoken. Standing, he shoved his clothes into his other arm, extending his hand to help her up. Not that she needed assistance. She hopped from the bed apparently refreshed from her long nap. He, on the other hand, felt too tired for speech. She followed him out into the hallway, where they parted ways. He made his way to the bathroom, leaving Perry to rustle around the kitchen in search of something to feed him.

Stripping down, Ethan turned on the shower, waited a moment for the water temperature to level out, and stepped into the wide stall. He lifted his face to the spray and closed his eyes as the warmth streamed over his body, permitting himself to be soothed by the gentle bombardment and the darkness behind his lids. Once again, life had taken quite the strange turn for him. He just needed to slow down and breathe and set a course of action.

He had been keeping his existence consciously and deliberately manageable. Sailing into storms with all canvas blowing had not been his style for some time now. In fact, he had only developed that mode of behavior from necessity. He had always been the person to step in and help when needed, yes, but in the end his life and his marriage with Cindy had called for more crisis intervention than prevention.

Opening his mouth, Ethan let the steaming water fill the cavity around his tongue, then he turned his head to spit out the last residue of foulness from the earlier episode outside Perry's house. The shower streamed over his hair and down his face. He bent his head, letting the pulsating flow work its way into his taut neck muscles.

Ghost-hunting in his youth had been one thing; this roaring need to protect Perry from whatever appeared to be haunting her was another. The constant flux of adrenaline was beginning to wear him down. As for Perry herself, well, she had certainly upset the balance he had created in his life, with or without her ghosts. She had taken him quite by surprise. To be honest, he hadn't anticipated feeling so close to someone again. He knew the swiftness with which his emotions had grown should be scaring him a little. Yet, despite all that wanting Perry seemed to entail, the fear, that fear, remained non-existent. Other things had unsettled him, but not Perry. Not really. When he thought about her, every time he thought about her, something in him seemed to settle, to drift into place, gently filling a void he had forgotten existed.

Hearing a noise, Ethan opened the stall door, listening. He thought he heard Perry's voice and wondered if she was talking to him or to herself.

"I'm in the shower," he called. "I can't hear you."

A second later Perry knocked on the door. She stuck her head in.

"I'm sorry," she said. "I didn't mean to answer your phone. Force of habit, I guess."

"Who is it?" he asked her, closing the shower door to keep the water from running onto the floor. "John?"

"No, it's a Maggie Barnes asking for you."

Groaning in irritation, Ethan grappled the soap from the dish and began to lather it between his hands. "Would you do me a favor?" He lifted his head so she would hear him clearly over the running water. "Tell her who you are and that I'm in the shower, and that you and I both thank her very much for the information she provided."

After a brief hesitation, Perry agreed and shut the door. Less than a minute later she returned.

"May I come in?"

"Of course." He smiled into the water, detecting laughter in her voice.

"Your friend was a little put out by your message," she advised dryly. "I take it that's the pretty lady from the historical society whose picture was in the paper with you?"

Ethan grimaced, wondered where Perry had seen the photo. "Yes."

"Hmm." He heard her near the sink and wiped the condensation from the door to peer out. Although blurred, he saw her at the mirror studying the bruise on her cheekbone. Biting the flesh inside his own cheek, he turned away.

"So basically what I just told her, in not so many words," she went on conversationally, "was to get lost, that we are friendly enough that you take a shower when I'm around, and you are otherwise involved and not interested. Correct? Oh, and you were thanking her for something. That, at least, appeared straightforward enough."

Ethan chuckled, soaping his body with vigorous strokes. "Yes," he said. "To all of that."

For a moment she remained silent, followed by a distinctive and rather unfeminine snort. "Had there been anything going on there?" she asked.

"Not on my part," he answered.

"Good," she said. His lips curved in response.

When she did not speak again right away, Ethan peeked out the shower door, wondering if she'd left. He located her standing in the middle of the floor, her head tipped to one side, the bruise on her cheekbone glaringly evident, her gaze meeting his as he blinked water from his lashes.

"Are you going to tell me what this information is for which I just thanked Ms. Barnes?"

"Of course. When I'm finished here." He shut the door again. "I'll just be another couple of minutes."

"I think," he heard her say from right outside the shower stall, "you may be longer than that."

Once more the door opened, splattering another watery half pint across the floor. Perry stepped in minus the men's boxers and tee shirt she had been wearing while sleeping. He took a step back, keeping his eyes on her face.

"Perry, I don't—"

"Yes," she interrupted, "you do."

She took the soap from his hand. "I have never seen a man looking more mentally and physically exhausted than you do now. Turn around."

"I—no. Wait a minute."

With a grip on his arm, she urged him to face the wall. "Do it," she said in a tone that made him smile and comply, turning his back to her. As she began to run her hands along his back, kneading tired, tense muscles, he put his arms on the tiled enclosure, leaning his weight into them. Although well aware she was nude and glistening wet from the water spray behind him, the massage soon drew his mind away from that image.

"This is wonderful. Thank you."

"Shush," she chastised. "No talking."

"Okay," he said with a grin.

She took her time completing a circuit over his back and shoulders, loosening knots created by the stress of the past couple of days as well as those resulting from the daily labor to which he had become accustomed. His breathing evened out and he wished, in a vaguely retained thought, they were lying in bed so he could just drift off to sleep.

"That's nice," he murmured. "And so are you."

"Hush," she said.

Her hands dipped to his buttocks, kneading the flesh and muscle there. He groaned, reveling in the remarkable sensation. When she moved to his thighs and calves he thought he had died and gone to heaven, and said as much. Once again she told him to stop talking.

"As you wish." He closed his eyes, nearly drifting off while standing upright, like a horse.

Abruptly, he sucked in a mouthful of water as her hand slipped between his thighs to cup his balls. Coughing, he turned his head aside from the shower fixture, but he knew better than to speak. She slid her soapy fingers along the hardening shaft of his penis and he was instantly and fully erect in her hand.

"Dear God," he moaned. She didn't chastise him for his speech now, but laughed instead, a pleasantly joyous sound. "Are you sure you want this?" he managed.

"Yes."

He could feel her warm breath racing over the skin of his thigh. Unable to bear any more of her stroking, he grabbed her hand and turned around, precariously balanced as he swung his leg over her head. Closing his fingers about her upper arms, he lifted her to her feet, forcing her to release him.

"If you want all of it, you're going to have to stop doing that," he advised quietly. She looked up at him from beneath her wet lashes and said nothing. The shower splashed over his shoulders and onto her face and breasts in glistening droplets, clinging to her hair, the tip of her nose, her mouth, poised to fall from her hard nipples. Holding her still with his hands, he bent and extended his tongue to capture first one drop, then the other, before they slid free. Despite his gentle restraint, she thrust her breasts forward toward his mouth, wanting more.

Delighted by her reaction, he slid his tongue

along the roundness of each breast, collecting water droplets as he went and avoiding the ridge of blue-black bruises, returning to her nipples again and again when the water accumulated there, licking one and then the other, divesting them of the trembling fluid beads. She breathed quick and shallow above his head, watching him through slitted lids. Impossible as it seemed, his arousal increased tenfold. Whatever happened, he couldn't let her touch him again. He felt like a skyrocket ready to burst into a thousand shimmering sparks.

Cupping a breast in his open palm, he lifted it, holding her for a long moment as he toyed with her nipple with the ball of his thumb, glancing up to view the ecstatic response flowing across her features. He bit her then, ever so carefully, tugging on the nipple with his teeth as he slid his tongue over the tightened flesh. Her fingers pushed into his hair and she made a noise that was nearly his undoing.

Releasing his hold on her arm, he grabbed her hip, pulling her near, then dropped to his knees before her. She became still, her whole body one thrumming, vibrating string of an instrument waiting to be plucked. He was almost regretful of his next move, wanting to keep her for as long as possible at that perfect, fevered pitch, poised on the edge of climax. The evidence and extent of her arousal were plain to view as she waited breathlessly for him to take her into his mouth.

When he did, her knees gave out, and he lowered her to the shower floor trembling and crying out in ways that made him nearly insane, but he would not release her. She was his in this most intimate of ways, powerless and powerful, making him want to never come back from this place where he had brought her and to which she had conveyed him, soaring virtually out of control. He could not begin to imagine how many times she climaxed or if it was only once without end, and then she struggled upright and away from him, reaching to take him into her hand again.

Tipping his head back he drank water from the shower, then he wrapped his arms around her and pulled her down on top of him. He slid into her without a word and her mouth came down onto his own, open and demanding, and the noise that welled up from somewhere deep inside her vibrated into him, into his head and his heart and every bone of his body. An answering call escaped him as he drove himself deep, feeling her muscles contract around him as she came again, and then he was lost. He didn't know when he'd last made such a cry of transport in ejaculation, or if he ever had. It didn't matter. He came as hard as she did, breathless, heart pounding, any other thought driven from his mind.

## Chapter Twenty-Eight

Perry rose slowly from the shower floor, fully sated and moved, oddly, to tears. Ethan looked at her questioningly and she smiled at him, stepping into the lukewarm flow from the shower head to bathe. From a seated position on the opposite side of the double-wide stall he watched her, one arm across his raised knee, his own expression complacent and contented.

"I'll bet your hungry now," he said.

"I am, at that," she answered.

"I'll cook, then," he told her as he stood. "How do you like your omelettes?"

"What are my choices?" she asked, turning off the water once she had completed his ablutions. He brushed the beaded water from his skin with an angled hand. Perry slipped her fingers into the hair on his chest, where the water still stood like diamonds against the short, dark strands. He raised her hand to his lips, kissing her fingers softly.

"Cheese or no cheese, I guess," he said against her knuckles. " I haven't much else to offer. I really do need to get to the store."

"Ah yes," she agreed. "I don't suppose you were anticipating a house guest, were you?"

"Not one like you, at any rate," he said. She warmed beneath his fond and somewhat libidinous gaze.

Reaching out from the stall, Ethan grabbed a towel from the rack and proceeded to dry her, despite her protests. She ceased her objections, accepting his affectionate attention. When he finished, he kissed her lightly on the tip of her nose.

"We really shouldn't do that again," he whispered.

Disconcerted, Perry frowned at him.

"Without a condom," he explained.

"Oh." Feeling somewhat chastened, Perry picked up her discarded clothing from the floor and got dressed, aware of his eyes on her. "You know, in romance novels they always skip that part."

He laughed. "I've always been careful about that," he went on in a gentle, even tone. "In fact, I can safely say I've not had sex without one since I've been widowed. I know you don't want to hear this, and I'm not going to start talking about any other women in my life—there really haven't been that many, by the way," he added. "But it's a precaution that should be taken in this day and age."

"I understand." A reasonable conversation to be having, she knew, and she felt grateful for his sensitive approach to the subject, but she felt slightly—well, cheapened by it. She wondered why he could not have waited until the afterglow had faded.

"If it makes you feel better at all," she stated, "despite the fact Jack and I drifted apart long before we actually admitted it and divorced, he wasn't the type to cheat. What I mean is, he was the last man I was with and likely safe." She turned to look at him. "That was nearly three years ago. I don't think you have to worry about me."

He paused with his shirt over his head, then slowly pulled it down, tucking the hem into his pants. Hooking his hand around her neck, he drew her closer and pressed his lips to her arching eyebrow.

"I wasn't worry about you. I'm sorry. I didn't mean to upset you. Honestly, I wasn't thinking about the transmission of anything. Not with you. I was thinking more about the possibility of getting you pregnant. After all, I have no idea if you're on the pill. It's not something we've discussed."

Perry paused. She scrubbed her fingers across her forehead. "Crap, I'm not."

She sensed a minute tensing in his muscles, swiftly flown. "We'll just have to be careful, then, won't we?" he said in dismissal before taking her hand and dragging her off to the kitchen for the promised eggs.

They split a microwave-baked potato, toast slathered with strawberry preserves and omelettes with cheese. Perry ate across from Ethan at the kitchen island beneath the glaring overhead light, barely subdued by the frosted glass fixture. Nevertheless, to her at least the meal felt absurdly romantic and if it tasted like anything less than the best gastronomic feast, Perry didn't notice. Every so often she would find herself overcome by warm heady memory followed quickly by a humbling stillness in which she would look across at Ethan and think, *thank you.*

Whom or what she thanked she couldn't be sure, but she'd begun to recognize the staggering options chance presented, and the resultant designations by fate. The slightest alteration in events would have made a vast difference in her position. If Ethan had opted to return to his office when he found her unavailable for her appointment, who knows what might have happened to her in the creek. For that alone she would ever be grateful, never mind all he had done since to help her. And what if circumstances had otherwise spun them into different circles so they did not meet, ever? He seemed so much a part of her life now, as if they had never *not* known each other. She had difficulty fathoming an alternative.

"Are you all right?"

Perry nodded. She felt a little wistful, oddly a little sad, and more than a little bit in love. She didn't say so.

"Dessert?" Ethan asked, clearing the dishes.

"What did you have in mind?"

At her tone, he glanced back over his shoulder. He grinned and her stomach rolled. His smile had done that to her from the very first time she had witnessed it. She had a feeling it always would.

"Up to you," he drawled.

Perry pressed her lips together, but was unable to keep the smile from forming. She arched her eyebrows at him.

"Now?" he asked.

"Up to you," she said.

He laughed, a rich and earthy sound, and slipped the plates and utensils into the sink without haste, running water over them briefly. Then he turned and walked back across the floor. Once again the way he moved struck her speechless. Confident and with unconscious grace like an animal in the wild, a wolf or a feral cat. She lifted her head. He placed his hand, palm open, on her throat, his thumb pressed lightly beneath her jaw. His warm mouth kissed her so deeply she felt herself disintegrate into liquid flesh and bones.

The phone rang. They both turned to look at the disruptive instrument in dismay. Ethan dipped to press his lips to her forehead.

"I really should answer this," he said.

"Are you sure you don't want me to do it," Perry queried sweetly, her voice only a little unsteady, "to deter another of your lady friends?"

He made a face at her. Striding over to the phone, he lifted it from the wall.

"Ethan Taylor," he said.

Not wanting to appear to be eavesdropping, Perry dragged her gaze away from his lean, muscled height, the attractive, restrained energy in his stance, and made a conscious effort to draw her body back into solid form. Her heart rate had just steadied when she saw him glance back at her after listening for several seconds without speaking. He looked away. She sat up straighter, lifting her hands and placing them side by side on the counter top.

"What do you think that means, John?"

Ethan continued to listen. Through the earpiece Perry discerned John Gooden's voice, though not the words. Making no bones about eavesdropping now, Perry turned to watch Ethan, attempting to read his reaction in the way he held himself. She couldn't. She realized he was a man very much in command of himself and used to giving little away. The fact he had repeatedly let down his guard over the past several days to consciously supply her with small portions of who he was felt suddenly very dear.

"Uh, yes. We were just going to discuss that," he said. "I agree. It's very important. No. No.

Goodnight then. We'll see you first thing in the morning."

Pushing the button to disconnect the call, Ethan stared for several seconds at the phone in his hand, before slowly placing the landline into the cradle. He returned to the island, taking up the seat he had vacated. Perry could see straight away any thoughts regarding lovemaking had fled his mind.

"We need to talk about what John and I found out this evening," he stated. A small alarm went off inside her brain at his tone. She forced a smile to her lips.

"From the lascivious Ms. Barnes?" she teased.

"I wouldn't call her that," he said.

"Oh no?  You must not have taken a good look at the photo of the two of you in the newspaper," she taunted without rancor. His expression had once again increased her pulse, but in a manner having nothing to do with lust.

Ethan's brows lowered over his dark eyes. After a moment he made a face, wryly amused. "Just when did you see this photo?"

"On-line, yesterday," she confessed. "I was trying to find out a bit more about you. Sorry."

He waved her admission aside. "If you must know, she made certain assumptions about me I didn't encourage. May I go on?"

"Please," said Perry, her unease growing.

Ethan lowered his forearms onto the counter top, his long fingers interlaced. He appeared to be searching for words. Having never witnessed this difficulty in him before, Perry lowered her own hands into her lap, clutching her fingers into a knot.

"Go on," she said. "Just tell me. I'm ready."

He smiled a little at her hesitation, loosening his right hand to stretch it across the counter. Perry lifted her left from her lap, slipping her fingers into his. *Goodness*, she thought, *this is going to be bad.*

"You remember the Bible I took from the attic?" Ethan said.

Perry nodded. She released her breath as quietly as possible.

"John has it now, looking through it. The name in the front of it, the Bible's owner, is Edward Nicholson. Sound familiar to you at all?"

Thinking hard, Perry had to admit it did, although she didn't know why.

Across from her Ethan looked at her strangely. "He was the minister at the local church."

"When?" she responded. "And which one?"

"Apparently from 1809 to 1829. As to where, in that little church you own."

Perry wrinkled her face in confusion. "The little church I own?" she echoed. "What are you talking about?"

Ethan rose from his seat and went to take two small bowls from the cabinet. Opening the freezer, he removed a half gallon of ice cream. He glanced over at her.

"Chocolate syrup again tonight?"

His idea of dessert had definitely altered since the call. Perry nodded, thanking him. "But just a little. Of both. You're going to make me gain ten pounds."

"Well," he said, leaning forward to scoop ice cream into each bowl, "the church in question is that tiny stuccoed building the State is supposed to maintain in preservation. Where your property crosses over to the other side of the road across from your place."

Frankly baffled, Perry echoed, "Crosses over to the other side of the highway? I wasn't aware Nana's land went over there. I don't remember that when I was a kid. Are you sure? You're talking about that abandoned church that's about the size of your living room, right? With the overgrown graveyard."

"That would be the one," he said, carrying both bowls to the granite island and setting one before her. "You had no idea?"

"None. How is that possible?" She lifted a spoonful of chocolate ice cream into her mouth, talking around it. "Aren't churches owned by, well, the church entity or something?"

As she ate, Ethan recounted for her his conversation with Maggie Barnes regarding the stipulation. Perry frowned.

"The estate lawyer has been hounding me to come to his office to discuss further details of my inheritance," she said. "Maybe this church business is one of them."

"Very likely," Ethan concurred.

"A church," Perry murmured. "How odd."

"Perhaps you should meet with the attorney sooner rather than later. I could go with you, if you'd like."

Perry gave his offer a split second's consideration. "I would like that. Thank you."

He rolled ice cream around inside his closed mouth, letting it melt. Perry witnessed the smile in his eyes at her response, pleasure perhaps at having his offer accepted so readily.

"No one mentioned any clause to you regarding that portion of the property, maybe when you were younger and your grandparents were still alive?" he asked, after swallowing.

"No."

He studied her a moment, a frown forming now between his brows. "You really have been distracted by this whole situation, haven't you?"

Knowing precisely to what situation he referred, she blushed. "I suppose I have," she said.

"You've let a lot go by since moving back into your grandmother's house that needed taking care of. I can't even begin to imagine where your head has been due to all of this. Honestly, I'm not sure I would still be sane at this point."

"Maybe I'm not," she retorted.

"Oh, you're sane, sweetheart," he declared. "Because if you aren't, then neither am I."

"Two crazies together?" she said.

His lips curved in a close smile. "I don't know. Are we?"

"What? Crazy?"

"No," he said. "Together."

Perry brought her hand up to her face, curving her fingers against her mouth as she gazed back at him. It might have been the aftermath of sex making her want to cry. or maybe something else altogether.

"I think so," she said, her voice muffled by her hand. "I really do think so."

He smiled again, an out-and-out grin, and shook his head, pushing her neglected dessert closer to her. "Finish this," he said. "I hate to see good ice cream go to waste."

Blinking away the moisture that had managed to evade the power of her dubious will, Perry picked up her spoon. She sniffed, once and very discreetly she thought, but apparently he noticed. His hand came across the island and squeezed hers again, lingering a moment before he pushed back his chair and stood. Taking his nearly empty dish to the sink, he ran the water to make it hot and prepared to wash. Perry joined him there, leaning her lower back against the counter as she finished her bowl's contents. The dishwasher at her left matched the cherry cabinets to either side. She wondered if he ever used it. Probably not, living alone.

"So," she said, "what about this minister?"

Ethan glanced sidelong at her. "Edward

Nicholson? Lily was Edward's wife."

The spoon slipped from her fingers into the bowl.

"Lily? Our Lily?" she faltered, staggered by the news and how quickly it had been uncovered. She had held minimal hope of any breakthrough whatsoever.

"Yes, our Lily," Ethan said, both his expression and his tone altering slightly. "And Edward's Lily. And apparently the Lily of his younger brother, as well."

Closing her eyes, Perry inhaled. She actually felt ill, shaken, cold and sick to her stomach. Lily and Edward. The unfaithful wife, the cuckolded husband. And the younger brother, the spirit who had chosen her, Perry, to replace his long lost lover? Was that what Ethan meant?

Remembering the captivating hours where lust and longing had battered her felt like a betrayal now. She didn't want to think about how *he* had made her feel. Indeed, she really felt quite sick.

Setting her dish on the counter, Perry retreated to the living room where she sat on the couch, bending forward until her head settled on her knees, her arms tucked tight across her abdomen. Ethan's shadow passed across the rug. The cushions shifted as he sat down beside her. His hand lowered across her neck, still heated and moist from his round at the sink.

"Is this some sort of classic scenario?" she

murmured without lifting her head. "Is there something about a triangle that ghost hunters, or whatever you call yourselves, have come to expect?"

His breath escaped him. Through his nose, she thought, like he'd tried to prevent it. "Nothing is expected when it comes to the supernatural. The only 'classic scenario' as you say is that of untimely death and unfinished business."

Perry nodded, or tried to. The awkwardness of her position precluded success. She sat up. In his dark eyes she witnessed struggling emotions and his attempt to master them.

"And in this case?" she asked.

Emotion snaked through his jaw. "I don't know. It would seem Lily and Daniel departed the area, leaving Edward to face his congregation and his own phantoms."

"Daniel? That's his name?"

"Yes."

She saw it again, a dilation of the pupil, an alteration of focus, and then he returned his attention to her. His hand on her nape continued to move comfortingly, but she wasn't certain he had any awareness his appendage performed the task.

"Why is he there?" she asked. "Why does he haunt the creek? What would cause a spirit to return to such a place?"

"I don't know." Still with that cautious look, something inside him tightly held in check.

"Is it Edward in the house, then?"

"I think so. This is all speculation, Perry. We can't be certain of anything."

Ignoring the reply's rigid phrasing, Perry plunged on. "It is Edward," she said. "That would make sense. Edward, who once hurt and shamed his wife as punishment for her transgression, and made you do the same to me. How is that possible? I don't understand."

Ethan's hand stilled, and then slowly his fingers curled to tighten about the back of her neck. A shudder coursed her spine, a remembered fear, recalling his attempt to overpower her, to restrain her while he thrust himself into a place she had given him no permission to go, his voice mingling with another, damning her, calling her a whore.

Abruptly he pulled her to him, up against his shoulder. His other arm went around her waist. He crushed his mouth to her crown and held it there, voice rumbling up from deep inside, harsh with regret.

"I'm sorry," he said. "God, I'm so sorry that happened. I wish I could erase it, from my memory as well as yours. Whatever else Edward Nicholson was, if this is really an indication of his character, he was a cruel man. If he ever truly loved his wife he would not have done such a thing to her, no matter her actions. Whether he viewed her behavior as mortal sin or hurtful or just a deadly wound to his ego, such a vindictive act could never be justified."

"But he made you—"

"No!" Ethan said. "It won't happen again, Perry. I promise you nothing like that will happen again."

Her unconscious preparation to fight or flee vanished. The tension in her shoulders eased. She pressed her forehead against the pulse in his throat. Her hand strayed to his hip, her fingers slipping into the pocket of his jeans.

"Am I ever going to be able to go home?" she asked.

"As far as I'm concerned, you could stay here until the moon turns blue, but I know you want to be back there. It is your home after all, and we're working on it, John and I. You'll go home again. I promise you that, as well."

Perry smiled against his neck and kissed him where his pulse beat steady and strong. She understood already how powerful his promises could be.

## *Chapter Twenty-Nine*

Sitting with his back against the headboard, Ethan watched the eleven o'clock news. He had muted the volume and sat observing the reporter's silent gestures as he tried to decipher what she was saying. He only wanted to see the weather at this point, but that wouldn't come until near the program's end. In the meantime, he engaged in a little lip-reading and his own interpretation of the video being presented.

The storm moving up the coast worried him. Although he kept works in progress tarped and secure against the elements, and extra precautions had been started against the promised high wind and torrential rains, he hadn't finished with them. What he needed right now was the most accurate timetable available in order to get his crew out before the weather turned bad to finish the work begun. Mentally he calculated man-hours and which men would be available, thought about how much more water the ground could take without flooding, whose roofs might still be open, anything at all. Normally, he could perform this exercise in his sleep. He knew concentration on upcoming work served only to skirt another issue far more troubling. He needed to distract himself. He couldn't go over again in his mind his conversation with Perry about the Nicholson brothers and their vicious soap opera.

His gut wrenched at the memory anyway, at the questions she'd asked. About the questions she hadn't.

Hearing a sound beside him, he glanced down. Although Perry had offered to sleep on the couch, perhaps a little uncertain about what was happening between them, Ethan had refused her offer. She lay curled up against him in his bed, her head on his arm heavy in slumber. He'd pulled the sheet up over her bare shoulders. Her hair curled in a tangled, cinnamon mass down her back.

Carefully easing his arm from beneath her, Ethan pulled her closer. She murmured in her sleep without waking. Bending his head, he studied the lashes curving over her cheekbone where the bruise showed in a dark, mottled blue, like the blush on a concord grape. He knew it had to be hurting her, yet she'd made no complaint. .

Clenching his teeth in memory of its cause, he let his breath out slowly. She slept on, undisturbed by the scrutiny.

Tomorrow, John planned to delve into his subconscious searching for any possible reason Ethan might have manufactured in those depths to turn on Perry in such a manner. Both knew there would be none, but the more he'd thought about it the more Ethan wanted to be absolutely certain. For his own sake, as well as Perry's.

Closing his eyes, Ethan leaned his head back against the headboard. Initially, after Cindy's death, he'd had a problem with repressed anger. It had affected everything he did, including his ability to grieve. But he had worked through that. He had no reason to expect he would be acting on such anger now. Not in that way. The occasional outburst, maybe, but not such a deliberate and cruel act designed to humiliate and inflict pain. Mutual consent was one thing, force quite another. The abusive berating that had spewed from his mouth still shocked him in recall as well, but he also felt thankful for it. If not for the words that were so alien to him, his doubts regarding the impetus behind his actions would have taken a firmer hold.

Lily. Lily Madson. He could only speculate at what dark emotion the woman had felt, married to one man and wanting another, and that man her husband's younger brother. And yet, there had to have been some joy in the mix, hadn't there? Why would she have risked her husband's wrath, being ostracized by her community, condemnation, if there had been no happiness for her? Still, it baffled him. It must have been an extremely difficult situation for all.

Lifting his lids, he glanced down again at Perry's sleeping form. He knew, of course, how he felt, the unnecessary jealousy snaking through his blood when he thought about the interaction between Perry and the entity in the creek. How much worse would it have been to be Edward Nicholson, a man of God, respected in his community, cuckolded by his wife and learning that the man with whom she was sleeping outside their marriage was his own brother. Maybe Ethan's unconscious empathy had made Edward, if indeed it was Edward, choose him as a conduit for an anger which should, by rights, have died along with the man himself nearly one hundred and seventy years earlier.

That made no sense either. At the time the incident occurred, Ethan possessed no empathy. He'd possessed no knowledge who Edward Nicholson was at all.

Releasing another pent-up breath, Ethan shifted his hips on the mattress to ease the stiffness caused by too long in one position. As if sensing his discomfort Perry moved too, resting her head and one hand on his thigh without waking. Ethan stared at her profile in repose. Her lips were parted as she breathed, slightly irregularly as if she might be waking or dreaming. Her teeth's pearly edge reflected the flickering illumination from the television screen. Extending a single digit he traced her curving mouth, then pulled the sheet back up around her naked shoulders, settling his hand into the bountiful red-brown curls tumbling along her back.

She could, he mused in reverie, do some sweetly entertaining things to him with her mouth. Not the least of which the way she kissed him. Remembering her mouth's gentle insistence stirred him to an immediate erection, lifting the sheet not far from her head. Willing himself to think about something else, he returned his focus to the screen where there appeared to be some discussion regarding shady dealings by certain members in the mayor's office in the city. He had heard enough about the investigation over the past several days to have a fairly good idea the content of discussion, but he stared at the television nevertheless hoping to run interference with his thoughts.

When she touched him, he leapt against her hand and she giggled like a sleepy child.

"Down boy. That was an accident," she murmured.

"You're awake," he said. Unnecessarily.

"I am now." She swept the hair back from her brow as she sat up with the sheet tucked under her arms. She scooted back to sit next to him, her spine against the headboard. Mutely he handed her a pillow, which she tucked between her back and the wood.

"What are we watching?" she asked, blinking at a fast-moving commercial.

He smiled at the 'we'. "The news," he said.

"Huh."

She sounded slightly disoriented. She tipped her head to one side. "What time is it?"

"About 11:15, I think."

She nodded and blinked, sinking down a little onto the mattress. With a stifled yawn, she slanted a glance at him. "Can't sleep?"

"Waiting for the weather."

Nodding again, she stretched beneath the sheet. He observed her arching body from beneath his lashes, suppressing a grin at the pleasured noise she made loosening her muscles. Then she reached for his tee shirt, which he had tossed at some point earlier onto the bottom of the bed. She sat up and slipped the garment over her head, smoothing it down over her naked body.

"I need to use the bathroom."

As she scooted from the bed she tugged his shirt to cover her bottom. The hem fell to mid-thigh when she stood up. He liked the way she looked with his black tee shirt hanging loosely around her.

Still, it seemed odd—yet endearing—to find her so shy she felt the need to cover up before heading into the hallway, when her inhibitions were limited to nil in passion's pursuit.

He waited until she'd exited the room before turning up the volume slightly to hear the remaining broadcast. The weather was coming next.

"Damn it," he said upon the report's completion.

"What's wrong?"

Perry crossed beyond the foot of the bed to climb back in beside him. She didn't remove his shirt. Instead, she raised the neckline to her face and breathed. Breathing in his scent, he figured. Something elemental in that. Something that stirred him deeply.

He looked at her with a smile, quickly sobering when he realized what he was about to impart. "They're moving up the start time for that storm they've been tracking. Sometime after midday tomorrow, rather than the next morning. Some areas might get four plus inches of rain. I'd hoped for more time. Water getting into jobs we're in the middle of could cause major damage. They're already prepped, but not the full precautions. I'll have to get a jump on finishing it first thing in the morning."

She bit her lip. "The creek will rise. I'll need to be home."

Startled, he pivoted his body toward hers. "Surely it won't flood all the way to the house?"

Perry shook her head. "No, of course not. I've never seen the water come to the house, but it has run into the barn. And the basement does get wet, just from ground seepage. When it rains like you're saying it's supposed to, it'll really fill up. I'll need to make sure the sump pumps are operating, at the very least."

"You've handled this sort of crisis in the past, have you?" he asked. It both worried and pleased him to find her so self-reliant. He suspected she could be stubborn because of it, and the present situation couldn't afford stubbornness.

"I'll send a guy over to take care of that, with a generator in case you lose the electric again," he said.

"I could meet him there, I guess. Yeah. That would work. Thanks."

Ethan shifted his arm around her shoulder, pulling her closer. "I'd rather you didn't go there at all. That's why I suggested one of my guys take care of it."

"I know."

"You do."

"Yes."

"So you'll stay here?"

Silent, Perry pulled her legs up and shoved them under the sheet.

"I have to go home sometime," she said.

Ethan turned off the television, setting the remote down on the bedside table. He switched the lamp on low. "I'm worried about your safety. The situation has gotten progressively worse. There's no guarantee you won't come to harm in some fashion. You've seen—we've both seen—what can happen."

She shivered beneath his arm. Her eyes closed, the auburn lashes fluttering. She drew a deep breath and let it out before turning to meet his gaze.

"I realize that and I remember."

He bit cheek. Of course, she remembered. He knew she would. How could she actually forget? And how could he? Those few moments when passion had turned into something ugly that had nothing to do with sex would be forever etched into his brain. Guilt was the least lingering issue.

"Ethan, it is my home, the only one I've got. I have a responsibility I can't ignore."

"I'm not asking you to ignore any responsibility, but it seems to me you'd be better off staying away until—"

"Until what?" she interrupted, touching his hand with her fingertips. "Until when? Maybe it's just something I need to face, without fear. Maybe fear is what feeds the situation. I admit I am a little frightened by the progression of events at my house, but—."

"A little frightened?" he echoed, incredulous.

"All right, a lot frightened, although it doesn't feel nearly as hair-raising when I'm here with you, I assure you." She butted her head lightly against his chin.

"Glad to hear you say so. You're safe with me, Perry, I swear."

But she hadn't been. Her momentary silence meant she remembered that fact, too.

"You're safe now," he amended. "I won't let anything like that happen again."

As he said those words, he meant them. Meant them with every fiber in his being, trying to push down the niggling doubt, the concern, the uncertainty as to whether he could prevent such an occurrence a second time. Knowledge as power, knowledge as a shield, would be all he needed to keep the entity at bay. He wanted to believe that. He had to believe that.

His grip on Perry's shoulders tightened. She pulled away a little, tipping her head to look up at him.

"Ethan," she whispered. "It's all right. This whole haunting business is territory I've never walked on before, so I don't pretend to understand it. I'm glad John's come to help. He seems to know his stuff. However," she added, almost reluctantly he thought, "there's no guarantee you'll find anything which may help me. Is there? I mean, eventually, I'll need to learn to deal with the situation on whatever terms are necessary, or else...well, I don't want to think that far ahead. That's not what I'm suggesting for tomorrow, at any rate. I only need to go home for a little bit to see to some things. And I don't plan to do it alone, if you really will send someone to give me a hand."

Ethan forced himself to relax. "Someone will accompany you. Or me, depending on how the morning goes."

"Fair enough," agreed Perry with a nod, "but I'll pay the fellow you send out."

"No," he said. "You won't."

Her brows arched, then drew together. His retort had altered something in her. He wasn't sure what.

"What I mean is, it's not necessary," he explained. "Someone's got to be out and about anyway, and it'll only take a few extra minutes to stop by your place. I'll already be paying for their time."

"All right," she said, after a moment.

During their conversation, they'd gradually drifted lower onto the bed. He sat up again, twisting to draw her eye to his.

"Look, Perry, if I'm overstepping some boundary, I'm sorry. I'm not intending insult or implying you owe me anything in return. If I want to help you, and if it means taking advantage of the my men's good graces, then let me do it, would you? Please. We're not strangers. You're not my client, I'm not your contractor. Or at least, that's not all I am. I hope.”

“You hope?  Sleep with your clients often, do you?”

He smiled. “I care about you and what is going on between us means a lot to me. I tend to take care of the people who are important to me.”

Her auburn lashes lifted as her pale eyes locked onto his in the dimly lit room. Raising his hand, he pushed the hair back from her brow, smoothing it over her head.

“I care about you, too,” she said. “What’s begun between us is absolutely wonderful.” She hesitated, studying his face. Ethan felt his smile seep away.

“What?  What’s wrong?”

Perry’s lips twisted. “We don’t really know where we’re headed, do we?”

“Does anyone ever really know in the beginning?”

“I suppose not,” she conceded. “Even so, I can’t hang out in a place that’s been yours, unfettered by the intrusion of the likes of me, without some fixed time limit. Don’t you think it might start to cause some friction between us?”

No, he wanted to say, I don’t. But he remained silent.

“We don’t know each other that well,” she added.

“Not yet,” he agreed.

“Heck, the sex alone could wear us both out.”

He chuckled despite the sinking feeling in his stomach. "What's wrong with that?"

Her lips curved, but she didn't smile. "Nothing's wrong with that. And I know you're afraid for me. I'm afraid for me, too, but I can't let whatever is happening run me out of my own house indefinitely. To be honest, when I think about it, I feel lost. Maybe because I can't go back and I can't really go forward. Situations have developed I didn't expect days ago, a week ago, a few months ago. Some are intensely bizarre, as you must admit. And one of them is probably the best thing to happen to me in a good long time."

The discomfort in his gut dissipated. "I feel the same way."

Her pale irises darkened in the gloom, the gray more like storm clouds and shielded partially from his view by her lashes. He took her hand in his and kissed her knuckles.

"You're not going to cry, are you?" he said. "Because you'll get me started, too."

"You are a romantic."

"I've never denied it."

"Well, don't worry, I won't spill a single tear." She spoke with quiet vehemence, waving her hand and issuing a small, humorless laugh. "God only knows, I'm not going to be responsible for that, as well."

He frowned. "As well as what?"

"Since you've met me," she stated, "you can't tell me you haven't been troubled by the things occurring between us. Not this," she elaborated, indicating the bed, "but what takes place at the house. I see something in your eyes that wasn't there when we first met."

"Don't assume that's a bad thing," he countered softly.

"You know what I mean."

Ethan shook his head. "I do know what you mean. And you're not responsible for any of that, Perry. Hopefully we'll soon uncover whatever is responsible and see if something can't be done."

"What? Like exorcism?"

He could see through her weak joke. "If necessary," he said, "yes."

Perry sighed. "Thank you. For everything."

"And John. We mustn't forget his assistance."

"Of course not."

He pulled her forward, breathed in the light scent in her hair, sweet with shampoo fragrance and her own heated skin. Her pulse beat steadily where his fingers lay against her neck.

"Will you tell me something?" she asked against his shirt.

"What's that?"

For several seconds she said nothing. Ethan waited.

"How," she asked at last, "did she die?"

"Lily? We don't know. Hopefully in a ripe and happy old age, but as she took off with her lover there's no local record regarding the date of her death or anything else."

"Not Lily," said Perry quietly, pulling away once more to look up at him. "Your wife."

The air rushed from his lungs as if she'd struck him squarely in the chest. Lifting his hand, he ran his fingers through his hair, hooked them behind his neck. Only then did he note Perry's glance across the room. Turning his head he followed her gaze.

"Oh."

The evening the picture had been taken came back to him clearly. A good day. For Cindy, a good day. One of the best, he had to admit, that she had known in many. Her mood had been even, her smile not bright, but calm, contented. They'd gone to the Jersey shore that week and he won a stuffed dog for her in a game throwing balls at stacked bottles on a shelf. He would have wagered the game fixed, until he actually took them down with a hefty pitch. The prize she'd  chosen had been the most God-awful pink shade, like the stuff you put on horses to keep away the flies. But she loved it, and he had taken her picture with the animal in her arms. After the photographs from their vacation were developed she had pulled that one out and had it framed for him.

I'll always remember this day, she had said to him each time she looked at it. More often than he could number. Obsessively, he realized now. He sighed.

"She killed herself, Perry. Took her own life while I was at work one day."

## Chapter Thirty

For an entire minute and a half Perry said nothing. Her instinct to express sympathy seemed shallow and unnecessary. Compassion went without saying. No one received news like that and said, so what? She knew he didn't need her pity or her curiosity.

She felt sorry she had asked, for with the answer her question appeared entirely inappropriate. Even so, she raised her gaze to the photo on the chest of drawers, the one to which her attention had been drawn on and off all day. She knew having it there wasn't the same as having a former spouse's picture as a reminder of better times. That would have been enough to send her racing for a motel or some other place to stay. But the fact he kept his departed wife's photograph in his bedroom's intimate setting had made her curious and a little uneasy. It had made her wonder if she could ever live up to the memories he possessed. Now that she knew Cindy had died and how, the somewhat natural uncertainty exploded into tiny fragments, leaving her baffled and at a loss.

As for Ethan, she could only guess what thoughts ran through his head, what roosting emotions she had shaken from their repose. Something in the way he answered her led her to understand this to be a subject he seldom spoke about. Given half a chance and an instrument sufficient to the task, she would have sewn her lips shut rather than dredge up past pain for him.

Too many awkward seconds passed. "I shouldn't have asked. It's not my place or my business," she said.

"It is your business," Ethan said, sounding firm in undertone. "It is very much your business. I brought the matter up, after all, in the attic. I wanted you to know. You have every right to your questions."

Perry slipped her hand into his. After an abbreviated hesitation his fingers closed tightly around her own. He turned his head to gaze at the photograph, his dark hair in disarray. His long lashes lowered, hiding his eyes. However, she couldn't mistake the tautness in his jaw. When he swallowed and turned back to her, his expression had become guarded.

"Cindy and I were married shortly after graduation from college," he said. She nodded, having assumed as much from the photo she had viewed on-line. Young, they had been terribly young, and had looked very much in love.

"She told me straight out, shortly after we started dating, that she suffered from bi-polar disorder. It didn't seem reason enough to discontinue seeing her. Not as far as I was concerned. She was on medication and doing well. Even had she not been, in time I cared enough about her that I would never have turned my back on her."

"Of course not," said Perry. "You loved her."

To Perry, she'd made a simple, factual statement. Yet the muscle suddenly leaping in Ethan's jaw told its own story. His grip on her hand tightened fractionally, then relaxed.

"This is difficult," he whispered.

Perry understood. She kept silent.

"We—we had decided not to have children. There's a genetic predisposition to the disorder. I suppose I should have taken the responsibility of reducing the risk, but I didn't. She got pregnant. And when she did, knowing what the medication might do to the fetus, she stopped taking it."

Lowering her mouth to his shoulder, Perry lightly touched her lips to the place where bone curved into the muscle on his upper arm. He pulled her against him, talking softly above her head.

"She miscarried. It had nothing to do with anything she'd done or not done, but she blamed herself. The lack of medication didn't help her frame of mind. When we finally got her back on the medication the routine that had been so helpful to her was canted and she never really recovered. When she felt good she would stop taking the meds without telling me, although it would not be long before I realized she was off. It was a constant battle. More than once she became suicidal, but we always managed to head her off and get her back on track."

"We?"

"Me," he clarified. "Her family. Mine. Understand that not everyone who is bi-polar suffers to such a degree, but those who do are at constant risk. In the end, the depressive stage of the disorder was so deep she succumbed to it. And somehow, that time I didn't see it coming."

Ethan lapsed into silence, shaking his head in negligible movement. As to how Cindy had taken her life, what pain and guilt and anger his discovery of her death, perhaps even of her body might have caused him, he said nothing. Listening to his respiration's staggered cadence, Perry imagined he had endured all those emotions and more, living constantly haunted by her passing, the existence they had shared before, his own since. Like the effect caused by water constantly dripping onto stone, she suspected part of him had worn hollow with it, a permanent indentation in which memory pooled in waiting for the next drop to stir the calm surface to animation.

She touched his wrist, closing her fingers around it. "Ethan, no matter what happens between us I want you to remember you can always come to me if you need to. If nothing else, you've shown me true friendship and I won't forget that."

He shifted on the mattress, setting her a little away from him. His dark eyes held hers.

"You sound as if you've made a decision. Have I scared you off?"

"Not even close."

He smiled, his mouth's curve both sad and hopeful. He kissed her lips with gentle pressure. "Tomorrow promises to be a long day," he said. "I think we should get some sleep."

Perry agreed, drawing him down into her arms after he turned off the light. He lay with his head on her breast, one arm draped across her waist. She ran her fingers through his hair several times, smoothing the dark locks back from his brow. Nestling her hand against his neck, she closed her eyes, her other arm behind her head on the pillow.

She had awakened an old and deeply rooted pain for him, and she regretted it. Had it been at all possible to go back and withdraw her question, she would have, for his sake. Yet for her own she was relieved to have an answer. To be happy about the answer had never really been a requirement.

As she lay there, his breathing evened out, his head heavy on her breast. Perry's fingers unconsciously stroked the short, curling hairs at his nape. His skin felt warm, her fingertips fitting perfectly into the hollow at the base of his skull, moving in the same direction again and again in gentle, abbreviated strokes. She wanted to tell him she was sorry, even though she had told herself a short time ago her condolences were too late and unnecessary, that her empathy went without saying. Opening her eyes to look at him, her lips parted to speak even if he wouldn't hear her.

In the darkness, the upturned shadow of his lashes revealed a minute reflection in the peat-colored iris beneath. She jumped a little at finding him awake and watchful.

"I'm sorry," she whispered.

"You didn't wake me," he said, a breath, no more.

Her tone had not been designed for apology but sympathy. If he chose to misinterpret her words, so be it. He understood her sentiment, despite his response. His arm tightened momentarily on her waist.

"May I ask you something now?"

She studied him in the darkness, the dark, unruly hair curling into the black fabric on her breast, his furrowed brow as he lifted his eyes to her face, the fine high arch of his cheekbones, the faint hollow curving into his shaded jaw, and hesitated.

"Sure," she said, hoping he didn't notice. He deserved so many answers. She only hoped his question wouldn't break her.

"You asked me not so very long ago if I believed in ghosts," he said. "You made that query on blind faith and trust, of a man you barely knew. You could have asked that question of anyone, anywhere, and received a totally different response than the one you received from me. And there's a reason for that. A reason you asked it of a man who would not turn away from you for asking."

Perry's released her breath, stirring the hair across his brow. "Perhaps I sensed you would understand."

"Perhaps," he said. "But you trusted me, Perry, as if you already knew me. Does it seem strange to you our relationship has advanced so quickly?"

"No," she said after a moment's thought. "Not at all."

His teeth gleamed in a flashing grin. "If you hadn't moved back into your grandmother's house, hadn't called me for refurbishment, if I had turned and walked away from the house when you didn't answer the door instead of letting my curiosity get the better of me, what do you think would be happening right now? To you, and to me?"

He had asked several questions, all skirting the heart of the matter, she felt, but spiraling nearer.

She wondered if she could steer him clear. "Well, you would probably be doing just what you did tonight. Watching the news, turning off the television, going to sleep. Well, not to sleep, obviously. Perhaps there would have been someone else in your bed."

"Not likely."

"No?"

"No. I haven't been inclined toward female company of late. Maybe I was waiting."

"What? For me?"

"Maybe."

"Fate?"

"I don't know."

She held her breath.

"But what about you?" he asked.

"What do you mean?" She knew exactly what he meant.

"What would you have been doing?"

She shook her head, turned away. He reached up, drawing her back, making her look at him.

"One reason I don't want you going home is your safety," he said. "My concerns for your well-being are sound. But a part of me is, well, to be direct, jealous as hell. And I'm not a jealous type of guy. Never have been before, anyway. Yet I can't help but wonder, when I think about what you told me, if you can fully turn away from...from what it, he, offered."

"That's not fair," Perry whispered.

"I know it's not," he said.

Perry bit her upper lip. She ran her tongue over her front teeth. She exhaled. All for delay. She couldn't help but wonder, dread, despair over what he might ask next.

"What is your question, then, Ethan? Ask it. Do you want to know if I would run to a creature of air and God only knows what else for gratification instead of you? Is that it?"

"Not exactly," he said.

"What, then?"

"I know you trust me," he said, rising up onto his elbow. "What I want to know is if you trust us. If you trust and believe in us, in what has begun here, enough to allow me to see you through anything that might arise from this investigation, this haunting in your life."

"Oh, Ethan," Perry breathed, her voice catching, "the responsibility is not yours."

"I'm aware of that," he said. "I'm asking it to be, nonetheless."

Perry's mouth twisted, her lips drawing in as she fought back tears. Her thoughts went to Cindy, to Ethan's loss and his self-blame. "Ethan, you have nothing to make up for."

"Maybe not," he said. "Maybe yes. It doesn't matter. This request has nothing to do with my past, Perry, but it has everything to do with our future."

Our future. She liked the sound of that. She said as much.

"Me, too."

"Even so, you might not be able to make this right for me."

"I'm damned well going to try, though," he answered.

## *Chapter Thirty-One*

*How many pieces of fine linen paper had he covered in his carefully practiced script only to crumple them and toss them away before the words came right? He could not recall. He could not even recall the words now. But it had only taken the one sheet of fancy paper to damn them both. Just the one.*

*Why had she been so neglectful with it? So careless as to leave the note that was his heart made plain where his brother might find it? Where Edward went daily as was his wont and preference, to prepare his sermon for the Sunday to come?  She knew. It seemed to him her negligence had been a deliberate act, so that Edward would learn the truth without the need for telling it. But there was a difference between words flown from the lips and those wrought in ink. You couldn't take them back, couldn't say they were misunderstood.*

*Rising from his knees he moved toward the fall of water. As always he could see the moon, nearly round, pristine and pale. He stretched out his hand toward the steady, unmoving orb, opening his palm, curving his fingers, remembering the feel of her breasts, their weight , her skin's scent, its texture. He recalled the curl of his tongue around her nipples, reminding himself that sometime before the spring to come her milk would flow, giving sustenance to the child that was yet such a tiny being in her womb.*

*Until he had found the note, Edward had believed the child to be his own.*

*Or so Lily said. He wondered, sometimes, at the sequence of occurrence. Clarity ofttimes eluded him and he could not distinguish the events of one day from those of the last, nor his thoughts from his actions. Lily was the only true memory he had, steadfast and constant. She belonged to him. Her body was his from which to partake, like a feast to which he returned again and again.*

*Remembering her taste, he closed his eyes. How exacting a price he paid for his pleasure.  How dear and precise a price. He wondered if Lily knew. She must, of course, for a woman could sense even if she had no true knowledge.  Yet she said nothing of it. Ever.*

*Lily wept each time in passion. That alone was enough. He made her happy, where Edward did not, where Edward failed again and again. He could not remember what it was that had made him question her, doubt her, accuse her of faithlessness. It was nothing, nothing. Just a momentary lapse.*

*Yet, where was she?  Where was his Lily?  How long did she expect him to wait for her here?*

*Forever.  She wanted forever.  That was what she had told him.*

*Yet when he had offered her forever she had refused him.*

# PAST SINS

## Chapter Thirty-Two

As a normal precaution, Ethan placed tarps and plywood over all jobs in progress, but with the coming weather further steps were necessary to prevent water damage. He had been of two minds about leaving Perry without waking her to tell her exactly where he'd be, but as she hadn't been inclined to stir when he climbed from bed he wasn't disposed to disturb her unnecessarily. Instead, he left a note for her on the nightstand before he headed out with John. He'd called him to come by earlier than anticipated with the truck so he could see to business. John sat in the pickup now, making phone calls. Watching him across the driveway, Ethan knew John must be talking either to his wife or eldest daughter. His animation was obvious.

Smiling, Ethan turned back to his work. A dedicated family man, John Gooden missed his family terribly whenever he happened to be away from them. Ethan wondered in a fleeting 'what if' what type parent he might have been had the opportunity presented itself, and dismissed the thought with a mental shrug. He wasn't likely to find out at this stage in life.

Turning, Ethan waved to Tom on the rooftop. Tom arrived at the shop a few minutes after he and John had, looking a little rough around the edges. Ethan knew he'd woken him up when he called. As a single man with a propensity for spending one or two nights a month with his buddies at the local bar, he probably hadn't been feeling on top of the world. Still, he was the best climber Ethan had, agile and with uncanny balance.

At Ethan's signal. Tom let loose the tarp, the heavy blue expanse covering the one already in place with several feet overage to either side. Ethan scaled the ladder to secure the ends while Tom made his way down the roof, distributing sandbags along the edges. Pausing after setting the last in place, he eyed Ethan critically. Ethan squinted up at him against a swiftly vanishing sun.

"Same one?" Tom asked.

"What?"

"Same woman who kept you up the other night?"

Ethan's brows arched. "You know, you're pretty damn nosy for a man who's expecting me to pay his salary come Friday." Still, memory made his skin warm.

Tom laughed, taking the threat in stride. "Anyone I know?"

Ethan opened his mouth to make a hasty and discouraging reply, but instead shook his head. "Not yet," he said. Although not the closest friend, Ethan had known Tom for nearly five years. Somehow, they had not socialized outside work except on specific occasion. Nevertheless, they had forged a decent relationship. Tom deserved his consideration. "One day soon I'll introduce you."

His uncharacteristic his reply obviously shocked Tom. To the man's credit, he quickly masked his surprise with a smile.

"Thank you," he said. "I'd like that."

Tom's artless response affected Ethan more than he cared to admit. He realized in that moment just how much he had been distancing himself from the people to which he was or should have been closest. He tugged on the tarp's edge, considering all the invitations refused, the lapsing exchanges in communication, and felt suddenly and intensely grateful to John in the truck below, who had not turned away despite Ethan's neglect. As for Tom, the man had stood by him through a great deal more than the ups and downs in his profession. If he had given it any thought at all, he would have recognized the man's past remarks were not those of someone seeking a blow-by-blow description regarding any sexual escapade, only an offer in friendship.

Ethan looked up again. He raised a hand to shield his eyes. "Maybe this week we might all go out to dinner. You did mention you were seeing someone, didn't you?"

Tom looked even more shocked than he had a minute ago. "It's pretty casual at this point, but sure. That would be great."

Ethan nodded. "We'll figure out where tomorrow or the next day. Once we see what this weather brings."

"Sure. There's an Italian place just opened up. Supposed to have good food."

"That could be it, then." It occurred to Ethan he had no idea if Perry ate Italian. Most people did, though, making it a pretty safe bet.

"Hey, Taylor," Tom called as he made his way back up the roof, "your buddy in the truck is trying to get your attention."

Turning, Ethan spotted John hastening toward him from the pickup, waving Ethan's phone back and forth.

"It's Perry," John shouted up. "She got your note when she woke up."

"Perry?" This from Tom. Ethan glanced up at him to find the man's face creasing into a grin.

"Yes, Perry."

"The woman whose house you went to look over sometime last week?"

"Yes," Ethan said again. "The same."

For a full three seconds Tom said nothing, and then he whistled, a low, single tone. "Quick work, boss."

"Shut up and get off the roof," Ethan growled, suppressing a laugh. He clambered down the ladder to take the phone from John.

"Perry, hi."  Although he would have liked to temper the fondness in his voice he realized how futile the attempt would be, and unnecessary. "How are you this morning?"

Smiling, John moved away.

"Fine," she answered, "and you?"  If she had been a cat, she would have been purring. He could almost see her face against his closed lids. When he opened his eyes he found John watching him with a peculiar expression, very nearly smug. John turned and continued on his way back to the truck.

"More than fine," said Ethan. "I'm finishing up here and then John and I are heading to your house to check the instruments."

"I'll meet you there. If you don't mind, would you bring that generator? I just watched another report on the weather. They act like we're in for the storm of the century before this day is over. Could be hype, but I'd rather be safe than sorry."

Ethan hesitated. Despite their conversation's outcome last evening, he really didn't want her going back to the house. She had to know that. To him, his expectation seemed reasonable, even though it was Perry's home. He knew how strongly she felt about not being run out of it. Try as he might, though, he could not banish the images from the past several days in that house from his mind. Not the episode in the creek, nor in the attic, nor the mist creeping off the porch toward him. He hadn't even told Perry about the last. John had advised him not to. With his penchant for understatement, he had warned Ethan Perry might become alarmed. Ethan considered using the information if he had to anyway, to convince her about her risk.

"Ethan?" she interrupted his contemplation. "How about in an hour? Does that give you enough time to finish what you're doing?"

Blowing out his breath, he agreed. "Give me an hour and a half. Don't go over any earlier than that, all right? I don't want you there alone."

In an hour's time he and John would be at the house well before Perry to check things over, as well as being able to finish their discussion about the findings in Edward Nicholson's Bible. If Ethan perceived any danger he'd have Perry out of the house so fast her adorable little head would be spinning.

"All right," she said. "An hour and a half."

"Promise me."

"All right. I promise. I'll give you an hour or so and then start driving over. Fair enough?"

"Fair enough," he said and she hung up.

Ethan cast a quick eye around the property to make certain they'd left nothing lying out of place, then he called to Tom.

"That's it, Tom!  Time to get your hung-over ass back home and tucked into bed!"

Collapsing the ladder, Ethan carried it to the truck and secured it in place. As Tom had not yet come around from behind the barn with the second one, Ethan went to help him. Rounding the corner he stopped short, skidding in the loose dirt. He had his phone out and ready to dial for emergency help before he reached Tom's body lying on the ground. Fingers probing for the pulse beneath the man's jaw, Ethan's held breath exploded in relief when he saw Tom's eyelids flutter open.

"Ouch," Tom said, moving his head.

Shoving the phone back into its holder, Ethan slipped his arm behind Tom's shoulder, hesitating to move him further until the man had given a more informative accounting as to his pain.

"What happened? Is anything broken?"

"Mmm. My ankle, maybe," Tom answered, lifting his leg from the ground. He seemed to be concentrating on moving his foot, but it remained immobile. The man grimaced in pain.

Ethan eyed Tom's head through his tumbled, sandy hair. His cap lay at a short distance, dirty and crushed. Ethan saw no blood, but that didn't mean anything. "Did you hit your head?"

Reaching up, Tom probed his scalp above the hairline. "Yeah, I think so. I'm not sure though. It hurts like a son of a bitch." His eyes closed again, then opened slowly.

"Your head or your ankle?"

"Both."

Ethan swore beneath his breath. Tom swore out loud.

"What happened?" Ethan repeated, glancing up the ladder for any malfunction.

"You told me to get off the damn roof," Tom muttered, trying to roll over to sit up. Ethan helped him, frowning at his words.

"I told you—"

"I'm joking. I stepped wrong on the ladder, about half way down. I've never done that before." He laughed, then groaned as he clutched his side. "Shit. I think I broke a rib, too."

"Oh, hell," said Ethan.

Tom struggled to rise, using the ladder as support. Ethan hoisted him upright. The man's body slumped against him. "Can't put any weight on the ankle."

"We're off to the hospital," said Ethan, half-carrying him toward the driveway out front. "I'll come back for the ladder later. Just take it slow."

Tom eyed him sidelong, pain making his skin pallid. "This puts a damper on your plans with the little lady," he commented through clenched teeth.

Ethan smiled. Grimly. "I wouldn't be calling her 'little lady' to her face if I were you. She's liable to throw you off a roof herself."

Tom laughed and groaned again, finishing up for good measure with some barely intelligible profanities. Ethan helped him slowly around toward the truck. John hastened to assist, taking Tom's other side. Once they were in the truck and on their way to the nearest emergency facility with all haste, Ethan asked John to give Perry a call to explain the situation.

"Tell her I'll ring her when we're ready to leave the hospital."

A minute later Ethan heard John leaving a message. John glanced at him around Tom's head with a puzzled expression.

"Don't worry about it," said Ethan. "She's probably in the shower or just not answering the phone. My pal Maggie phoned last night. Perry might be avoiding picking up another call."

John chuckled.  Ethan turned his attention back to the road. He would try again himself from the hospital, just to make certain he spoke to her before she made plans to leave.

## *Chapter Thirty-Three*

Wrapped in a towel and trailing watery footprints across the floor, Perry hurried to the ringing phone, pausing to check the number on caller id. Not recognizing the digits as belonging to Ethan she hesitated to pick it up, expecting it might be a repeated call from Maggie Barnes. As she faltered, the phone ceased ringing. A few seconds later the light on the base began to blink, indicating a message on voice mail. She could only hope it wasn't for her, because she hadn't a clue as to the password to access the telephone system. Why on earth did the man insist on this old-fashioned landline anyway? Cell phones were so much easier. If he'd called her cell, she could have been sure it wasn't a Maggie communication.

Unconcerned, she went to dress and dry her hair. More than once her gaze drifted across the room to Ethan's wife's photograph on the chest of drawers. She went closer, tilting her head to study the image, extending a finger to slide the frame back and to the side a little for a view unobstructed by the window's reflection.

She remembered the picture on the website, and how plainly happy they both seemed. The woman in this photo was different, somehow, haunted perhaps by the loss of her child and the decision to have no more, as well as the depression inherent to the particular extreme of her condition. Knowing Cindy Taylor's story made Perry feel almost guilty about her own place in Ethan's life these past few days.

Tapping the frame with her fingernail, Perry returned the photo carefully to the exact space it had been, aligning the edge along the mark in a barely discernible dust line. She considered the peculiar circumstances which had thrown her and Ethan together for more hours straight than most people barely met would spend in each other's company over several weeks. More than anything, these events had a great deal to do with their relationship's forward momentum. She wondered if they would burn themselves out too quickly, like a fire and lighter fluid, or if a return to normalcy would toll the bell to end a premature, frantic rush of shared communication and, well, lust.

She hoped not. No matter how guilty she felt standing before the photograph of Ethan's deceased wife, she really wanted what she and Ethan had to last.

She glanced at the clock on the bedside table. No point in trying to get any work done before she had to leave. Instead, she picked up her mother's diary from the place Ethan had set it down the night before. Grabbing the orange juice she'd poured herself before her shower, Perry carried both out onto the back deck and sat in an Adirondack chair. A weak sun shone like a white disc through the thickening cloud cover. The wind blew fitfully, tugging at her hair and her clothes, an intermittently chill harbinger to the approaching storm. She smelled rain in the air already.

Perry felt an urgency to be home, almost in her bones, to be home and taking care of those things for which she was responsible rather than lounging in Ethan's house as if she hadn't a care in the world. But she had promised Ethan and therefore she would wait.

For some time now, since long before moving into her old home, Perry had been caring for herself, her own needs, her own obligations. To have someone else looking after her was an unfamiliar experience, although not unpleasant. Her heart and skin warmed thinking about Ethan's safeguarding her, his tender care, his amorous attentions. She smiled, leaning her head against the chair back.

He had hinted at fate, at destiny, and it did seem their relationship was influenced by something beyond themselves. Their paths might easily have never crossed. Instead, they'd become intertwined on numerous levels. Perhaps when they needed each other most.

Her mind skittered nervously around the connection with the ghostly residents in her home and their direct link to her past and to her present, and then veered away. She did not want to consider the implication that shades of past deeds in some way influenced what she and Ethan had now.

She let her gaze rove over Ethan's pretty landscaping, finding herself returning again and again to the possibility. Both she and Ethan had been controlled, to an extent, by ideas or memories or replays of past incidents, right? Conversely, wouldn't that mean if they made deliberate choices not to be influenced, they could avoid a repeat? Somehow, she didn't entirely trust the theory, nor did she want to put Ethan to the test. When she went home, it would be a quick trip to check the sumps and have Ethan hook up the generator, then they would both get right back out. No sense taking unnecessary risks.

She found herself speculating about the equipment John and Ethan had set in place, curious as to whether any activity would have been picked up in their absence. Would there be any, or was she the catalyst? She, and now apparently Ethan? In that likely scenario, showing up with Ethan for a few minutes could be a problem. And yet, as she'd told Ethan the night before, she couldn't let herself be run from her home indefinitely. Although she was direct in line, many distant relatives would have been more than happy to have the house, and Nana knew it. For reasons known best to her, and therefore a mystery, Perry's grandmother wanted her to have the house.

Deliberately, Perry turned instead to the book on her lap. A little distraction would come in handy.

"Hi, Mom," she said as she opened the diary. Goodness, how long had it been since she'd said those words?  Sixteen, seventeen years. Yet her utterance in that moment seemed familiar and as if no time had passed at all.

Biting her lip, Perry flipped through the pages, trying to locate the place she'd left off before dozing. Frustrated in her attempts, she randomly picked a place to start again. She saw no date at the top, but by the tone she felt certain this entry had been made a few years after the last she'd read.

Reading for a few minutes about a date and a party, a new teacher at school and her mother's newly cut hair, Perry leafed a few pages further to find more of the same. Impulsively, she turned to the back, flipping in reverse to the last entry.

*I've missed my second period*, it read. *I know I'm pregnant. I don't know what to do.*

And that was it. Blank lines filled the diary's remaining pages. Perry stared at the yellowed paper with its faded blue lines and felt a hole open up in her, a gaping void. She wanted to weep, fought it, but tears soon welled up in her eyes, slid down her cheeks. Those three simple sentences tore at her soul, embodying all the fear and uncertainty her mother must have felt at the realization her life forever changed by the hasty choice she'd made. No further words to indicate how she might have vacillated between options, or if she ever had. Or even if she had from the beginning determined to give birth to Perry and raise her alone.

She hadn't quite been alone. Nana had been very good about that. Perry's mother had always made it clear to Perry how much she wanted her, that there had never been any doubt in her mind. Somehow, as an adult, Perry had come to believe a teenage girl in her mother's position couldn't be so strong and decided. What she just read had given no indication anything had been different, in either direction. Perry had found only a scared young girl's words, a girl who had chosen to write no more after, as though sharing her thoughts within a journal's private pages had suddenly become a child's pastime. Childhood had passed away at such an early age.

Of course, Perry might be viewing the whole thing through her own insecurities. Sheila Madison might, indeed, have decided from the exact moment she set her pen to paper to smake the entry that she would never look back in regret, that she would get on with her life.

In this regard, mother and daughter differed.

There had been a time during Perry's marriage to Jack when he had expressed a desire to start a family. Although his expression in that direction had been short-lived it had, for a time, been earnest. Perry had held back, the one who had been afraid to take that leap into total responsibility. Afraid of other things, too. What, exactly, she didn't know. Perhaps that Jack would leave her, as her mother had been left. Or merely that the responsibilities required in caring for another living being would be an overwhelming, somehow foolhardy endeavor, at a time when she was not so very certain about the caring for herself. Independence had come late to Perry, after Jack, when necessity had become the mother of, not invention, just growing up, once and for all. Other women, new mothers themselves, told her they possessed the same doubts and worries she expressed, but once their children were in their lives adjustment came naturally, although not always easily.

In the end, she supposed it was just as well. Jack lived God-knew-where with his new wife and Perry didn't believe he would have had the time or the inclination to give a child what he or she would need, even from a long-distance parent. But suddenly and perhaps unreasonably, Perry wished she'd possessed her mother's courage. She wanted to know the joys and heartaches, to share moments like the ones she had shared with her own parent, to form that special bond.

"Well," she said out loud, dashing away the tears rolling down her cheeks, "that's rather selfish of you, isn't it?"

One didn't want a child just for the experience, the companionship, the love...did they? Or was that part, too, and so much more besides?

Picking up her glass, Perry drank the juice down in several great gulps. Wiping her mouth with her hand, she decided to go back further in the diary. With nothing after the pregnancy revelation, at least she might determine where her mother's head had been beforehand.

Randomly picking a page, she started to read, trailing her finger for a few seconds along the curling, slanting script. At the third paragraph in the entry, she froze and re-read it very slowly.

Tearing her gaze from the page, she looked up and around Ethan's well-tended backyard, then down again at the words marked by her fingertip on the yellowed paper. A chill crept along her skin, lifting the hairs on her arms, her neck.

*I've never seen the ghost of the minister's wife. I don't believe she exists. It's just a story the girls tell, to scare each other at slumber parties. They don't know who he might be. But I've seen him. I've seen him, right by the waterfall down at the creek. Nobody else can say the same. I don't think they believe me anymore than I believe them. But it's true. I saw him just the other day again. He moves like a bit of sunlight and you can't really see him until he's in the shadows behind the rocks. But then he looks very sad, looks right through me actually, and disappears. The last time I thought I saw his hand lift. I got a real funny feeling when I saw that, way down low, like I was going to be sick. It made me feel like I should run away, more than just seeing him did. I don't think I'm going back there again.*

Keeping her finger in the page, Perry flicked ahead in cautious haste, careful with the brittle paper, anxiously searching for another mention. The entry immediately following had been several days later, the one after that seemed to have been written after several weeks. The next three were consecutive days, with no ghostly mention, no apparition by the creek. Could her mother have so easily dismissed him? What age had she been when she wrote this?

Perry located another reference, what appeared to be a month later, following several paragraphs in which her mother had agonized over her first menstrual cycle. Perry herself had her first at twelve, but she didn't know for certain when her mother had begun. Surely not much older than that. Maybe thirteen years?

*I have decided I am very brave. I saw him again today and called to him, daring him to speak to me. He will not. I don't know why. I suppose ghosts can't talk, but I had hoped he would. He must be very lonely. I thought I could help him, maybe send him back where he belongs.*

Perry scanned more along that vein, childishly romantic theories about unrequited love and a lost soul longing for the woman who had scorned him. The passage where her mother wondered about the possibility she might kiss the "spirit of the waterfall" caused Perry a vicious, irrational possessiveness, jealously even, before recognition rushed in to cool her veins.

He hadn't just contacted Perry, although from what she could see there had been no physical intimacy between her mother and the entity to whom she, herself, had submitted so willingly. Perhaps the difference in age or sexual experience factored in, or maybe something more subtle, maybe even more sinister, enabled him to manufacture the bond between himself and Perry.

Suddenly the orange juice soured in Perry's stomach. Memory surfaced, dark and bubbling like rising swamp gas from murky depths.

"Oh, God," she whispered.

Daniel Nicholson's spirit—if indeed it was he—had actually spoken to Perry, a long time ago. Vivid flashes returned to her from that day, or was it days? In sudden clarity they careened around her mind. She couldn't have been more than twelve, a precocious child aware of the changes in her body. She had gone to the creek on a miserably hot day, longing for the chill water on her skin.

Perry leaned over the diary, fighting the nausea roiling in her stomach. How had she forgotten? Pushed the memory down so deeply that not even recent events had brought it forth? It had taken her mother's written word, a child's words, to dredge up recall.

She needed to tell Ethan and John what she had discovered, that the spirit had not only come to her, but to her mother. Yet, she needed to read on in order to understand what her mother had experienced.

The next ten pages were filled with Sheila Madison recounting her excursions to the creek bank, to the falls themselves, sometimes viewing the spirit, sometimes not. It became quite apparent her mother's fascination with the creature grew with each visit, despite lacking reciprocation. It seemed as if, so the diary revealed, the spirit had taken no notice of her at all.

What difference, then, between Perry and her mother had enabled the boundary to be transcended? In turning the next page, Perry understood. Shock numbed her hands and made her skin shiver beneath the wind's shifting chill.

*Mama says I am not to go back there. It is forbidden. She said she should have told me sooner to stay away, and would have, if she'd known that was where I wandered. I asked her why the spirit haunted that place. I asked her what it wanted. And she said, very matter-of-fact, as if she had only been waiting for me to ask, "He does not want you, child. He waits for another. You must be grateful for that and never go there to seek him again."*

Perry slumped against the chair back, closing the volume slowly.

Nana had known. God, Nana had known. How?

She recalled again her mother and grandmother's early warnings about the creek, intimating danger by drowning. Why hadn't they informed her straight out? Why? Of course, because they knew she would never have believed them and would have been more determined than ever to venture to the place which had drawn her irresistibly from her earliest memories. When she had been frightened off, when he had told her to leave him, that she was just a child, they must have known they could relax their vigil. It seemed to her in retrospect the stern admonishments had ceased at that point in time, or shortly thereafter.

Why hadn't they all just moved away? And what? Left it for the next resident to do battle? No, no, something eluded her. Some reason for silence she couldn't begin to imagine.

Perry opened the diary again. This time it fell without restriction to the last page she had been reading.

*He does not want you, child. He waits for another.*

He waits for another.

And he had found her.

Perry stuffed her shaking hands under her arms. She tipped her head against the chair back, closing her eyes. An irregular rhythm, not in her heart, but in her mind's inner fabric, began to beat, making it difficult to breathe. The diary felt abnormally heavy on her thighs. She wanted to push it off her lap, toss it across the grass into the bushes at the lawn's edge, and yet despite the urgency she knew she wouldn't do it. Although providing revelation, her mother's diary hadn't caused her present situation. She had. Somehow, she had.

If Nana had known the danger, why had she left the house to her, ensuring her return? Or had Nana in her elder years pushed the knowledge aside in the same manner Perry had, until the episode had ceased for her to be anything more than a figment born from a vibrant imagination? And even that, in time, forgotten.

Gasping as if she had been running, Perry leaped up from her seat on the deck, snatching up the diary in one hand and her empty glass in the other. She hurried into the house, deposited the glass in the sink and went straight for her shoes. According to the clock she had been a good deal longer than she'd meant to be, lost in reading words that had unnerved her far more than any encounter with young Daniel's restless shade. She needed to show the diary to Ethan and John Gooden. See what they made of it. What she should think of it. She felt too disturbed by this particular family secret to know what to think on her own.

She grabbed her keys and her purse, tucked the diary into the latter and headed out the door, locking it behind her. As she started across the gravel drive she heard the phone ring and stopped short, skidding in her sneakers on the loose stone. Nothing she could do about the phone, even had she been of a mind to answer. She didn't have the key to get back inside.

Determined, she marched on toward her car.

## *Chapter Thirty-Four*

A discordant note, like an inner alarm bell, went off in Perry's head when she pulled into her driveway and couldn't locate Ethan's truck. Sweat broke out under her palms on the steering wheel. Rechecking the time, she silently berated herself for having hurried from his house without calling him first, especially since the last call might have been him, telling her he had been delayed.

Yanking her cell phone from her purse, she checked it for any calls from Ethan, still finding none. This didn't make sense. She quickly dialed

Ethan's cell, having committed it to memory last night. Straight to voice mail. Maybe the problem was he'd left his cell somewhere, and if he couldn't remember her number, didn't have access to it from her paperwork, perhaps he had called his home hoping to get her. Or maybe something had happened…

"Stop overthinking things," she said aloud, as if hearing her own voice might steel her nerves to leave the car. No such luck. The act only served to make her feel more nervous and alone.

She glanced over at the diary sticking up from her purse. How could the two people she loved most in the world keep such a secret from her? At the very least the action had been uncharacteristic, and at the worst, dangerous. Perhaps they hadn't wanted to frighten her or confuse her or burden her unduly with the knowledge a ghost haunted the women in the house. And why only the women? Well, the answer to that question was obvious. But he had sought fulfillment only with her.

He waits for another...

The knowledge she had apparently filled that niche held no comfort.

Perry leaned her chin on fingers clutched tightly around the steering wheel. She stared at the porch, the walls, the windows, their curtains barely visible behind glass. With the marked decrease in sunlight, each pane looked like pewter. The facade had always been dear to her, but it suddenly seemed menacing, or at the very least as though the house belonged to a stranger. Her feelings for it had been canted further by the diary's revelations as well as what lurked within the aged walls. She stared for a long time before forcing her left hand to release the wheel and move over to the door.

"It's *my house*," she said, hooking two fingers around the handle.

"It is *my* house," she said again, pushing the door open with her knee.

Standing in the graveled drive, Perry took several deep long breaths. Her eyes lifted toward the roof line and the attic concealed beneath row after staggered row of hand-hewn slate. In the journal pages recently read there had been no mention as to anything unusual in the house itself. Perhaps Edward Nicholson had been disinclined to make his presence known until the entity that seemed likely to be his younger brother had become more active, until Perry had begun her strange descent to meet him in that nebulous, altered reality.

No, corrected Perry. Not accurate. To be perfectly candid, Edward had not made an appearance until Ethan had made his.

Shaken by the realization, she told herself she should also be reassured by it. Perhaps it meant that with Ethan away from the house she could enter without worry. Determined, she marched toward the side yard and the kitchen door, hesitating halfway across the lawn.

If such were true, then she would not have experienced the episode in the woods, awakening as if she had been walking in her sleep to find herself on the trail and the mist, whatever it had been, the sensed animosity, blocking the path leading back.

Remembering the struggle under the water and Ethan's timely rescue, Perry eyed the kitchen window askance. She moved a few steps away into the oak tree's shadow on the grass. A wooden swing, at least as old as she, hung from thick ropes tied to a branch overhead. She sat on it, bending her arms around the ropes and clasping her hands together near her waist. Pushing back once with her heels, Perry set the swing into motion, her sneakers dragging over the earth. She stared at the plastered stone wall as if she might bore a hole through to uncover the secret life of the occupants within.

Perry couldn't help but wonder if some purpose existed here beyond her ability to fathom. Recent events seemed too interconnected to be coincidental, and that offered no comfort either. What was this all about?

Perry continued to stare at the house where she had grown up, returned, left and returned again. The house her grandmother had bequeathed solely to her possession, ghosts and all. Remembered conversations, looks exchanged between her mother and grandmother, wisped through her mind like the ghosts themselves. They'd thought her safe. She needed to remind herself they hadn't abandoned her to fate. They'd thought the ghost had dismissed her. Which he had, but only for a time.

The swing creaked to a halt. Perry stood.

"This *is* my house," she said, for the third time. Maybe therein lay the point, after all. Maybe someone with the connection to the spirit and the will to reclaim what should be hers by right might be all that was required to finally end the conflict.

Striding once more across the lawn, Perry went straight to the kitchen door, extending her hand with the key at the ready. Slowly her hand dropped to her side.

The door stood open.

Although only parted a few inches, she could see past the door to the kitchen floor, littered with natural debris as if a blasting wind had blown the detritus from her untended lawn inside. Yet, if that had been the case, wouldn't the door still be standing wide? Frowning, Perry shoved the wooden edge with a single finger, effortlessly pushing the door inward on its hinges. Something rushed out at her.

A cry parting her lips, Perry jumped back and away, throwing her arm up. The bird flew past her head, taking wing to the sky and freedom. Heart pounding, Perry watched it a moment before returning her attention to the jamb. She could see no sign entry had been forced. She knew she would have felt better if she had.

Stepping over the threshold, Perry planted both

feet side by side just inside the doorway. Silently she looked around the kitchen. The place's air of abandonment came from more than the debris strewn across the floor. She had a nearly overwhelming sense that if she spoke, her voice would echo as though off barren walls despite all her possessions plainly in sight.

A tendril of Virginia creeper wrapped around the doorframe. Perry frowned at the leaves, poked them. Sleeping Beauty came irrationally to mind, the castle lying entranced for a hundred years, everyone asleep inside a structure barricaded from the world by rapid and expansive growth. Yet except for the vine at the door, nothing littering the room was either green or living, but as brown and dead as if summer had departed and autumn arrived.

Reluctantly Perry crossed the floor, realizing after several steps she'd been placing her feet with deliberate concentration and as quietly as possible. She paused, listening, annoyed and unnerved, then moved on.

Through the open access to the living room she spied John Gooden's equipment standing eerily silent. She studied it, teeth in her lip. If the machinery recorded something, she couldn't tell. Not all the devices produced noise when in operation. John had told her so. But some did. Still, she heard nothing. A good sign? She had no idea.

Leaves had caught in the rug's heavy weave and lay scattered across the sofa cushions. A single leaf clung to a curtain panel well above her head. On the shelves, the tables, the fireplace mantel, everything placed there by her grandmother over the years had not been moved. Perry's own stereo still maintained its place in the cabinet. Everything might have been a little more dusty than she'd noticed, but otherwise all was untouched.

If someone had come to rob the place they'd left everything behind, including the expensive infra-red camera set to be triggered by the unusual. She had expected nothing less. She knew no burglar had entered here. By definition of the unusual, however, the camera should have tripped, catching something.

Without turning her head, Perry reached for the phone on the wall. Her cell phone had dropped to the bottom of her purse. She didn't want to take the time to search for it. Holding her grandmother's old yellow piece in a position where she could see it peripherally while not removing her gaze from the equipment in the living room, she depressed the buttons with a shaking fingertip, dialing Ethan's cell phone again. Each tone sounded astonishingly loud. She held the phone to her ear.

"Hello?" Hearing his voice, rich in timbre, she briefly closed her eyes. In swift reversal, she jerked her lids open again, staring into the living room.

Dust motes disturbed by an unfelt air current danced like silver flecks in the deepening gloom.

"Ethan, where are you?"

"At the hospital," he said.

"The hospital?" She checked, startled. "Are you all right?"

"I'm fine. I'm not hurt. I tried to call you. Tom fell off the ladder. My foreman. Where on earth are you?"

Perry drew a steadying breath, stilling her quaking knees. "Home," she said.

Silence greeted her statement.

"I thought you would be here." She wished, wished so badly he had been.

"Shit," he said, followed by a hasty apology to someone standing nearby.

"Is Tom all right?"

"Tom? What? Yes. He'll be all right. Some broken bones, though, it looks like. What's going on? I really don't want you there alone."

"I know you don't. I'm sorry. I'm here now, though."

"Are you all right? You sound odd. Perry? You still there?"

"Yes. I...Ethan, I found something in my mother's diary I want to talk to you and John about. It's important. Apparently they both knew. Both my mother and my grandmother."

"What do you mean?"

"They knew about him. He approached my mother, too. Not the way he did me, but she wrote about it in the diary. My grandmother spoke to her about it afterward, and told her he was waiting for someone else. God, Ethan, that someone was me."

"Perry, stay calm."

Considering her day thus far, she thought she sounded remarkably calm. Scuffing a leaf with her foot, she glanced down at it, then back up to the room before her.

"The house is...different."

"Different?" Ethan echoed, uneasy. His voice channeled strangely into her ears, slightly muffled like the tones were wrapped in a heavy vapor. "How so?"

She swallowed hard, struggling to speak. "There's stuff everywhere. Debris from outside. The door was open, but except for all this mess, nothing's been disturbed. Still, it doesn't feel the same—"

"Get out."

"What?"

"Get out of the house, Perry. Now. Please."

It took her a second to realize she'd begun nodding her accord in short, rapid movements, unable to speak. In the living room a monitor had jerked into life, sharp bands evident on the paper spewing out the side like the register of an EEG machine or a lie detector.

"What is that?" Ethan's voice cut in. "What is that noise?  Is that the equipment?"

"There's a paper readout showing some sort of activity," Perry managed. "Is it because I'm standing here?"

"No. God, no, Perry, it's not!"

"I didn't think so."

She didn't hear what he said next as her attention jerked away to the joists creaking in the attic far above. A steady, progressive sound. Heavy footfalls striding across the floor. Clutching the phone tightly, Perry lowered it against her thigh and began to back away from the entrance to the living room. She visualized, as clearly as if it appeared to her, something on the attic staircase making its way to the second floor. The hair on her arms stood straight up from her skin.

In the living room the dubious light dimmed further beneath a shrouding, coalescing fog. The leaves at her feet trembled, fluttering upward to fly against her face, her arms, to blow through the open kitchen doorway. Her gaze remained riveted to the place where she knew the staircase existed beyond her sight on the wall's opposite side. Where the wind struck the gathering mist, it swirled, took shape, broke apart and attempted vague shape again, all the while spinning not toward her, but toward the stairwell, as if the elements were being called to some focal point.

"Get out of my house," she growled through clenched teeth. "Get out of my house!"

Ethan called to her through the phone, muffled against her pant leg. She had no time to spare for him, no energy to divert.

"Get out," she said again, louder but breathless,

unable to fill her lungs with much needed air. "Get out of my—"

*Lily.*

The voice boomed through her skull, robbing the oxygen from her lungs. She stumbled to her knees. The phone clattered across the floor.

She couldn't understand how she had ever mistaken these tones for Daniel's when this voice had been telling her the things it could make Ethan do at its bidding. The difference was now glaringly and frighteningly clear. Clutching the counter for support, Perry struggled upright. Loosened from the barrette at her nape, her hair whipped into her eyes, stinging them to tears.

Perry continued backing toward the open doorway, pushing the hair away from her face with both hands. Her drumming heart vibrated her shirt. She thought she might strangle on the blood pumping too swiftly through her veins.

"Go away," she ground out. "Get out. You don't belong here."

*Lily.*

"Shut up!" Spinning on her heel, Perry ran for the back door. She thudded up against the wooden barrier, closing it painfully on her arm. Jerking free, she scrabbled for the knob, yanked the door wide again.

*You'll not leave me again.*

"The hell I won't," she spat, digging her nails into wood. The rage inside her head deafened her.

Debris from a wind with no source battered her flesh. Outside, the storm finally erupted against glass and stone, its origin seeming not nature's caprice, but the hatred and fear that made her knees quake and her skin crawl. She fought to push through to the porch outside, her car within sight, resisted the urge to turn and view whatever she could sense nearing her.

Until a hand circled her arm.

## *Chapter Thirty-Five*

Windshield wipers slapped hard, barely clearing the wind-driven torrent from glass. From the truck's handling, Ethan knew its tires had not actually touched road surface for the past fifteen minutes. He had no plan to slow down. As long as the vehicle remained in his command the gas pedal would get no relief. And neither would John. On the cab's opposite side he sat mutely, expression grim, one hand clutching the seat edge for support, the other hooked through the handle on the doorframe.

Ethan's conversation with Perry had been cut off by what sounded like the phone hitting the floor. He had tried dialing back as he rushed John from the hospital after a hasty word to Tom, but to no avail. After his fifth attempt to get through, Ethan phoned the police. Unable to give them a concrete reason for his concern, they had still offered to stop by the house at their earliest opportunity. With the current weather, Ethan did not expect the opportunity to present itself anytime soon.

Before they reached the truck the rain had begun falling in torrents across the hospital lot, drenching them both to the skin. Now midday had darkened like a sunless evening, the sky split by vivid lightning, the resultant thunder vibrating along the truck body. Ethan had not bothered with speech since he began to drive and John made no attempts to engage. Ethan's mood was obvious, his worry even more so. For the moment no further explanation was needed. John knew where they headed.

"Tell me again spirits cannot hurt the living," Ethan demanded abruptly, not taking his eyes from the roadway. Beside him John made no comment.

"There was some sort of read-out while we were speaking," Ethan continued, although he knew he had spouted out that information in their race across the lot. "The phone went dead after."

"You said it sounded like she dropped it, didn't you?" John reminded him.

"Yes."

"Perhaps that's all it was, then. Maybe she broke the phone. You won't help her, Ethan, if you don't ever make it there. I would suggest you slow down just a tad."

With enormous effort, Ethan backed off the gas. Broken branches laden with slick green leaves littered the highway, waving madly in the wind. Given the ground saturation from recent storms, the runoff from the fields and the road itself had quickly filled the shallow drainage ditches and covered the roadways clear across. John was right. He had to take care not to run them off the shoulder, because they wouldn't regain the road without assistance.

He wished he believed John's explanation, that nothing had taken place at the house to cause concern. Perhaps, had he been standing in different shoes, he would have been able to call to mind various case studies for reassurance. Instead he remembered the attic and how he had hurt Perry, nearly quite badly; recalled, too, dragging her from the creek and the bruises on her chest. His mind filled with the things the spirit had told her, reflecting the thoughts in his own mind, making them seem malevolent somehow.

"Try the number again, would you?"

"Of course." John dialed the number. After a moment he shook his head.

Ethan's teeth came together, hard. "We're nearly there anyway." He expected to feel better saying the words aloud. No such luck.

Maneuvering along the driveway was nearly as laborious and treacherous as the road had been. Wear had reduced the driveway's unpaved surface until it lay completely under muddied water several inches deep. The trees hung lower than when dry, scraping the truck. A sapling had fallen over, uprooted when soil washed from its roots. Ethan drove right over it.

When he pulled up before the house, he spotted Perry's car through the rain. His stomach rolled. He had been hoping to find the graveled parking area empty and Perry gone.

Jamming the truck into park, Ethan jumped out without troubling to turn off the engine. A prudent, expeditious, move. If he had his way they would be leaving immediately.

John exited a moment later. Ethan heard the truck door slam followed by the man's feet splashing through water. He caught up, head ducked low against the pounding rain. Ethan made straight for the kitchen door. Recalling Perry's explanation, he gave the lock and jamb a cursory inspection as he turned the knob. He stepped over the threshold and stopped short.

John sidestepped him to avoid collision, pausing to look around, frowning, pushing his thin and sodden sandy blond hair back from his brow.

"What the devil happened here?"

Ethan didn't answer, taking in the kitchen's disorder through narrowed eyes. He turned away, heading for the living room.

"Perry! Perry!"

Leaving John to inspect the equipment, Ethan

bounded up the steps to the second floor two at a time. He called Perry's name again, throwing open closed doors, peering into every room in rapid succession, finding nothing. When he reached the narrow attic stairs the door already stood wide.

Ethan hesitated at the bottom, jaw tightening, breath whistling through his nose. He forced himself up the staircase and into the dimly lit space beneath the roof. The roaring rain on slate nearly deafened him, preventing him hearing anything else.

"Perry? Are you here?"

He hurried across the attic, glancing into the clutter for any sign she'd been there or still was before making his way slowly back to the stairhead, checking every shadow. He couldn't imagine she would come up here alone after the other day, but he had to be certain. As he searched he fought to regain his composure, knowing he would do no one any good in his agitated state. Satisfied she hadn't hidden in the attic, he set his foot to the first step, his hand on the narrow rail. Below him, the door slammed shut.

He jerked back from the darkened well. Somewhere near his left hand he knew he'd find a light switch to the bare bulb hanging from the ceiling below. He felt along the roof joist for it, located the switch, flicked the tab up.

Empty. The stairs were empty. Ethan hurried down. Below him, the ancient doorknob started to turn. He braced himself, hastening to the bottom where he pushed the door, hard. It door struck something solid. On the other side John swore.

"Sorry," Ethan apologized, stepping down and out into the hall. "You spooked me a little when you slammed that door."

"I didn't slam it," John told him, rubbing his elbow. "A draft caught it when I was coming along the corridor. The kitchen door is open. The police are here."

"Perfect timing."

He met two officers in the kitchen, one who had been eyeing the equipment in the living room in patent speculation. The other kicked at the debris on the floor while accumulated rainwater sluiced from his raincoat onto the linoleum. When Ethan entered he held out his hand.

"Officer Clark," he said by way of introduction. "Are you the guy that called?"

Ethan gave the officer's hand a brief shake. "I am. Thanks for coming out. I'm sure you've got your hands full in this weather."

"Not a problem," responded the officer. "What happened here?" He indicated the kitchen's state with a tilting chin. As he spoke, he pulled a slim notebook from his pocket.

"I don't know. It was like this when we got here. However, I think my friend—the woman who owns the place, Perry Madison," Ethan expounded, seeing the officer taking notes, "found it in this condition as well. Nothing appears to be missing at first glance, but I wouldn't be the one to know that for sure. I was speaking with Perry on the phone and she said the place was littered with debris from outside. Shortly after, the phone went dead. It sounded like she dropped it first."

The police officer nodded. "Is that the phone?" he asked, pointing with his pen.

Ethan turned, locating the kitchen landline in its cradle. He walked over to it, tilting his head to study the scuff on the shiny plastic. He couldn't tell if the damage was new.

"When she phoned me she said she found the door open," said Ethan, feeling suddenly defensive.

"And what did you tell her?"

"I told her to get out of the house."

"Maybe she took your advice," suggested the officer.

"Her car is still here," Ethan stated. "If someone had actually broken into the house, they might have been inside when I was talking to her. I've searched the house with no sign of anyone. Except the basement. I haven't checked in the basement."

"We'll go look," Officer Clark said. "You stay here, sir. Where is the basement?"

"The only access is outside through the double metal doors," Ethan said. "Watch your heads, it's not as deep as you might expect."

He noted the recognition they would have to go

back into the rain register in both men's eyes as they donned their hats once more and departed, pulling the door closed behind them. Ethan grabbed some paper towels to blot the water from the floor where the officers had been standing. Cupping his hand to catch the overflow, he tossed the soiled toweling in the trash. Silly. Silly thing to do. He wasn't thinking straight. Giving the can's lid a violent spin, he frowned in anger.

"Damn it, John, where can she be?"

"Well," said John from the living room, "if these officers really thought there was a possibility Perry had interrupted a burglary in progress, they'd be treating the place like a crime scene. Before I came upstairs for you, I saw them checking the front door and the windows on the porch on their way around to the back of the house. I don't believe there's any forced entry. All this might have blown inside when the wind picked up prior to the storm," he said, indicating the floor. "Or not," he added, pointing to the equipment. "I don't know. I think other things would have been disturbed as well if the wind had blown through with that force. But I don't think any burglar or mischief maker would trash the house with leaves and twigs and grass, do you, and then leave everything of value inside?"

Ethan shook his head. No, he did not. Precisely the point. "She didn't leave, unless she went on foot, and why would she do that? Wherever she went, though, she pulled the door shut behind her. It was closed when we got here, right?  Hell, maybe she's just out in the barn. That's why she came here today, to make sure the pumps would be working if the creek rose high enough."

John threw up his hand in that direction. "Let's go, then," he said.

Ethan started across the floor, interrupted from his goal by both officers returning. Shoving a small mat toward the door, Ethan opened it. The men stepped inside.

"Nothing," said the one who had not introduced himself. "Some water down there, though. Might want to keep an eye on that."

Officer Clark spoke. "Do you want us to treat this like a missing person? Unofficially, at any rate. Could she have left with someone? A boyfriend maybe?"

Ethan stared levelly at the man. "That would be me," he said.

"Husband?"

"She's divorced."

"I'm sorry, but there doesn't seem to be any evidence of a crime here, Mr.— Taylor, was it?"

"Yes, Ethan Taylor."

Apparently, the radio dispatcher had not given the officers his first name, because Clark jotted that down, too. "May I have your home phone number and address?"

Growing impatient, but understanding some protocol needed to be followed, Ethan provided both. "Look," he said, "I'm going to check the barn. I'm sorry to have bothered you. Shall I call to let you know everything's all right?"

"Sure, that would be helpful. Maybe she went to a neighbor's to borrow something and is waiting for a lull in the storm?"

"Maybe," agreed Ethan, starting to edge toward the door. He wanted to check the outbuildings and then the creek. He didn't believe she would have gone there, either, but she had before, seeking safety. As it had turned out, she hadn't been safe at all.

"What is all that stuff?" This from the other officer, who seemed unable to contain his curiosity any longer. "You guys making a movie or something?  Looks like a lot of sound equipment and the like."

"It is sound equipment," John answered as Ethan made his move to exit. "These instruments are for recording sounds beyond the normal range of human hearing. These others are for detection of atmospheric changes, electromagnetic fields, and various other indicators."

"Indicators of what?" the officer asked.

Although he would have loved to hear John's explanation and the reaction from the two men, Ethan had no time for it. He headed outside and across the water-logged grass, head bowed against the onslaught.

## Chapter Thirty-Six

*The moon had been unchanging for so very long that the darkness seemed deeper still because of it, like velvet draping the bed in an unlit chamber. He understood now what had happened; remembered it and wept in pain. But it did not matter. Time had come full circle. She was here with him again in the darkness that was theirs alone. She would not leave him. She had accepted forever and would rejoice in it. This final battle was not Edward's to win or lose.*

*Outside the creek was rising, just as it had, just as it was meant to again. He could hear the change more than see the mounting water, for the sound from the falls had altered as the drop lessened. Still musical, still voluminous, but the tones were deeper, like the reverberations of a church bell after it has rung.*

*Slowly he turned away from the tumbling water, making his way back to the narrow cleft in the stone. Soon the water would enter in, but there was still time before that happened.*

## *Chapter Thirty-Seven*

Perry rolled her head, opening her eyes onto blackness. No, not total blackness. Somewhere beyond her feet she witnessed movement, like intertwined shadow in the darkest night. It seemed very far away. Slowly, Perry dragged her hand along damp stone to her hair, fingering the strands absorbing water from beneath her like the wick in a lamp. She pressed her fingertips to the ache in her skull, alarmed by the lump's size and its tenderness.

When she lifted her head, nausea rolled in her stomach, making her gasp. Beneath her skull, her spine, she felt a ceaseless vibration. A roar, a tumbling roar came into the place she lay, overwhelmingly loud.

Oh God, she breathed, recognizing everything.

*Have no fear, Lily. You are safe.*

Perry closed her eyes. His voice evoked an uncanny response in her. But now she hated it.

"How did I get here?"

*You came willingly, Lily. Edward knows. This time he knows your choice.*

"I made no choice."

*You did. My love, you chose me.*

She did not remember being presented with any options from which she had to choose. All she remembered was—

*Yes. Edward wanted to hurt you. You had to come with me to prevent it. The baby in your womb belongs to me. He must accept that now.*

"What baby?"

She felt confused, disoriented, ill. She realized how cold her body had become. Her clothes were soaked and gritty with sediment from the creek.

*The babe we have made. Inside of you. In here.*

Without preamble, he cupped her crotch through her sodden pants. An intimate gesture which once she had welcomed. She moved and made a small noise, but whether of protest or welcome she was uncertain. Her body and her mind floated on separate planes.

Ethan, she thought, where are you?

The phantom caress stilled.

*Who do you call?*

The spirit possessed a strength she had not previously known and she wondered if she had crossed over a boundary that made him somehow more real, and she less so. She felt as if she had, as if she were not wholly within her body.

*Not Edward. You have never wanted Edward. It has always been me.*

Shaking her head, Perry closed her eyes again,

fighting another nauseous wave. Her soaked blouse moved, lifted, was pushed aside. In the past he had not possessed the ability. She had been the one to remove her clothes.

His mouth closed on her breast in the familiar pattern of manipulation, one he knew would arouse her instantly. Lifting her arms she shoved on his shoulders, expecting no resistance, expecting her hands to go right through. Instead, she found him nearly solid.

Fear shuddered through her body. "Am I dying?" It seemed a reasonable question.

*Soon.*

"What?"

*Soon. Soon the oblivion of forever will claim us both. This time will be different. This time we are together.*

The air rushed from Perry's lungs. "No."

*You have chosen.*

"No," she said again. "I have made no such choice. You are mistaken. I am not Lily."

For a moment a silence gathered in the deafening noise. In the silence Perry realized two things. One, she had somehow become separate and apart from the physical world. Two, she wanted very much to live. How?

*You are she. I know you in my soul. I will always know you. I have waited long for you to return to me, Lily.*

Struggling up onto her elbows, Perry faced the

spirit. He cupped her breasts in his hands, bending to tease her nipples. She pushed him away. Hard.

"You are wrong, Daniel. I am not who you seek."

*You gave yourself to me. How could I not know who you are?*

Despite the darkness surrounding them, she realized she could see his face clearly, as if some fey light emanated from within. She saw the planes forming his cheekbones, his mouth, the close-cropped hair curled above his ears. The pain in his brown eyes went straight to her heart.

"I'm sorry," she whispered. "It's over. You need to move on. You don't belong here any longer."

Bewilderment altered his expression, and then he smiled, slowly, sadly.

*I know I do not belong in this place. Soon, we will be gone from it. Can I not have you once more?*

"No."

*Before the end. Before the water fills the hillside and takes us both. Do you not remember, Lily?*

Remember? Remember something that had passed between him and Lily? Of course, she didn't—

No! The creek was rising! Yes, yes, she had nearly drowned crossing over the swollen watercourse. She remembered that. Her memory, not Lily's. How had she gotten inside? How had she struck her head?

"I don't remember anything," she cried.

She needed to get out. It might already be too late. In flood stage, the torrent raging down the narrow watercourse had the strength to move trees. She could never hope to swim against it. She would be dashed against the rocks, sucked down into the current. Envisioning the water filling her lungs, Perry gasped and struck out. To her surprise, the ghost staggered back.

But the movement had its price. Perry leaned over and vomited, her head spinning in sickening circles.

*You see? It is the babe making you ill.*

Perry pushed the hair from her eyes. "There is no baby. I'm concussed. It is concussion making me ill."

*You told me you were with child.*

"I did not. Not me."

*Lily, you did. You were so happy you wept with joy.*

Perry closed her eyes again. Tears seeped out between her lashes. Whatever had taken place between the ghost of Daniel Nicholson and the long departed Lily must have broken his heart and his mind.

"I am not Lily," she whispered, determined to make the spirit understand. "I am Perry Madison."

*Yes. Lily Madson was your name before you took my brother's.*

Turning her head slowly, she stared at him. "What did you say?"

He ignored her question, his hands taking hold of her as if to force her once more to lie down. She pushed him away. He grabbed her again, one hand reaching down to stroke between her legs. She blocked his movements.

"Leave me alone. I am not Lily. There is no child. What passed between us could not have manufactured one, I assure you."

Another sudden silence echoed in her head. He released her immediately, pulling away.

*How dare you? Do you think to tell me again that you carry Edward's child in your belly?*

Perry blinked. In an instant the situation clarified itself. On impulse she reached out to him, closing her hand over his groin.

"You are barely erect," she said. "It has always been this way. You have used other means for pleasure with me. You cannot make a child like that, Daniel. Your seed was never expended. Not in me, for certain. Nor, I suspect, in Lily."

In an angered gesture, he flung her hand aside. The force caused her to rock back onto her elbows again. Smaller stones ground into flesh and bone. Perry tumbled onto her back. She lay prone, gasping with pain. Waning consciousness shimmered before her eyes. She fought to maintain awareness, watched him from beneath lowered lids. He seemed to have gained solidity, mass, strength. But he was still the ghost of a man who had lived nearly one hundred and eighty years earlier. She would do well to hold onto that fact.

"I thought you had forgiven me, Lily. When you came back, I thought you had forgiven me."

Perry shuddered in fear. His voice no longer sounded only in her head. It echoed through the cavern. The falls had hushed, no more than rushing water. Perry rolled onto her side, retching again. She attempted to slide away from him. Her feet touched chill liquid several inches deep. The creek had come inside. She might only have moments, now, to gain access to the cleft in the hillside before the cave behind filled with churning brown water.

Seeming to realize what she attempted to do, the spirit grabbed her arms again, dragging her back. He threw himself down on top of her, his face close to hers, her arms pinned beneath his chest. She couldn't budge him.

"Tell me you forgive me, Lily. You must, or all will be lost."

His mouth latched onto hers, hungry, all gentleness gone, and she turned away from it. His lips moved with urgency along her throat.

"Forgive you? For what?" She struggled against him for time, for her life, feeling the cold water licking along her calves now. "What did you do that has damned you to haunt this place?"

Abruptly, he rolled off her, onto his knees with his hands at his sides. The grim light that had been emanating from him seeped away to a pale, spectral glimmer. He bowed his head, reaching out to touch her throat, curving his hand around the slender, all too vulnerable column.

*I killed you, Lily. I did not mean to. You were going back to him and I could not let you.*

Perry lay still, sensing his hand on her throat without pressure. The water had risen nearly to her waist, tugging at her shirt hem. Her legs had gone numb.

"I am not Lily," she stated softly. "But it appears you may have killed me, too."

With a howling cry, the spirit lunged toward her. She braced herself for the inevitable, but rather than attack, he shoved his hands beneath her arms, ineffectually, weakening. It appeared he wanted to move her.

*There is a place at the back which is higher than the rest. Perhaps you will survive if you go there.*

Obediently Perry summoned the strength to drag herself in the direction indicated. She jammed her body into a place where the cave floor sloped up to a shelf. What good it would do, she didn't know. The water would rise here, too. Lapping, swirling, it had already filled the cave. Daniel's ghost crawled up beside her, laying his head against her thigh. She stroked the feather-light hair back from his brow.

"I forgive you," she whispered. If she had to die, it was the least she could do.

## *Chapter Thirty-Eight*

Horrified, Ethan stared at the creek. Brown and frothing, the water rushed by below him tumbling logs and debris. The spume sprayed high into the air. For the moment the rain had stopped. Only for a moment. The sky remained dark and threatening. The storm had dumped several inches in an hour's time. More would be coming.

He'd found the barn empty, the smaller outbuildings as well. After assuring for Perry's sake the pumps were operable, he had gone back to the house. The policemen had already left, exiting along a driveway completely underwater, having been called away by an emergency. An emergency. This was an emergency. They just didn't realize it.

Now John stood at his side, shaking his head.

"She wouldn't have gone in there."

"Why not?" Ethan argued.

"She wouldn't have made it across."

"Not if she went in right after the rain began. She could be in the hillside now."

"Let's hope not, Ethan." John's low voice carried over the thundering flow, due, Ethan suspected, to the enormity of its content. "She won't survive it."

Ethan's fists clenched at his side. He couldn't breathe.

"Call the fire department, John. Go back to the house and call them. If I'm wrong, then I'm wrong, but they might possess the equipment to gain access. I can't just let her die, if she's there. I can't do that again. I can't."

John's hand fell on his soaked arm. "You didn't let Cindy die, Ethan. She made that choice on her own."

Ethan's jaw tightened. He dashed a hand across his eyes, his face, wiping away moisture dripping from his hair, from his eyes. Whether or not he'd been at fault when Cindy died, he'd blamed himself for a good long time. Now, Perry's life was in danger. He couldn't live with himself if he didn't do his best to save her. If she hadn't gone into the cave, all well and good. He would look elsewhere after he had ascertained that fact for himself. But if she'd gone in there—God if she had...

"Please, John, go back to the house and call